"Do you believe?"

"No… Yes. Well, maybe. Let's just say my dreams aren't usually so vivid." Cassie looked once again at her surroundings, and still couldn't believe what she was seeing. "What are you, anyway—some kind of cosmic cop?"

"Be quiet," Morgan said suddenly.

"Look—"

Morgan's hand clamped over her mouth so quickly she had no chance to elude it. The small shake he gave her to emphasize his point only succeeded in making her more aware of him. Hauled up against his chest in the shelter of a lengthy second-story shadow, Cassie felt his heartbeat and the strength of his muscled body. This man had a strange power over her… which scared her to death.

"This isn't a game, Cassie. Your life is in danger, and like it or not, I must protect you."

"That's what you think, Morgan. I'm very capable of taking care of myself."

"Remember what century you're in. And remember this is the home of Jack the Ripper…."

Dear Reader,

What else can be more romantic *and* more mysterious than traveling through time to meet the man who was destined to share your life? We're especially proud to present TIMELESS LOVE, a unique new program in Harlequin Intrigue that will showcase these much-loved time-travel stories.

So journey back with Jenna Ryan to the dark, mist-filled alleys of Edwardian England—and come face-to-face with the notorious Jack the Ripper. Who was he, really? As Jenna said after her trip to England, "Wouldn't it be fascinating to go back and learn the truth?" Join us and find out.

We hope you enjoy *When Night Falls*... and all the special books coming to you in the months ahead in TIMELESS LOVE.

Sincerely,

Debra Matteucci
Senior Editor and Editorial Coordinator
Harlequin Books
300 East 42nd Street
New York, NY 10017

When Night Falls

Jenna Ryan

Harlequin Books

TORONTO • NEW YORK • LONDON
AMSTERDAM • PARIS • SYDNEY • HAMBURG
STOCKHOLM • ATHENS • TOKYO • MILAN
MADRID • WARSAW • BUDAPEST • AUCKLAND

To those people who still believe

ISBN 0-373-22265-3

WHEN NIGHT FALLS

This edition published by arrangement with Harlequin Enterprises B. V.

Printed in U.S.A.

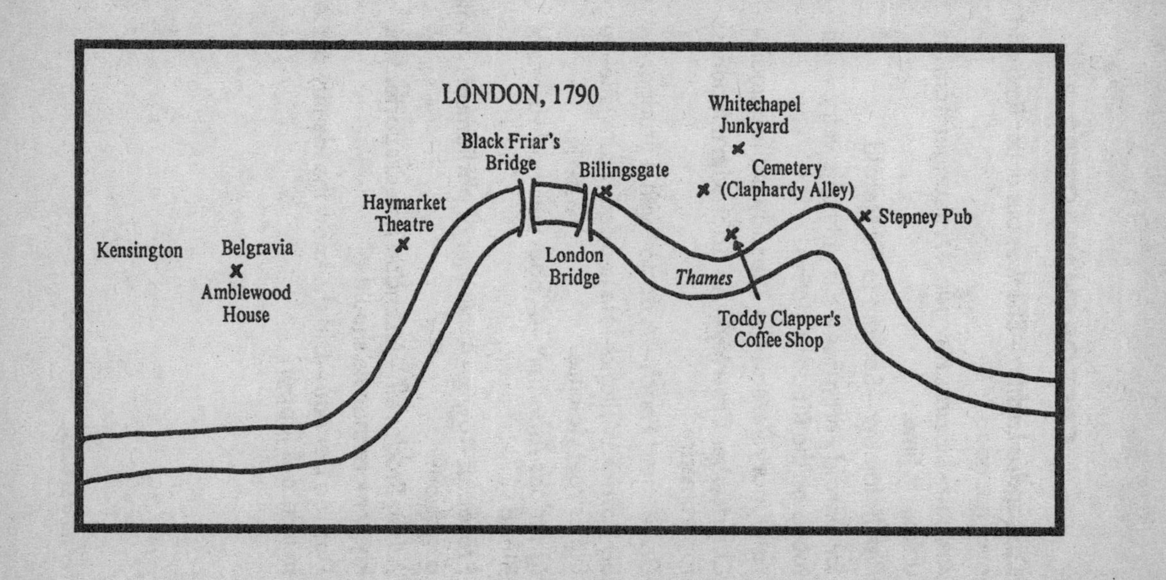
LONDON, 1790
Kensington
Belgravia
Amblewood House
Haymarket Theatre
Black Friar's Bridge
London Bridge
Billingsgate
Whitechapel Junkyard
Cemetery (Claphardy Alley)
Thames
Toddy Clapper's Coffee Shop
Stepney Pub

CAST OF CHARACTERS

Cassandra Lachlin—She was out of her time and over her head.

Anthony Lazarus Morgan—A stranger from an unknown time.

Bartholomew—Servant to Sir Gerald.

Sir Gerald Peregrine—His gifts of jewelry were found on the Ripper's victims.

Lady Mary Peregrine—The lady of the manor.

Christopher Crowley—An actor with a fondness for women.

Dr. Samuel Peach—A doctor with a grudge.

Sir Patrick Welland—He headed a committee to fight street violence.

Ignatious Athelbert—A poet who had visions of blood.

Procopius Rowe—A member of parliament . . . with a mission?

Julian Stockwell—A *London Times* reporter who knew more than he should.

Desirée Deveau—Did she know the identity of the murderous Ripper?

Prologue

London, England
December 3, 1993

Mr. Pit was a curious man. He'd owned a curio shop in Camden Passage for forty-three years, filling it in that time with every knickknack, ornament and odd bit he could lay his skinny fingers on. But tonight's find might just be the best he'd made since he opened his shop.

Brushing aside thick cobwebs in the rafters, he wedged out a small book with a peeling black leather cover and gold Florentine trim. A diary, by the looks of it, and unless he missed his guess, at least two hundred years old.

Scurrying down the ladder, he called to his friend. "Mr. Flint, I believe I've found something."

Mr. Flint had owned Amblewood House for the past six months. Once a grand manor, its late occupant, Mr. Flint's great-aunt Clara, had closed up all but two of the rooms in the west wing where she and her three cats had lived. It was evident she hadn't come near the old kitchen for fifty years or more. The rooms adjoining it where Mr. Pit stood now were in an even worse state of disrepair.

"What is it, Mr. Pit?" asked his friend, a portly man in his late sixties, wearing mismatched clothes and a dusty bowler.

"It's a diary, I think. Possibly belonging to one of your noble ancestors."

Mr. Flint snorted and rubbed his wool-gloved hands together. "I can see my breath in here, Mr. Pit." The two men always addressed each other formally. "Let's go into the parlor and have a look, shall we?"

Mr. Pit scuttled along in his friend's wake, stopping just long enough to scoop up a bottle of wine from the barely functional kitchen.

Though Mr. Flint had decided to convert Amblewood into a rooming house, he had opened up the second floor only last week. Already he had two tenants. Another was due to arrive later this evening.

"Mrs. Rudyard's offered to cook Christmas dinner," Mr. Flint said, closing the parlor doors to keep out the draft. "I'll have to get that old kitchen fixed up for her."

"You still have more than three weeks," Mr. Pit reminded him. "It's only the second of December."

"Third," Mr. Flint corrected. "And the holiday season's a bad time to have renovations done." He stopped in front of the window. "My heavens, look at that snow come down, will you. The Thames will be an ice rink by morning. Pour us some wine and let's sit by the fire. I thought you might find some chipped bric-a-brac in those old rooms. I never expected you'd turn up a diary."

Mr. Pit handed the worn black book to his friend.

"Real gold filigree," Mr. Flint observed, flicking at the border with his thumbnail. "Looks like a diary Lady Mary might have kept in the 1700s. I wonder what it was doing in the servants' quarters?"

Mr. Pit drank his wine, spilled a little and wiped his chin on his coat sleeve. It was too cold to go back into the kitchen for a napkin, and the fire in here was quite delicious. "Should we have a look inside, do you think?" he asked.

With a grin that produced dimples in his pudgy cheeks, Mr. Flint removed a thin silver stickpin from his lapel and fiddled with the ancient catch. "There, that's got it," he said at length. "Now, let's see who did what to whom, and when." Removing a pair of bifocals from his baggy jacket pocket, he began to read. " 'December 10, 1993.' " Frowning, he stared at the entry. "That can't be right."

"Are you sure you're reading it correctly?"

For an answer, Mr. Flint laid the book on the table between them. "See for yourself, Mr. Pit. 'December 10, 1993.' It's as plain as the nose on your face."

"But that's impossible," Mr. Pit objected. "That date hasn't happened yet."

"Black ink," Mr. Flint remarked absently. "Looks like a fountain pen to me. Yellowed parchment, though." He fingered the heavy pages. "Parchment's the genuine article, at any rate. And it's written in the style of the day, lots of squiggles or flourishes, as old Aunt Clara would say. It looks like a man's hand to me. Where did you find this, Mr. Pit?"

"In that room just off the kitchen, the one that looks out on the garden. I could see the snow coating the mulberry bushes from the window."

Pushing back his bowler, Mr. Flint scratched his scruffy head. "It baffles me, Mr. Pit. Look at this, will you. 'I arrived in a snow-covered London on December third and, as luck would have it, found I could rent a room at Amblewood House.' "

"What?" Mr. Pit choked slightly on his wine, blinking at the unlikely entry. "Surely there isn't another Amblewood House in London, is there?"

" 'It feels good to be back,' " Mr. Flint continued, his plump brow furrowed, " 'although in defense of Manchester it wasn't the city's fault that Jack chose to wreak his homicidal havoc at such a turbulent point in time. Labor rebellions, fires, fog and scarcely an oil lamp to light the streets after dark.' "

A frown crossed Mr. Pit's weasely features. "What does it all mean—labor rebellions and fire? This is gibberish, Mr. Flint. The man must have been a loon."

Mr. Flint shook his head, clearly perplexed. "It is confusing, I must say. 'I don't know what made Jack decide to come to London now,' " he read on, " 'but I'm certain he's here. He's already killed twice in the seven days since I arrived, and once before that, I suspect. Scotland Yard is completely frustrated, an understandable state of affairs where Jack is concerned.

"'Since this is a belated entry, I won't recount here all that I've done to catch him. Suffice it to say I know Jack's handiwork when I see it. The method of death is consistent without exception, his victims here in London the same as the ones he stalked the last time he visited this city.'"

Intrigued, Mr. Pit edged closer to his friend. "Is there more?"

Mr. Flint nodded, flipping through the pages. "A great deal more. Shall I go on?"

Bobbing his head, Mr. Pit poured more wine. Snow continued to fall, burying nighttime London under a blanket of white. Inside Amblewood House, however, it was quite warm and cozy by the fire just as it must have been back in the days of Mary Peregrine, the first lady of the manor.

Mr. Flint cleared his throat and settled back.

"'I have a feeling Jack's going to kill again, possibly tonight. If he stays true to form he'll be prowling Lambeth after dark. So will I. Still, it's a big area, and for all his brutality Jack is a clever man. It will take more than luck to catch him. I almost wish old Nathan Kroat hadn't quit and dumped this mess in my lap. However, since he did, I'll do what I must to finish the job. I'm leaving for the docks now. Instinct tells me that one way or another, this will be the last entry I make in this particular year...."

Chapter One

December 10, 1993

"She's dead, all right, just like the others. Her throat's been slashed, she's been disemboweled, and the contents of her purse and pockets have been laid out neatly at her feet."

With her eyes locked on the frozen victim, Cassandra Lachlin listened to Inspector Keegan's weary assessment of the murder scene.

"A constable found her on his beat, outside the knacker's yard." A pause, then, "Lambeth again. Down by the river...."

Shifting her troubled gaze, Cassie watched one of her counterparts on the London police force kneel in the snow to photograph the dead woman. He obviously was disturbed by what he saw through his lens.

"Bastard," she whispered softly, her breath evaporating into the frosty night. "What kind of monster could do this?"

"A sick one," Inspector Keegan answered, sighing. "What are you doing here, Cassie? I thought you were off to the Highlands for a week."

"I am." She shifted her stuffed leather backpack as proof. "I decided to visit Joelle Terry's parents before I left. They only live a block from here. It was hard to miss the commotion of your arrival." Cassie turned her attention back to the dead woman. "How long do you think she's been dead?"

"An hour or two maybe. It's hard to say with the cold and the snow."

"Was she a prostitute?"

The inspector nodded. "Keep the busybodies away," he snapped at the local constables behind him.

"Morbid curiosity," Cassie said mildly, glancing at the sea of speculative faces that surrounded them. "You can't blame people for wanting to know. It was all I could do to keep Joelle's parents from coming with me."

The inspector stomped his feet in the snow to warm them. "You still feel badly about her death, don't you?"

"She was a friend."

"She was a prostitute."

"I liked her, Inspector. And don't hand me that old she-took-her-chances-working-the-streets-at-night line." Cassie flicked a disgusted hand at the bloodied snow. "Whoever could do something like this should be hanged by his—"

"Inspector!" one of the officers interrupted anxiously. "Call for you, sir."

With a sigh, Keegan patted her shoulder. "Go to Scotland and try not to think about this, Cassie. Photograph some pretty scenery instead of corpses for a few days."

Cassie closed her eyes for a painful moment. Try not to think about it? Her friend Joelle had been brutally murdered three days ago—the second, possibly third, victim of a homicidal madman uncomfortably reminiscent of Jack the Ripper—and Keegan wanted her to forget about it. As a police photographer, she'd been forced to photograph Joelle's body, and the one before that. How could anyone not think about something as horrible as that?

And there was that first woman, too. No one was sure about her. Like the next three victims, her throat had been slashed and her abdomen cut open. But the abdominal incision had been incomplete, as if the killer had been interrupted before he could carry out his ritualistic task.

Shivering, Cassie turned away, balling her fists in the pockets of her lined suede jacket. Snow crunched under her boots; the city breathed heavily around her. She could hear the jingle of sleigh bells in the distance.

Resolutely, she opened her eyes. Keegan was right, she shouldn't dwell on this grisly scene. She couldn't change what was, and she certainly wasn't equipped to catch a twisted murderer. That job was best left to the inspector and his detectives.

As she started away from the body, her attention was captured by a vaguely familiar sight.

It was him, the man in the long black coat and high boots. She was certain she'd seen him twice before. Well, once for sure. In fairness, she'd only caught a glimpse of someone who looked like him the night Joelle had died. But she was convinced it was the same man. Something about his calm bearing stood out in her mind, even if she'd never gotten a good look at his face.

She saw him in profile now. Snow swirled about his head, but he seemed not to notice. He stared at the victim's carefully arranged possessions as if trying to memorize the arrangement.

His long, very dark hair curled away from his face; he had a strong, straight nose and a full mouth, but nothing she would really call remarkable. He wasn't particularly tall—five feet ten, perhaps. Despite the bulk of his wool coat, she suspected an average build—not very muscular, but lean.

Cassie processed the details swiftly. She was more interested in his presence here than his outward appearance.

She edged toward him, torn between learned caution and innate curiosity. It surprised her a little that none of the officers paid attention to him. As she watched, he frowned and pulled a small black box from his coat pocket, glanced at it, then snapped his head around.

A word she couldn't hear formed on his lips. Turning, he slipped through the crush of onlookers and started for the street.

Cassie caught one of the officers' arms. "Who was that man?" she demanded.

"The one in black?" The constable shrugged. "I don't know. Why, did he do something?"

Yet even as he responded, Cassie found herself following the man, uncertainly at first, then with increasing urgency as he easily outpaced her.

He was heading for the cabstand in front of a run-down pub and a collection of similar old-brick stores with crooked chimneys.

"Oh, no, you don't," she whispered, determined not to lose him. She ran up to the next car in the line, tossed her backpack inside and pointed over the driver's left shoulder. "Follow that cab."

"What?" The driver stared at her.

"You heard me. Follow it, and hurry."

"Bloody Americans," he grumbled, starting off.

Cassie continued to hover at his shoulder. The snow blew harder as they drove across Lambeth bridge into Westminster. "He can't be going to Scotland Yard," she said, frowning in perplexity. "I'm sure he's not a cop." She prodded the driver's heavy arm. "They're turning left." Then she frowned. "Wait a minute—this is Belgravia."

"Posh," the driver remarked with a hint of sarcasm.

"Just drive," Cassie told him.

He did, and without further comment, until they turned off Chesham Street. A row of dark, stately houses stood well back from the curbs. Only a few lights burned in the mostly shuttered windows.

"Posh but gloomy," the driver amended as the cab before them halted. "You want me to wait?"

"Please." Cassie paid him, trusting that he would give her the correct change. The man in black had climbed from his cab and was making for the side of one of the larger houses.

Slinging her backpack over her shoulder, she trailed him along the cobbled walk, past bushes buried under a carpet of white, toward what appeared to be the cellar entrance. He opened the door, stooped to pick up a bag and disappeared inside.

She shouldn't be doing this, Cassie told herself as she slipped through the door after him. For all she knew, this man could be the killer.

A narrow set of stairs, concave with age but surprisingly sturdy, led down to a cold, musty cellar.

Ignoring the sticky strands of cobweb that plastered themselves to her face and hair, she crept downward. He had a flashlight, she realized, pushing aside a huge web. She could see the beam cutting through the murk.

"Odd color," she murmured, pausing on the last step and rubbing her fingers on her jeans.

A silhouette against the deep purple glare, he took a covert look around, straightened, then stepped into the light. And promptly vanished, Cassie noted in shock.

"Hey, wait a minute." She didn't stop to think, which was perfectly normal behavior for her. "Where did you go?"

Launching herself from the last step, she plunged into the glare. Rather than a flashlight beam, it appeared to be some sort of doorway.

She decided to walk through.

Her skin began to tingle the instant the light touched her. It seemed almost crystalline, and it was fading. She could see the particles winking out around her. No, not winking out, pressing in, enfolding her body in an icy cocoon.

Her insides went cold, then hot, then cold again. Her feet absolutely refused to move.

The fear she should have experienced had no chance to erupt. She felt the first tendrils of terror in her stomach, then suddenly nothing. A numbing purple haze swept through her mind, driving out panic as a pleasant sort of dizziness set in. She was floating, comfortably, yet very fast, shooting through a brilliant void.

Or were the impressions of color and speed products of her imagination?

At this point Cassie wasn't sure she cared. Images swam before her eyes, Christmases in New Hampshire with her family, her sister's wedding, her father's funeral, her mother moving to Scotland to live with her sister in a tiny village near Loch Ness.

She saw herself at twenty-one, taking pictures in London, finding a flat, learning to drive on the left. She didn't want to be a county coroner like her father, or a pathologist like her mother or a student of forensic medicine like her sister. Not Cassie Lachlin, no sir. She would photograph dead people instead. A giggle bubbled up inside her. What a morbid family they were.

The light that enveloped her intensified; the sensation of speed decreased. Now it was a cloud she rode, a fat purple cloud with strong, billowing arms. It deposited her onto a hard surface, gently, but she stumbled even so and bumped her head on the floor.

Like a London fog, the cloud lifted, leaving her alone in a dark place that felt familiar yet different somehow than it had before.

She'd tumbled into the center of the cellar. Had she dreamed the colorful tunnel? she wondered fuzzily, sitting up and rubbing her bruised temple.

"I must have," she said out loud. "I'm still here." She looked around at the thick shadows. "Wherever *here* is."

An uneasy feeling coursed through her as she climbed shakily to her feet. Hoisting her backpack onto her shoulder, she let her fingers stray to the dusty strands of hair that had escaped their braid.

"Cobwebs," she murmured, squinting into the darkness. "That's what's missing." And the smell of must, her attentive mind added. But they couldn't have just disappeared.

Uncertainly, she backed toward the staircase, groping behind her for the saggy railing. Absorbed in thought, she missed the sound of footsteps descending from above. But she didn't miss the rough hand that caught her from behind, snatching her up by the scruff of the neck.

Before she could react, the hand jerked her around. "Caught you, bloody urchin!" a woman's voice roared. Then, in one swift motion, her other hand slammed hard into the side of Cassie's head.

"Let me go! Who are you? What are you doing? Stop it!"

Cassie struggled ineffectively with the woman behind her. The smell of flour and lemon assailed her. The hands of her captor were red and chapped, and her hair—what Cassie glimpsed of it—looked black and coarse.

"March," the woman ordered, pushing her. "We'll see what Mr. Morgan has to say about you scoffing apples from our fruit cellar."

"I wasn't scoffing apples," Cassie protested, stumbling. The woman held her fast. The sound of a long dress swishing about her ankles reached Cassie's ears. "Look, I'm not a thief. If you'll just let me explain . . ."

"Explain to Mr. Morgan."

"Damn," Cassie swore under her breath.

She was shoved unceremoniously through a door at the top of the stairs, into a kitchen unlike any she'd ever seen before.

A huge fireplace comprised at least half of one enormous wall. Orange coals glowed beneath a collection of heavy black pots that hung on hooks from the brick mantel. Candles—dozens of them—burned in wall sconces and on every available countertop. Something charred and crisp roasted on a spit, there were piles of vegetables on the island table, and there wasn't an appliance in sight. Two women in period costume gaped at her as she was thrust across the threshold.

"Mind your business, the pair of you," the woman behind Cassie snapped. "Where's Mr. Morgan?"

A plump girl with fuzzy blond curls peeking out from beneath her floppy cap recovered first. "He's upstairs with Sir Gerald. Shall I fetch him?"

"Bartholomew!" the woman bellowed.

Taking advantage of the distraction, Cassie gave her arms a final wrench and broke free. "What is all this?" she demanded. "Why are you people dressed so strangely..."

She trailed off when she finally got her first good look at the woman who'd been hauling her about.

"What are you staring at?" the woman snapped.

Her captor had a strikingly severe look. Her black hair, half pinned up, half hanging around her face had the consistency of unraveled hemp. She was solidly built, very solidly built, a little shorter than Cassie's five-seven, fifty-some years old and glowering out of eyes that resembled olive pits. Her face looked as though it wore a perpetual scowl, her skin was leathery, her stance formidable.

"Nothing," Cassie answered quickly. "Um, why are you all dressed like this?"

"Like what?" The woman placed impatient hands on her heavily skirted hips.

Cassie again regarded the white ruffled cap, the limp old-fashioned dress and smudged apron. "It's like something out of the French Revolution."

The woman's lips thinned unbecomingly. "Don't you compare us to Frenchies. Bartholomew!" she thundered. "You're a fine one to be talking about clothes, anyway." She drew closer, her eyes narrowing in suspicion. "Hell's teeth, you're not even a boy, are you?"

Cassie straightened, offended. "Of course I'm not a boy. What kind of a crack is—"

Her question was cut off by the appearance of a short man with long brown hair. He was dressed like an old-fashioned peasant and carrying a heavy black pot. The moment he spied her, his brown eyes widened in alarm.

"Oh, dear," she heard him whisper.

"Come here, Bartholomew," the woman snarled. She gave Cassie an unnecessary shove. "I found this...*girl* in the cellar, getting ready to make off with our winter veggies."

"Oh, for heaven's sake," Cassie began, exasperated, but the woman silenced her with a sharp slap to the back of her head.

"You speak when you're spoken to."

"Now wait just a minute—"

"Mrs. Dickson," the little man interrupted, setting his pot down. "I think we should let Mr. Morgan deal with this."

The woman leaned forward, ner stance taunting. "Then go and fetch him, Bartholomew."

"Yes, ma'am."

"And you two." She raised an arm to the pair still gawking from the far side of the table. "Get back to work. It's late and you know Sir Gerald likes to feed his guests well."

It wasn't until that moment that Cassie, too outraged to react properly, noticed the cloudy gray twilight through the single high window in the kitchen. She stared, not liking the sensations that crept over her. "What happened to the darkness?" she said mistrustfully. She whirled on the woman called Mrs. Dickson. "It was dark when I went into that cellar."

"So you admit you were down there!"

"I never denied it. Look," she said, taking a deep breath and spreading her hands as she backed away from the lot of them. "I don't know what's going on here, or why you're dressed the way you are, or why you don't have a stove or a fridge or even electric lights. All I know is that there was a woman murdered on the docks tonight, and the man I followed from there to here went into your cellar ahead of me."

"There wasn't any man in the cellar," Mrs. Dickson maintained flatly.

"What's a fridge?" one of the girls asked.

Cassie sent her a startled look. This had to be some kind of bad joke. She glanced at the window and the snow that fell in large white flakes beyond it; at least that much was the same.

"Are you getting ready for a costume party?" she questioned carefully, setting aside the fridge question.

"A fancy-dress party, you mean?" The blonde's plump face broke into a smile. "Good heavens, no. Lady Mary doesn't go in for that sort of thing anymore." She leaned over her kettle. "What are *you* wearing?"

"Hush, Susan," Mrs. Dickson ordered. Folding her arms across her ample bosom, she sauntered speculatively around Cassie. "Dresses like a boy in funny breeches and a funny coat. Talks funny, too." She stopped and smiled, but her eyes were filled with distrust. "Where are you from, girl?"

"New Hampshire," Cassie replied cautiously. Maybe it was all a dream. It didn't feel like one, though.

"Where's that?" Mrs. Dickson demanded.

Cassie opened her mouth, but the answer never emerged. A door opened above a short set of stairs that led into the kitchen, and she turned to look.

"She's for it now," the girl with mousy brown hair murmured.

"That's her." Cassie heard Bartholomew's cockney accent and squinted up at the shadowy threshold. A man in black stood there—but surely not the same man she'd followed into the cellar. It couldn't be him. This one wore buttoned knee breeches, black stockings and black buckled shoes. She glimpsed an embroidered velvet waistcoat or vest beneath the black frock coat that fell to his knees, a white cravat tied with perfect late-eighteenth-century precision and ruffled cuffs at his wrists.

Speechless, she lifted her gaze again to his face. It *was* him. Strong nose, full mouth—currently set in an unpromising line—dark curling hair, dark brows and very, very dark eyes. How on earth had she thought him unremarkable?

"I found this scrap in the cellar, Mr. M." Reaching out, Mrs. Dickson gave her another shove. If she hadn't been so engrossed by the man, Cassie would have shoved her back this time.

He wasn't especially handsome, but there was something compelling about him, an air of undisputed authority.

He came slowly down the stairs, his expression closed to her, each movement measured. She noticed then what she hadn't before. He had a long ponytail, much longer than the rest of his curls, tied back with a black satin bow.

Her frown deepened. "It's like stepping back in time," she whispered to herself.

"Quiet," Mrs. Dickson ordered. Her leathery face broke into a smug grin. "Shall I send for the bailiff, Mr. M.?"

A slight head shake was his only response. His eyes never left Cassie's face. She noticed that the blond kitchen maid had quickly tidied her hair when he'd appeared.

"I'll take care of this, Mrs. Dickson," he said, his gaze steady on Cassie. "You get back to your meal preparations. This way—miss." A wooden screen partially set off the kitchen from a cramped eating nook. He motioned her toward it. "Bartholomew, bring us some tea."

He had a nice voice, Cassie noted, a proper British accent and a highly polished manner.

"Look," she tried again, not budging. "I don't know what you people are playing at, but it isn't funny. I admit I'm trespassing, but that doesn't give you the right to get pushy.

"I saw you in Lambeth tonight, at the scene of a brutal murder. I've seen you before under similar circumstances. I want to know who you are."

The man regarded her, not quite frowning. "You followed me into the cellar, didn't you?" he demanded, not sounding so polished now.

Cassie lifted her head. "Yes."

"Of course you did." He sighed heavily. "And the light as well."

"What about it?"

"You passed through it."

"So?" Confusion gave way to an uneasy blend of frustration and anger. "What is this place? Who are you? And where did the night go? It was dark when I got here. Now it's just *getting* dark."

"Here you go, Mr. M. Hot tea." Bartholomew deposited a tray on the table and offered Cassie a small smile of encouragement. "This'll help," he told her.

"I wouldn't count on it," the man murmured a trifle sarcastically. He fixed her with an unreadable stare. "What's your name?"

"What's yours?"

"Anthony Lazarus Morgan." He gave her a meaningful look and she relented, absently accepting the cup Bartholomew pushed between her fingers.

"Cassandra Lachlin. Cassie for short."

"Scottish." Morgan said the word with mild contempt, his gaze sweeping over her red brown hair and brown eyes. "I should have known."

Cassie set the cup down hard. "What does that mean?"

"Nothing that matters. How long have you been here?"

"How the hell should I know? I thought maybe twenty minutes, but since I seem to have lost a night somewhere, I imagine it's been a little longer than that."

"Oh dear," Bartholomew said again. "So she did come through by accident."

Cassie was losing patience, and more than a little nerve. Before her bravado could desert her completely, she demanded, "Came through what by accident?"

"The door." Anthony Lazarus Morgan regarded her, his expression fathomless. "You haven't lost a day, Miss Lachlin. You have, in fact, gained approximately two hundred years."

In spite of herself, Cassie trembled. "Don't be ridiculous."

"I'm not. You stepped into a time corridor."

"A what?"

His stare didn't falter. It unnerved her that he could sound so rational when indeed he must be quite mad. "You walked through the light," he explained. "Except that it wasn't just a light—it was a doorway to another time."

In the background Mrs. Dickson barked at her underlings. Pots scraped across the counters and a cat Cassie hadn't noticed began yowling for its dinner.

Unable to control the spikes of fear in her stomach, she inched backward until her spine was pressed against the screen. "You're crazy," she accused weakly. "There's no such thing as a time corridor."

"Oh, but there is, miss," Bartholomew said. His smile was minus a top tooth. "Mr. M. here goes in and out of it all the time."

"That will be all, Bartholomew," Morgan said with a hint of impatience. "Look, Miss Lachlin, there's really nothing I can say that will soften the blow. You've traveled back in time more than two hundred years. Until I can reverse the temporal flow that will return you to the twentieth century, I'm afraid you're stuck here."

He might as well have kicked her in the ribs. "This has to be a dream," she said, pressing the fingers of both hands to her temples. "A nightmare."

It both startled and unsettled her when Morgan reached out to wrap his own long fingers about her wrist. "No," he said simply. "It isn't. The time is real and so are you within it."

She took a calming breath, willing her heart rate to slow. "I don't believe you."

His expression didn't soften. "Accept it," he repeated flatly. She sensed he wasn't the most patient of men. "The year is 1790. For a while, at least, you're going to have to learn to fit in."

"I'm not..."

"Yes you are," he said without inflection. "Because if you don't, Miss Cassie I-should-have-minded-my-own-business Lachlin, the only thing you're going to learn firsthand about this bit of British history is how easy it is to die."

Chapter Two

December 9, 1790

Time travel was impossible, Cassie's intellect knew that. Certainly it was beyond any reality she'd ever known. And yet within twenty minutes of Mrs. Dickson dragging her out of the cellar, every other part of her was prepared to believe. Eager to believe, in fact. It all seemed frighteningly real to her, right down to the horse-drawn sleighs that jingled past on the snow-covered streets.

For a time, she lapsed into silence, allowing Morgan to relieve her of her leather backpack. "Take this to my room," he instructed Bartholomew. "Tell Mrs. Salton to fetch a dress and a mobcap. Shoes, too. What size?" he asked Cassie with a meaningful arch of one dark brow.

"Seven," she replied levelly. "Listen, Mr. Morgan..."

Morgan waved a dismissing hand at the smaller man. "Mrs. Salton will know what's necessary. As for you..." Teeth gritted, he silenced Cassie when she started to protest. "You keep quiet. I'm going to sneak you up to the third floor where you're going to wait for Bartholomew. When you're dressed, I want you to come straight back to the kitchen. Do you understand?"

Cassie slapped at the finger he was jabbing in her face. "I'm not a damned servant, Mr. Morgan. I'm a police photographer."

"Not here you aren't."

"Oh, really?"

"Yes, really."

His dark eyes flashed, the first true sign of temper she'd seen; it suited him. In fact, once you got past the shock of it all, which she hadn't yet, this whole time period suited him. He might seem perfectly proper, but something told Cassie there was a great deal more to Mr. Morgan than met the eye, a quality of manipulation, or even deviousness, lurking just below the surface.

The house—what he permitted her to see of it—appeared large and lavish, as most any house in posh Belgravia would be. As they passed exquisitely upholstered damask sofas, carved cherry and rosewood tables and enough fine bone-china figurines to fill a shop, Cassie's muddled mind recalled what Morgan had said earlier. *Reverse the temporal flow.*

If she allowed herself to believe him just for a minute, it sounded as though he intended to send her back unharmed to her own time. A time in which she'd seen him staring dispassionately at a dead woman.

Fighting a ripple of fear, Cassie regarded his elegantly clad back. Could Morgan be the murderer? While the thought sent an icy chill up her spine, another calmer part of her said *no* with complete conviction. Still, she'd been wrong about people before.

With a sigh, she reached out and gave his coat a cautious tug.

"Yes?" He didn't stop or look back. His eyes continued to prowl the broad corridor.

"What were you doing in the twentieth century?"

"Hunting." He motioned with his hand behind him for her to stay close.

"Hunting women?" Cassie asked warily.

He glanced back, mildly irritated. "No, a homicidal maniac I call Jack."

Another chill crawled along her spine. "As in Jack the Ripper? But that's ridiculous—those murders occurred in the 1880s!" She swallowed the lump of inexplicable terror in her throat.

"No less ridiculous than your traveling back in time. Think about it, Cassie. If you can do it, *he* can do it. And does." Without waiting for her to comment, he led her up a set of broad, winding stairs to the second floor.

"Aren't there any back staircases?" she whispered.

"Several, but they're always jammed with servants. This is the least traveled route."

"Typical eighteenth-century indulgence," she noted, looking around at the family portraits.

He glanced back again. "So, you believe, then?"

"No—Yes. Well, maybe. Let's just say my dreams aren't usually this vivid. What are you, anyway—some kind of cosmic cop?"

"Be quiet."

"I am being quiet."

"For a Scot," he said under his breath.

"Look, Mr. Morgan—"

His hand clamped over her mouth so quickly that she had no chance to elude it. Hauling her up against his chest in the shelter of a lengthy second-story shadow, he gave her a shake. "I said, shut up. This isn't a game, Cassie. I'm not a cosmic cop. I'm a butler in a very large, very wealthy London household. That's my cover in this century. It's a good cover and one I've worked hard to establish. This happens to be Jack's favorite point in time, his home away from home, if you like. I know he's here. What I don't know is his identity. I also don't know whether he's planning to go on an all-out killing spree, or if this is just another of his—"

"Morgan, is that you?" A frail elderly voice drifted out of a nearby bedroom. "Stop for a minute, will you?"

Morgan released Cassie instantly, tugging on his waistcoat as a tiny female form appeared in the doorway. "Certainly, Lady Mary," he said with such charm that Cassie was left speechless. She'd never seen anyone change moods so quickly in her life.

The woman's keen gray gaze fixed on her bemused face. Immediately Morgan set a hand on her back, urging her forward. "Say good afternoon to Lady Mary, Cassie," he told her with a practiced smile that didn't look forced but had to be.

"Good afternoon, Lady Mary," she obliged, wondering if she was supposed to curtsy.

The old woman hobbled into the hall with the aid of a silver-tipped cane. A dark blue satin robe covered her bony frame. She couldn't have been more than five feet tall or weighed more than eighty-five pounds. A white wig cleverly interlaced with jewels and feathers sat regally atop her head. Her powdery face was thin and creased with a webwork of fine lines, but her eyes were as bright as those of a child.

"You wear strange clothes, girl," she observed. Cassie thought she sounded vaguely amused. "Are you a friend of Morgan's?"

Odd question. And since it had been directed at her, Cassie knew it was up to her to respond.

"Not really," she said slowly, with a quick glance at his impassive features.

Folding his hands in front of him, Morgan took over. "Mrs. Dickson found her," he explained smoothly. "In the cellar, hiding from the cold. She's just arrived from the colonies and has no place to stay. I thought we might put her up for the night."

Lady Mary hobbled closer. "Very pretty," she said, peering into Cassie's face. "And clean. Schooled, too, by the sound of her. Can you read, girl?"

"Yes, ma'am."

"And write?"

"Very well, ma'am."

"Good." The old woman gave her cane a satisfied thump. "Then you shall be my new personal maid."

"Ma'am?" Lady Mary's remark startled Cassie, but it was Morgan who reacted.

"Do you think that's wise?" he asked.

"I may be old, Morgan, but I'm not daft, not yet. What's your full name, girl?"

"Cassie Lachlin."

"Scottish?"

Cassie tensed defensively. "Of Scottish descent. I was born in America."

"Then you'll have plenty of spirit." The old woman waved her cane. "Go upstairs immediately and change out of those wretched clothes. Then come straight back here. I'll need you to help me dress for the party. Morgan, I want you to talk to Gerald for me. Tell him to stop sending for Dr. Peach every time I feel a little tired. First, though, I think you should show young Cassie here her room."

"Oh, damn," Cassie heard Morgan say under his breath. However, the smile he bestowed on Lady Mary held no trace of annoyance. "As you wish," he said with a small bow.

"None of your tricks, either," she warned, her gray eyes sparkling. "I don't want to hear that my new maid has suddenly been taken ill."

"Certainly not, ma'am."

"And don't you maneuver her into leaving on her own, either." She turned to Cassie. "He's very cunning, our Morgan, and charming when he wants to be. He fools my grandson and all of our friends, but he doesn't fool me. Do you, Morgan?" she said in amusement.

"No, ma'am," he agreed with a smile and another correct bow. "If you'll excuse us, I'll take Cassie upstairs and instruct her in her new duties."

The old woman gave them an imperious nod, and with exaggerated politeness, Morgan gestured Cassie forward.

In spite of everything, she couldn't resist a grin when they were out of earshot. "*Cunning,* Morgan?"

He slid her a dangerous sideways look. "When necessary."

"Bull," she said eloquently, though the look disturbed her. "You strike me as a man whose middle name is cunning."

"Yes, well, it's going to take more than cunning to get me out of this mess."

"I knew it," she said, battling her mounting uneasiness with disdain. "You're completely self-centered, aren't you? You're not after a homicidal fiend—you're out for glory. What do you do? Chase this Jack person through time?"

"Yes."

She hadn't expected the simple answer. "What?"

"I chase him through time." Morgan nudged her toward another, narrower staircase. "Up here."

Cassie stared at the polished steps, feeling overwhelmed suddenly. It was real, all of it. She wasn't going to wake up in bed; she knew that as surely as she knew her own name.

Panic pressed in on her. More things were possible than all the scientists on twentieth-century earth could envision. One only had to think about life in the 1790s to understand that. Who in that day and age would have believed that people would fly to the moon or make movies or be able to flick a few switches and wrap themselves in a cocoon of light, heat and loud rock music?

Her feet dragged as she mounted the stairs. Personal maid to an eighteenth-century aristocrat—what did that entail? How long would she have to stay? And how long, for that matter, had Morgan been here? Longer than her, obviously, which meant there was more to time travel than blundering through a door. She'd stepped into the light only seconds after him. Could seconds in a time corridor be translated to weeks of real time?

They stopped before a low plank door. Cassie began to shiver as Morgan looked covertly around the corridor.

Her head spun with the infinite possibilities. "I don't think I can pull this off," she heard herself murmur.

"Yes, you can," Morgan said, ushering her inside. "You have to."

"Couldn't you reverse the temporal field now and send me home?"

"Flow," he corrected. "And the answer is no, it's not a simple process. Now keep quiet and let me think."

"Just loaded with compassion, aren't you?" Cassie muttered, though not loud enough for him to hear.

She closed her eyes, willing calm. In the end, his lack of sympathy would undoubtedly be to her advantage. It meant she would have to tough out the situation alone. In her experience that was usually the best way.

The room they entered contained an oak armoire, a table and two chairs—expensive-looking furniture, considering these were servants' quarters. A thick throw rug adorned the polished wood floor. The walls were white plaster crossed with rough dark timber—Tudor-style, if she wasn't mistaken.

"George III is king, isn't he?" Cassie asked, sinking onto the windowsill. Two sleighs she couldn't see jingled past below. There were no streetlights to break the encroaching darkness.

Morgan nodded, tapping his thumbnail against his lower teeth as he paced the room.

"Didn't he go mad?" she persisted. "Or won't he go mad soon? Or was that the Prince Regent? No, it must have been the king. Gas lights were introduced in Regency England, and that hasn't happened yet."

"Be quiet, Cassie," Morgan said, still pacing.

"And then there was the Scarlet Pimpernel," she continued. Somehow talking helped. "Except he wasn't real. Unfortunately, the French Revolution was very real, but I don't know much about what happened. Still, I don't suppose that matters, does it, because women aren't supposed to think in this time."

"Oh, shut up," Morgan snapped, which made Cassie's frayed temper flare and her fists clench.

"Look, Mr. Morgan, I realize that I'm the one who stepped into *your* time corridor, but I didn't do it on purpose. While time travel might be old hat to you, it's a shock to my system. You might give me five minutes to adjust before you go biting my head off."

There was no apology in his absorbed expression as he passed her. She wasn't even sure he'd heard her.

"How much do you know about this time?" he inquired at length.

"You mean customs, inventions, that sort of thing? Not a lot." Permitting herself one final moment of fear, Cassie focused on her predicament. "I'm a fast learner, though. And highly adaptable."

When he didn't respond, she slid from the sill. Still pacing, he almost bumped into her.

"Don't you think," she said as reasonably as she could, "that we should work together? Obviously you want to catch a murderer, and my being here is a problem you don't need. But since I am here, maybe I can help."

He stared at her, his brow furrowing in faint astonishment. "Help me? Why?"

She turned away, pressing her palms together, not entirely sure where the idea had come from, only that it was there now. "Because he killed a friend of mine. At least, I assume he did, since her death was the same as the one tonight—or whenever." Blocking the picture of Joelle's savaged body from her mind, she continued. "It couldn't hurt to let me help. I *am* a police photographer. I'm also very observant."

"No." Then, holding up a conciliatory hand, he said, "Look, it's a generous offer, but I work alone."

She'd expected that. It didn't deter her, but she was smart enough not to pursue the matter immediately. Once Cassie Lachlin got an idea in her head, there was no stopping her. She was a loyal and determined friend. Joelle hadn't deserved to die, no matter what anyone thought of her profession. If Cassie could help bring her murderer to justice, then she would in this time or any other.

Bartholomew arrived with an armload of clothes, fine satin and charmeuse, and petticoats stiffer than anything Cassie had ever worn.

"Can you manage?" Morgan asked, giving the bundle a cursory inspection. "Or shall I send the housekeeper, Mrs. Salton, to help you?"

"I can manage. I want my backpack, though."

"Certainly." He gave her a small bow—a mocking one, Cassie knew. "Be in the kitchen in ten minutes."

"I thought I was supposed to report to Lady Mary."

"Not until we get a few things straight." He bestowed a succinct and completely false smile on Bartholomew's silent form. "Let's leave Cassie alone to dress, shall we? I'm sure she can find her way down the rear staircase to the kitchen."

Cassie's fingers stroked the pale green fabric that would complement her hair and skin nicely. "He's coming to the party, isn't he?" she said. "That's why you're not sending me back tonight."

Bartholomew gave the butler a startled glance. "But how can she know..." he began.

Morgan nudged him forward. "Never mind how she knows, Bartholomew. Ten minutes," he told Cassie. "And avoid the other servants as much as possible."

"You didn't answer my question."

"No," he said, pausing in the doorway. "I didn't. Jack isn't your average twentieth-century homicidal maniac, Miss Lachlin. He's a ruthless, sadistic time traveler with the mind of a genius and the cunning of a fox."

"Rather like you, then."

Morgan's only response was a narrowed look from under his dark lashes, but it was enough to make Cassie's blood run cold. He knew what it was to kill, she could see it in his eyes, a glint of malice he made no attempt to hide.

"Ten minutes," he repeated, and Cassie shivered deeply as the door clicked shut behind him. What on earth had she gotten herself into?

JACK. HE LIKED the name. It wasn't his real name, of course, but then he'd never much liked his own.

Ah, well, he was home now, he reflected pleasurably, back where he belonged. He traveled all through time, but this was the world he preferred, eighteenth-century London. The elegance of this age appealed to him. Then again, so did the late 1800s, the period of his most notorious—and still unsolved—crimes. Still, it was all a facade really—barbarism thrived in any age, and that suited him just fine.

Home... A sigh fell from his lips as he stood and looked out over snowy London. What a picture postcard these streets made. Pre-Victorian, but lovely just the same.

Flames crackled in the fireplace to his right. He could see the orange tongues licking at the Yule log. Like a woman's fiery hair, he thought, and felt his stomach tighten in warning.

But he mustn't.... He didn't want to.... Not now, not here. And yet he already had, hadn't he? He'd killed not once but twice in the space of a fortnight.

He hadn't wanted to do it. This was where he lived. One should never kill where one lived. That was the beauty of time travel. When the craving overwhelmed him, he could go someplace else to satisfy it.

This time in both cases, the women had made him do it. They'd teased and laughed and flirted and run. It really hadn't been his fault they'd died. It never was. Sluts, painted whores—they were vipers, the lot of them. They should all be killed.

"But not here," he whispered out loud. "You know how close he is to learning your secret. And he's good, very good. Better than that old fool, Nathan Kroat."

Jack turned to regard his reflection in the mirror. Out there in time he could keep his pursuer off balance. Here, the man was established, just as Jack himself was. Oh, he might not be quite so firmly entrenched in society, but they knew the same people, and that was dangerous.

He would be at the party tonight, Jack knew. Watching. Eavesdropping. Being the perfect silent butler....

A slow, sly smile curved Jack's lips. Well, fine. So be it, then. The day he couldn't outwit another from his time was the day he would hang up his knife. And he had no intention whatsoever of doing that.

From a hidden drawer he drew out a box lined with red velvet. Inside lay his stiletto. Such a beautiful weapon. One slash and his victim's throat was ripped neatly open.

He touched the silvery blade. Not here, he reminded himself firmly. Go to another time if you must. She'll be there. She's everywhere. A whore is a whore, now and forever, no matter how she dresses.

Closing his eyes, Jack slid the stiletto inside his sleeve.

"I DON'T BELIEVE THIS!" Morgan exploded to Bartholomew out of sight behind the kitchen screen.

He paced like a caged animal on the far side of the table. Bartholomew knew better than to speak. Morgan, when cross or disturbed, was not the kindest Morgan in the world.

Tapping his thumb on his tooth in a habitual gesture, he switched directions. "God, what are we going to do? Lady Mary wants Cassie as her personal maid, and she doesn't know the first thing about eighteenth-century life."

"I could teach her," Bartholomew offered.

Morgan treated him to an ironic sideways glance. "And just what do you know about women, Bartholomew?"

"Not much, but I know this century. I've been in it all my life."

"Keep your voice down," Morgan snapped. "She's going to start in on equal rights and all that twentieth-century nonsense. I know the type. You're not equipped to deal with that. No one here is."

"I don't know, Mr. M. She seemed pretty smart to me."

Morgan gave his hand an impatient wave. "She is smart—that's the problem, isn't it? Smart and pretty and a bloody Scot to boot."

"I thought she was an American."

Morgan ignored Bartholomew's comment. He went back to tapping his tooth and pacing. "No, I've got to think of a way to get her back to her own time without making Lady Mary more suspicious than she already is, and without missing my chance to search for Jack tonight. He's already killed at least once in the week I've been back. I have a feeling it isn't going to stop there."

Bartholomew propped his grubby elbows on the table, ignoring Mrs. Dickson, who bellowed loudly behind him. "So, you do think he'll be at the party, then."

"Of course I do. This century is Jack's second home. For all I know it might even be his real home. He'd have friends, maybe even relatives, if he was born here. He'll be hard to catch, Bartholomew, that's for damn sure. He could be any one of half a dozen people I know, assuming I'm not wrong."

Which he seldom was, Bartholomew thought. Whatever it was Morgan did, and whoever he did it for, he was good at his job. Much better than his predecessor, Nathan Kroat, another *traveler* Bartholomew had known.

Bartholomew's involvement in this messy murder business had started as things often do by him being in the wrong place at the right time. Before his shocked eyes, old Mr. Kroat had stumbled out of nothing into a dirty West London alley.

"I'm too old for this kind of work," Kroat had croaked, falling into a shimmering heap at Bartholomew's feet. "Close the door for me, whoever you are."

Bartholomew had been terrified. There was no door in the alley, and in the old man's hand, a funny black box glowed.

Tentatively, he'd touched a shiny button on the box. At that moment, the light winked out and the strange shimmer surrounding Mr. Kroat vanished.

He'd stared, transfixed, for the longest time. Thankfully, Mr. Kroat had revived and stood, apparently uninjured. Thus had begun a bizarre two-month relationship of questions never answered and mood swings so abrupt they'd frightened Bartholomew into total submission.

He hadn't liked old Kroat. He most definitely had not been sorry to see him shimmer off again through his invisible door. He'd hoped it would end there, with Kroat dissolving back into the night from which he'd come, but of course it hadn't. Six months later, on Christmas Eve, Morgan had arrived and, acting on Kroat's advice, come looking for Bartholomew.

"I'm after a killer," Morgan had explained, which was more than old Kroat had ever done. "He's vicious, unprincipled and probably mad. I'll need your help to establish an identity in this time."

Three years had passed since Morgan had said that to him, three unpredictable years during which Morgan had popped through his invisible door seven times that Bartholomew was aware of. Where he went, Bartholomew didn't know—nor did he want to. It was enough for him to understand that Morgan's job involved time travel and a twisted sod named Jack who led everyone brave enough to follow on a merry chase indeed.

Morgan wasn't Jack's only pursuer, but he was the best, the only one who physically tracked his quarry. Morgan explained that the others did their hunting with devices called computers and laser probes and a dozen other machines Bartholomew couldn't pronounce, let alone comprehend.

It didn't matter. He'd never met those people. He never would. His loyalty was to Morgan, a riddle of a man with a perfectionist's attitude and an extraordinary and clever mind.

"Maybe Miss Cassie *can* help you," Bartholomew said now, as Morgan resumed his restless pacing. "She's awfully pretty. Jack would probably like her."

Morgan glared. "Are you suggesting I use her as bait?"

"Why not? If she'll let you, that is."

"Because, my faithful mushroom-brained assistant, that would be an incredibly dangerous thing to do. No." He rapped his knuckles lightly on the table. "We'll have to think of something else."

Mrs. Dickson clumped past the partition, a sour expression on her face. "What did you do with the little beggar, Mr. M.? Threw her out, I hope."

"Nope." Reaching for the coat he'd discarded moments before, Morgan pulled it on. He reminded Bartholomew of a cat the way he moved—and a rat the way he thought. "She is going to be Lady Mary's personal maid."

"That thieving bit of fluff, maid to Her Ladyship? You must be joking."

Morgan summoned a smile. "Unfortunately, I'm not." He glanced at the frost-coated window. "She's late," he said to Bartholomew. "I'll have to intercept her. Go upstairs and check the ballroom. Let me know if there's anything that hasn't been done."

"Right, you are, Mr. M." Bartholomew gave a quick salute and obediently left the kitchen. He felt sorry for Cassie, starting off like this on Morgan's bad side; she wouldn't last five minutes in this century if she stayed there. She wouldn't last much longer if Jack ever caught sight of her.

Bartholomew knew a few things about Jolly Jack. For one, he was anything but jolly. For another, he hated women—redheads in particular and pretty redheads most of all.

Bartholomew wasn't sure about Jack's apparent prostitute fetish. He *was* sure about Cassie Lachlin. She had lots of long red-brown hair; her skin was smooth and unfreckled, her eyes the color of rich, dark chocolate. She had a really good figure, if a bit on the tall side. Put together, those things made for a striking combination.

Jack would notice her, all right, Bartholomew thought unhappily. And when he did, even clever Mr. Morgan might not be able to prevent the horror that would follow.

Chapter Three

"So who is she, Morgan? And what was she doing in our cellar?" Sir Gerald Peregrine rang for Morgan before he could locate Cassie. Even a phony butler knew where his duty lay.

"She was apparently taking refuge from the storm, sir," Morgan told the man who was only slightly younger than his own thirty-five years. He adjusted Sir Gerald's green velvet coat from behind.

Sir Gerald, vain to the point of conceit, surveyed himself in the cheval glass. "Spot there, Morgan." He pointed to his shoulder. "I heard from one of the maids that she was pretty."

Unruffled, Morgan wiped at the speck. "She is, sir. Very pretty."

"Educated?"

"It would seem so, sir."

"And a redhead." Sir Gerald licked his lips. "Ah, I love redheads."

"And blondes and brunettes," Morgan added, tidying his employer's cravat and white wig.

Sir Gerald smiled. "You know me too well, Morgan."

"Yes, sir."

Bored with the ritual of dressing, Sir Gerald turned to look out the window. The snow fell heavier now than before. "So what *is* she like? The staff's positively buzzing. I hear she gave Mrs. Dickson a damned good tongue-lashing, or tried to."

Morgan walked over to the sitting-room table and poured a glass of red wine. "I believe the report of her discovery has been slightly exaggerated, sir. She's just a girl from America." His composure intact, he handed Sir Gerald the glass. "I don't see her staying with us for very long."

"Long enough for me to meet her, I hope. Most of the women around here are about as interesting as a pair of old socks." Sir Gerald spread long, expressive fingers. He was a tall man with narrow, handsome features, pale brown hair under his wig and the same sparkling blue eyes as his grandmother. Fortunately for Morgan, he didn't possess her shrewd mind. "Some new blood would be just the thing to liven up the holiday season."

Morgan glanced over but said nothing.

"What time is it, Morgan?" Sir Gerald asked, too lazy to look at the mantel clock.

"Almost six-thirty, sir."

"Good, so there's no rush then." He stretched out on a blue satin chaise and reached for the *Times*. "Let's see what Julian Stockwell has to say about that new parliamentary committee."

Morgan stood to one side, hands folded in front of him. "He's not impressed, sir."

"Well I'm not, either, actually."

"And why is that?"

Sir Gerald flapped an indifferent hand. "Well, it's all rather pointless, isn't it? A committee to investigate violence—what good will that do?"

"Perhaps none, sir, but—"

"I mean, it isn't as if the peasants are about to revolt or anything. Good Lord, this isn't France. Anyway, it wasn't a peasant who butchered poor Baroness Roth—or Abigail Dexter Booth, for that matter."

"What?" Morgan's head came sharply up. He hadn't heard about the second woman.

"Abigail," Sir Gerald repeated. "Murdered a fortnight ago. Oh, that's right, you weren't about then, were you? Well, it was all kept very hush-hush. Word around town is that she'd been spending a great deal of time in Sir Patrick Welland's bed. Not that any of us care, but Sir Patrick's father is a pious old fool. Doesn't want his son sleeping with a married woman. Of course, it doesn't help that Sir Patrick was made the head of the parliamentary violence committee ten days before Abigail died. Still, I don't think anyone suspects him of killing her, not even her husband, so his committee involvement probably isn't relevant."

"Just ironic," Morgan said with a polite smile.

"Well, yes, it is that. The whole thing's a damned shame, if you ask me. Baroness Roth was a beauty, and you know yourself that Abigail possessed certain charms." With another dismissing wave, Sir Gerald drained his wineglass. "Oh, well, forget I mentioned the whole grisly business, Morgan, for old Lord Welland's sake, if not for Patrick's. Bloody loud-mouthed barbarian. Flogs his servants regularly, I'm told. And this from a man who's looking into violence on the streets."

Morgan poured a fresh glass of wine. "You're a pacifist ahead of your time, sir," he said with a measure of sarcasm he knew would be lost on his employer.

It was. Sir Gerald beamed at him. "Thank you, Morgan. Now go and check my grandmother, will you? Then come back and tell me what Dr. Peach has to say."

Morgan bowed. "Certainly, sir."

"She's too bloody old to be hosting parties. Her heart won't take it much longer."

Her heart was perfectly fine, Morgan knew. He also knew Sir Gerald. "Then, perhaps, sir, you shouldn't fight her so hard."

Sir Gerald stared blankly. "What?"

Morgan refrained from rolling his eyes and tried again. "If she wants to enjoy herself, maybe you should let her. After all, sir, you are her only heir."

Sir Gerald's mouth dropped open, then quickly snapped shut again. "That's right, I am." He said it as if only now realizing the fact. "Good Lord, and I've been coddling her all this time." A greedy light entered his eyes. He made an impatient motion. "For heaven's sake, Morgan, don't just stand there—go and get rid of Dr. Peach. I'm sure Grandmother doesn't want that old quack cluttering up her sitting room on the night of her annual Christmas party."

"Of course not, sir. Will you be needing anything else?"

Greed turned to lechery in Sir Gerald's blue eyes. "You might send up that new girl."

Morgan bowed again. "If at all possible, sir," he agreed pleasantly. "However, Lady Mary will undoubtedly have other plans for her tonight."

"Oh well, I'm sure there'll be other willing females at the party."

It was unfortunate, Morgan reflected as he exited the room, that one of those willing females would not be the wealthy Abigail Dexter Booth.

Apart from the obvious, Morgan didn't like the implications of his latest discovery. Abigail's death meant that Jack must have emerged from his time corridor at least two weeks ahead of him. That shouldn't have happened. Unless...

Closing his eyes, Morgan groaned silently. Oh God, no, not that. A malfunction in the time circuits was absolutely the last problem he needed right now. For one thing, it would seriously hamper his departure if Jack decided to take off to another time. For another, he had an uninvited guest who needed to be disposed of as quickly as possible.

Things were not going well today, he decided, tapping his tooth with his thumbnail as he headed for Lady Mary's suite of rooms. If he wasn't careful, Jack would kill again right under his nose.

CASSIE DIDN'T QUITE make it to the kitchen. A cockney scullery maid with straw for hair walked in on her while she was struggling with a row of impossible hooks to announce that Lady Mary expected her in her suite immediately.

"It's like slavery," Cassie muttered, adjusting her petticoats.

The woman eyed her up and down. "There are worse places to work, ducks. Lady Mary's a peach and Sir Gerald's too dense to know what's going on. Mirrors, wine and women are all he cares about."

Unbraiding her thick, curling hair, Cassie shoved the sides up under a white floppy-brimmed mobcap. "So who deals with the staff?"

"Mr. Morgan, of course. Or Mrs. Salton," she added with a disdainful sniff. "You won't like her much. She's an old prude. Strict, and a mean hand with a leather strap."

"Whereas Mr. Morgan's an absolute doll."

"He has a nice bum."

"I hadn't noticed." Cassie started out.

"Wouldn't do you any good if you had," the woman told her, making room. "Mr. M. only does it with ladies." She drew the last word out in an Eliza Doolittle drawl. "Bit o advice. Don't waste your time on tears around Morgan. I won't work. Lady Willam from Windsor can tell you first hand."

"Yes, well, I wasn't planning to use tears on anyone in this centu—house," Cassie substituted swiftly. "Uh, can get to Lady Mary's room down this other staircase?"

The woman nodded, and Cassie left. Unsure what to make of her new information about Morgan, she decided to make nothing of it. She concentrated instead on her sur roundings, moving about in clothing that must have weighed a quarter of a ton.

She'd forgone the corset, praying the waist buttons would fasten without it. She'd needed the small bustle to make he skirt billow properly, and a fichu about her shoulders and collarbone to hide any cleavage. She liked the flounced sleeves but not the restrictive fit.

When she reached the second floor, Cassie turned her at tention to the furnishings. Except for the bedrooms up stairs, the house was Georgian in design, graceful and no unfamiliar. Only the newness of everything felt strange to her. The furniture, primarily Chippendale and Hepple white, though lovely to look at, was not particularly com fortable to sit on. No matter, she could endure anything i she put her mind to it.

She was going to stay. She'd decided that upstairs. Mor gan didn't know it yet, and wouldn't be happy when h found out, but she felt confident she could convince him Not with tears, but through the use of simple logic. She had a certain amount of police training, certainly more than th police of this time. She also had a knack for figuring thing out. She could be aggravatingly observant when she wanted to be.

She could have told that scullery maid a few things about Mr. High-handed Morgan, things the woman probably hadn't noticed. True, he did have a very nice backside. He also had nice hands, a sinewy build and absolutely gorgeous hair. But it was his face that intrigued Cassie. He possessed an incredibly expressive mouth, and eyes that could convey a message without him speaking a single word.

His mannerisms were flawless. He *was* the quintessential eighteenth-century butler. But she had a feeling that he was in control of more things here than anyone around him could begin to imagine.

Cassie deliberately stopped there. She'd promised herself not to think about him, and it was a promise she intended to keep. At least for now.

Her knock on Lady Mary's door was rewarded with a husky, "Enter."

The woman seated near the fire like a finishing-school graduate was not Lady Mary, and this was obviously not Lady Mary's bedroom.

"Good evening, ma'am," Cassie said politely. "I'm Lady Mary's new maid. I understood she wanted to see me."

"Cassie, isn't it?" The woman smiled. "Lady Mary's inside with Dr. Peach. They won't be long. Lady Mary despises doctors."

Cassie thought of eighteenth-century medical techniques and shuddered. "I don't blame her."

The woman stood with a flourish. She was a beautiful creature, as tall as Cassie and elegant as the age demanded. Her long red hair, more of an orangy shade than Cassie's, hung in ringlets to her shoulders. She wore a lavender silk dress and a hat with flowers tilted stylishly forward from the back.

"I'm Desirée Deveau," she said, not extending her gloved hand. Of course, she wouldn't shake hands with a servant. "I'm a friend of Lady Mary's."

She had the kind of voice men called sultry, velvet with a whiskey edge.

But there was another edge, a tinge of uneasiness that had been present in her expression even as Cassie entered the room.

"Is anything wrong with Lady Mary?" Cassie inquired carefully.

Desirée's penciled brows went up. Her makeup was artful, dramatic and undoubtedly lead-based. Cassie tried not to think of what problems might arise from that in a few years.

"She's fine as far as I know. Healthy as a horse, if you want my opinion. But you didn't hear me say that, of course."

"Of course," Cassie agreed, grinning.

The sparkle that had appeared in Desirée's eyes vanished. "I do wish that doctor would hurry," she said, fidgeting slightly. "I want to ask him about the baroness. You've heard about her, haven't you?"

"I'm not..." Cassie searched for the right words, not wanting to blunder. "Which baroness is this, my lady?"

"Mrs. Deveau, please," Desirée said, reseating herself on an embroidered ivory settee. "I'm not an aristocrat, just a widow who used to be an actress and wishes she were again."

"Then, why aren't you?" Cassie asked.

A frown touched Desirée's full lips. "What are you suggesting?"

"Nothing improper. You just seem..." She hesitated. "Well, I'd say melancholy, but I have a feeling there's more to it than that. Something to do with the baroness, maybe?"

"Ah, yes." The frown became a deep release of breath. "Baroness Margaret Roth. She was a fond acquaintance of mine. So was Abigail."

"Who?"

"Never mind." Desirée linked her fingers together. "It's the death, you see. The violence." She shook her head. "He's a monster. There's nothing else he can be."

Cassie went to her knees beside the woman. "Who's a monster, Mrs. Deveau?"

"The man who killed them, of course." Desirée's voice dropped as her agitation mounted. "There's a rumor around town that he'll always choose women who have red hair. They say he wrote a letter to the police. In it he promised he would prey upon women with fire in their hair. The baroness had auburn hair. Abigail, whom I'm not supposed to talk about, had red-blond hair. As you see, my hair is also quite red. So is yours, I fear."

Swallowing the nervous lump that crept into her throat, Cassie reminded herself that Joelle's hair had been black. Well, more or less. She'd put several bright red streaks in it a few months ago. "Surely that's just a rumor," she maintained. "About the red hair, I mean."

"Possibly." Desirée sighed, pressing her fingers to her forehead. "Yes, possibly it is. I want to believe that, Cassie. It's just that I have a dreadful feeling he's one of us."

"You mean an aristocrat?"

"Not necessarily, but certainly in favor with them. The baroness was extremely—how can I put it?"

"Status conscious?"

Desirée smiled. The sparkle returned briefly to her dark eyes. "You're being polite. Let's be honest and call her selective."

"Let's be blunt and call her a snob."

Lady Mary's entrance surprised both women. She was followed by a large, heavyset man in an ill-fitting white wig and black coat. He carried a black bag and a walking stick and was currently in the process of mopping his perspiring face with an enormous handkerchief.

"Do go on, Desirée," Lady Mary instructed. "It's so seldom I have a chance to discuss current affairs. Half of London's convinced my heart will burst from the strain of simply breathing."

"Well, there is something to that," the doctor began, but Lady Mary cut him off with a sharp,

"Do shut up, Samuel. I allowed you to poke and prod me for thirty minutes. The least you can do is permit me to indulge in a little harmless speculation. This is my new maid, by the way—Cassandra Lachlin, from America. Cassie, Dr. Samuel Peach. Ring for Morgan, girl, to show the good doctor out. It's the cord next to the fireplace." She settled herself on the divan beside Desirée. "Now, please do continue, my dear. What were you saying about the late Baroness Roth?"

Desirée's initial amusement faded. She plucked at a long ringlet. "I was about to tell Cassie why I don't think the baroness would have gotten into a carriage with a man she didn't know. It would have been against her nature to consort with a stranger."

"Is that how it happened?" Cassie pulled the tasseled cord. She'd already deduced that the murderer they were discussing must be Jack, hard at work it seemed in yet another century. His home away from home, if she'd heard Morgan correctly. "Did someone actually see the baroness get into a carriage before she was killed?"

"It was a cab," Dr. Peach clarified. He scratched his stubby nose. "The driver's not been seen since."

"And doubtless never will be again," Lady Mary said.

"Could the driver have killed her?" Cassie asked.

Desirée shook her head. "There was blood on the upper seat as well as on the horses' reins. And two men admitted to having witnessed a struggle between the driver and his fare. The driver was knocked out. It was the other man who whisked the cab off into the night."

"With Baroness Roth inside," Lady Mary finished.

"Either unconscious or already dead," Cassie murmured, resisting the urge to pace. Personally, she tended to believe the *unconscious* theory. The Jack she knew was too vicious to kill his victims without torturing them first.

The doctor patted his fat belly. In his powdered wig he bore a strong resemblance to Santa Claus, minus the beard and red suit, of course. "No one knows precisely what the baroness's condition was at that point," he said. "But she was certainly in a ghastly state when her body was discovered by London Bridge the next morning. Be that as it may, however..." He straightened, easing his loose wig back with a pudgy finger. "I must insist that this kind of talk be stopped." He turned at the sound of a brief knock. "Ah, good. There you are, Morgan. Be a good chap and put a halt to this conversation, will you?"

Morgan entered the room, his response as deceptively understated as his arrival. "And what conversation is this, Doctor?"

Desirée's eyes brightened at the sight of him. "We were talking about Baroness Roth."

Cassie noticed a hint of flirtatiousness in the way the woman shifted her body, and felt her muscles tighten. But why on earth should she feel proprietorial about a time-traveling butler with an attitude?

Giving herself a shake, she returned her attention to the gathering.

"Murder is scarcely a topic for women to be discussing," the doctor insisted.

His pompous position got Cassie's full attention. "Don't be ridiculous." She assumed a defiant stand in front of him. "Why shouldn't women discuss murder? Especially when it seems the fiend who's committing them preys on women."

"Them?" The doctor knit his brow. "There's been more than one death?"

He was asking Morgan, but all Morgan did was spread his fingers. "Not that I know of, sir. I believe the point Cassie is trying to make is that whoever killed the baroness very likely won't stop there."

The doctor's cheeks mottled. "Rubbish," he declared. "For all we know, the man might have held a grudge against her."

"Possibly, sir," Morgan agreed with a warning look at Cassie, who longed to make a few more of her views known. "Nevertheless, she is dead—"

"And it's getting very late." Standing, Desirée deftly changed the subject. The tremulous edge was gone, supplanted by a note of regret. "I so wish I could be at your party this evening, Lady Mary, but my aunt and uncle will only be in London for one night. They don't enjoy socializing, and it wouldn't be proper for me to abandon them. Besides," she shivered, "as I recall, Baroness Roth was murdered after a party."

Lady Mary accepted the apology graciously, but added a forthright, "The baroness was a fool as well as a snob, Desirée. She shouldn't have gotten into a cab with anyone except her husband."

"Are you sure it wasn't her husband in the cab?" Cassie couldn't resist inquiring.

"Baron Roth was in France," Morgan informed her from the door. "This way, Doctor," he said with a small bow for his charge.

The smile Lady Mary bestowed on him bordered on affectionate. Her words, however, chilled Cassie's blood.

"It would seem," she said, setting her small, bony hands atop her cane, "that you can't trust anyone these days, not even your friends. The baroness exited her own carriage in favor of a cab, which suggests to me that she knew the occupant well. And who Baroness Roth knew, I also know. Which is to say, I fear, that whoever killed her is a person of my acquaintance. A person who in all likelihood will be present in my home this evening."

DESIRÉE CRINGED inwardly as her coach and pair glided through the Belgravia streets toward her town house. Home was a familiar and comfortable place, yet probably less of a haven than she liked to believe.

She knew who he was; she'd figured it out. And what's more, he knew she knew, or at least she assumed he did. He hadn't actually confronted her yet.

Maybe he never would. He was a twisted, savage man, not what she would call normal in any sense of the word. She'd seen him murder the baroness, had watched the horror unfold through a haze of nausea and terror. But not disbelief. If anyone had asked who in her circle of acquaintances was capable of such violence and depravity, she would have singled him out long before her eyes actually beheld the grisly scene. Now she didn't dare speak of it.

The horses' hooves crunched on the freezing snow that was a rarity in London, even in December. The air smelled like winter, cold and crisp; it should have been invigorating. Instead, she pictured herself lying on a bed of newly fallen snow in a pool of her own blood.

"No!" The fierce denial burst from her lips. Her breath formed a cloud around her. "I won't let him kill me. I'll..."

What? Kill him first? She rubbed her temple where it throbbed. Could she do that? Did she have the strength, or would he kill her first?

She couldn't go to the police. There would be no sanctuary there. They were a feeble, disorganized lot at best, and he was a man well thought of about London. He had many friends, more powerful ones than she did, certainly. Loyalty was an odd thing, too. Who could she really trust with her secret?

Lady Mary, perhaps, but she was an old woman. She had enough burdens to bear. She didn't need another one.

Morgan then? Desirée's heart lifted a fraction at that thought. Now there was a strong ally, and a sexy one to boot.

Anthony Lazarus Morgan, the perfect butler. Everybody wanted him—the men to run their households, their wives to get him into bed. He was the current conquest of choice. It was said that no one had ever touched Morgan's emotions. That made him a challenge. But which lady in London would get to his heart first?

Desirée had made a few fleeting attempts to attract his attention, but nothing serious, and heaven knew, now was not the time. Still, he was smart and reasonable and probably practical. For money he might be willing to help her.

There was also that new maid of Lady Mary's, Cassie Lachlin. She'd seemed nice, smart and strong—and opinionated. Desirée knew of one man, at least, who would hate her for that trait.

"Oh, I don't know what to do." Sighing, Desirée leaned back in her padded seat. A butler and two women against a fiendish genius who'd managed to deceive almost everyone around him into thinking he was, if not a great man, at least a respectable one.

The baroness had believed, and look what had happened to her. On the other hand, Abigail had sensed something grotesque in the man. Whether she'd told him so or not, Desirée couldn't say, but one way or another, Abigail was dead, butchered by a demon straight from hell.

"I won't wait around for you to kill me," she whispered aloud. "I can do things to make sure you get caught."

Chapter Four

"No," Morgan said flatly a full two hours into the party. "You're going back tomorrow."

Cassie opened her mouth to argue, but was forestalled by Mrs. Dickson, who stomped past the kitchen partition with a large wooden spoon in her hand.

"No cheek, girl!" she barked, although she couldn't have heard the conversation.

"I wasn't—"

"Be quiet."

Cassie gritted her teeth. Bartholomew gave her a sympathetic look while Morgan shepherded the disagreeable woman back to her smoking fireplace.

"He has a knack with the staff," Bartholomew said, opening a dusty case of port.

"So I've noticed." Cassie cupped her chin in her hands, thoroughly frustrated. "People must be easy marks in this century."

"Beg pardon?"

"Nothing." As she watched Morgan deal with Mrs. Dickson, she thought back over the ninety minutes she'd spent helping Lady Mary dress. Well, fumbling around at first, but she'd caught on soon enough.

"I favor wigs," the old woman had confided. "Not high wigs, mind you—too many vermin nest in those."

"Really?" Cassie stared at the powdered one in her hands, wondering if it was infested. "I suppose that's still—I mean, that would be a problem."

"Your bath is ready, ma'am," a trio of maids announced from a connecting room.

"Splendid." Lady Mary rose unassisted, smiling at Cassie's uncertain expression in the mirror. "Does it surprise you that we bathe in this house?" she asked.

"Yes— No." Cassie scooped up a bottle of rose water.

The old woman studied her. "Well, now that is odd, because it appalls many of our friends. Most unhealthy, you know."

"Bathing?" Even knowing how it had been in that era, Cassie didn't understand how such an idea could persist. "So people actually prefer to be dirty?"

Eyes gleaming, Lady Mary hobbled across the floor. "Many do," she said, then glanced back. "Is it different in America?"

"Very different," Cassie lied.

"Then I think Morgan must have been to America at some point."

"Ah." Comprehension finally dawned. "So this bent for cleanliness was his idea. I should have guessed."

"Morgan has many unique ideas."

"I don't doubt it."

"He's really quite charming when you get to know him."

"Like a snake," Cassie murmured. Then she smiled and offered an amiable, "He certainly seems efficient."

"We hired him without references. That's unheard of in London...."

Lady Mary had continued her monologue for a full thirty minutes, and always with that spark of amusement in her gray eyes. It made Cassie wonder just how much the old woman either knew or suspected about her butler.

She met Sir Gerald an hour later. He appeared at the door in a flashy green velvet coat and off-white silk trousers, smiled broadly in the direction of Cassie's breasts and said without preface, "Bloody Morgan must be made of stone."

"Not tonight, Gerald," Lady Mary reproached a trifle sharply. "Cassie, you may leave. Tell Morgan I said you should report to him rather than to Mrs. Salton."

Her grandson's grin widened. "Better yet, you can report to my bed—"

"Gerald!"

He relented and obediently kissed her powdered cheek.

Cassie wasn't sure she cared for the gleam in Sir Gerald's eyes, but it was probably typical of the time. Aristocrats needed to employ manners only with their peers.

"Right." Morgan returned and Cassie reluctantly dragged her thoughts back to the present. "Get that port out," he ordered Bartholomew. "Then help Mrs. Dickson load those glass trays. Go on."

"Right you are, Mr. M."

Cassie sighed, bored with sitting still. "I don't suppose you'll let me help."

The tolerant look he sent her contained the same measured edge of danger she'd glimpsed before. "No."

"Why not?"

"It isn't your place."

He was arranging glasses on a silver tray. "I want my backpack," she said, just to be difficult.

"I'll have Bartholomew bring it up later."

He had wonderful hands, Cassie noted again. And his hair was entirely his own. No wigs for this man.

Catching herself, she ceased her admiration and focused on the matter at hand. "Desirée's afraid," she revealed with deliberate bluntness.

He ignored her challenging tone. Raising his head, he frowned at her. "What do you mean, *afraid?*"

"She says the word on the street is that Jack has a penchant for redheads. I gather he wrote a letter to the police after he killed Baroness Roth admitting as much. Desirée's worried that Jack is in favor with many of the London aristocracy and that he'll eventually set his sights on her."

"I imagine he will."

Exasperated, Cassie glared at him. "Do you know the meaning of the word *compassion* at all, Morgan, or doesn't it exist in your futuristic vocabulary?"

He returned her stare with a dispassionate one of his own. "For someone who shouldn't be here, you're full of assumptions and accusations. What you see in me is all there is."

A lie, Cassie suspected, but she let him continue.

He did so, bracing his hands on the table and leaning forward with just a hint of impatience visible in his otherwise placid face. "You're going back, Cassie. Accept it. I haven't got the time or the inclination to deal with a nosy twentieth-century female. Honest to God, your kind never let up." He made an irritated gesture with his arm. "You'd be dead in five minutes if I let you run around loose." He aimed a finger at her face. "Now, I want you to eat some supper and wait for me here. I have to go upstairs and I don't want to have to worry about what trouble you might be getting into while I'm gone."

She liked his mouth, Cassie decided. Especially when he was angry or crabby, or whatever you called this controlled display of temper. Sometimes full-lipped, sometimes not, it varied with his mood and the set of his features. She'd met a lot of men before, but never one quite like Morgan.

She didn't offer a single protest to his orders. She even refrained from glowering at him as he left. But if he thought he was accomplishing a damned thing by telling her to mind her own business, he was sorely mistaken. Her curiosity mounted steadily as the jolt her mind had suffered wore off. Who was this strange man? What century did he come from? What exactly was his job? What would it be like to kiss him?

"Oh, no," she said out loud to the last question. "Not that, Cassie."

"Talking to yourself, miss?" Bartholomew returned with a stack of clean trays and a plate of meat and vegetables. "You really mustn't mind Mr. M. He has a temper and a sharp tongue, but only with people he trusts. So actually, you should be flattered. All that polite charm is just a clever fake. A means to an end, he calls it. Now, here you go. You eat this supper I've brought and start thinking about going home."

Cassie considered confiding in the little man, but decided against it. She sensed in him an unflinching loyalty to Morgan. Faced with a choice, he'd give her away in a minute.

To her surprise the supper was very good, if a little too nutritious for her taste. She had a stash of candy bars in her backpack along with a bag of Oreos; unfortunately they'd have to wait. Right now she wanted to explore.

Desirée thought Jack was in favor with the people upstairs. Morgan and Lady Mary seemed to agree. That meant he probably was here tonight. So all she had to do was figure out who the mad murderer was before Morgan shoved her back in the time corridor. And, she thought with a deep shudder, before Jack had a chance to notice her auburn hair.

"WHAT DO YOU MEAN, she's gone?" Morgan stared at Bartholomew with a blend of outrage and disbelief. "Weren't you watching her?"

"I tried to, sir, but she's fast and quiet."

"And a bloody idiot if she thinks she's going to get away from me. She's looking for Jack—you know that, don't you, Bartholomew? Honest to God, that woman's going to drive me crazy."

"I thought you were sending her back."

"I am, but I have to make the time calculations first. Here." Morgan shoved a case of wine across the table. "Take this upstairs and keep your eyes open. I'm going to look for her." He straightened his coat, shaking out the collar and, no doubt, a portion of his irritation. "I should have tied her up," he muttered. "Never get mixed up with a woman, Bartholomew. Especially not one like her. They don't listen to a bloody word you say."

Bartholomew sucked his cheeks in. "So you like her, then."

"Certainly not," Morgan snapped, rounding on him. "She's stubborn and completely unreasonable, and the sooner I can be rid of her the better."

"Yes, Mr. M."

Morgan shot him a dark look in parting. Bartholomew hadn't been able to keep the amusement out of his voice. He'd never seen anyone affect Mr. Morgan the way this new woman had. Maybe it would be nice if she stayed around for a while.

With a surreptitious look at the bustling staff, Bartholomew started for the small suite of rooms beyond the kitchen.

CASSIE HEARD THE SOUND of a full orchestra long before she reached the ground-floor ballroom. A minuet, if she wasn't mistaken.

She'd come up the back stairs and worked her way down a series of corridors from the rear of the house. It hadn't been difficult to get her bearings. The music grew louder with each corner she turned.

"Damned nuisance, really," a man's voice said, and hastily Cassie flattened herself against one of the paneled walls. "Half the time I can't even decipher my own notes. I wind up trying to recall a conversation I wasn't paying much attention to in the first place."

"In that case, I'd simply fill in the blanks from my imagination," a deeper, more booming voice replied. Both men sounded mildly intoxicated. And both were coming closer. Cassie inched down the wall.

"I can do that with most things," the first man agreed. "But not with this committee business. Sir Patrick doesn't like to be misquoted."

"Sir Patrick's an ass of the first order— Hello, what's this?"

Cassie froze as the men turned the corner. The one speaking was well over six feet tall, an uncommon height even for a twentieth-century male. Long, bright red hair flowed back from a broad forehead, falling well past his high collar. There were no deep curls as custom demanded, and unless she'd missed something, his long red beard was also outside the current dictates of fashion.

"Very nice," he said, his blue eyes glinting with appreciation. "There's a face for you, eh, Julian? How could words hope to describe that?"

His companion, a less ostentatious if no less daunting man, summoned a thin smile. "I'm a reporter, Procopius. I leave the poetry to Mr. Athelbert, thank you. What's your name, girl?"

Cassie was getting heartily sick of being called *girl*. "Cassie Lachlin," she said, lifting her chin. "Who are you?"

The tall, red-bearded man laughed out loud. His friend merely raised a dubious dark brow and said, "You're a servant here, I presume."

"I'm Lady Mary's personal maid." Although aware she'd made a large faux pas, Cassie refused to apologize. On the other hand, she was no fool. She relaxed her defiant stance. "I just started today."

"I see." He wasn't placated. "Well, in answer to your rather bold question, my name is Julian Stockwell."

"He's a reporter for the *Times,*" the man with the red beard confided. Reaching out, he caught up a strand of her hair. "Extraordinary," he murmured, while Cassie struggled not to pull away. "I'm Procopius Rowe," he added belatedly. "Member of Parliament from Hampstead."

"The most vocal M.P. in the Commons," Julian said with mild disdain.

He had dark, almost black hair, like the feathers of a raven, soft and sleek and worn in a single-length ponytail. No curls again, Cassie noticed, and no beard. His eyes, a vivid shade of blue, seemed to stare right through her. He was an exceptionally handsome man, narrow-featured though a good six or eight inches shorter than his companion. The word *beautiful* came to mind. However, Cassie doubted he would appreciate it.

But that was a side issue. Cassie's goal was to find Jack. She held still while Procopius continued to finger her hair.

"Scottish, I'll wager," he announced unexpectedly. He swayed a little but didn't stumble or release her.

Julian shook his head. "Wrong accent, my friend. Where do you come from, girl?"

Cassie forced a smile. "America, sir."

"You don't sound American."

Morgan wasn't the only one who understood the value of charm. She softened her smile. "You've been there, then?"

"Twice."

"How wonderful. You must be very worldly to have done that."

"Yes, well, I suppose I am." The suspicion in the reporter's slender features faded. "Come along, Procopius. Let's get on to our game of hazard before I get on to the story of my travels."

"It's a lengthy story," Procopius told Cassie with a wink. He still had hold of her hair. "Send us in some brandy, will you, love? There's a good... Ah, Morgan." He grinned past Cassie's shoulder. "Come to take your pretty robin back to her nest in the kitchen, have you?"

"Not at all, sir." Cassie could hear the practiced pleasantness in Morgan's voice. She had a feeling she didn't want to see his face. "Lady Mary's maid is Mrs. Salton's responsibility, not mine. However," he added, placing his hands lightly on her shoulders as Procopius, more drunk than she'd realized, stumbled toward her, "she does have certain duties to attend to before Lady Mary retires. Run along, Cassie," he told her, and there was no mistaking the order in his genial tone.

For once Cassie didn't object. "Yes, Mr. Morgan," she murmured, and with an apologetic smile at the red-haired M.P. eased her hair free.

"Don't forget—brandy first," he called after her. "We'll be in the library."

"In which case, I won't be," Cassie muttered once she was out of sight.

Since there was no point dwelling on the encounter, she forged a path down a new set of candle-lit corridors toward the ballroom.

Thick carpets muffled her footsteps. No one should be able to hear her coming. Of course, she wouldn't actually be able to join the party, but with luck she'd be able to do a little discreet eavesdropping.

She'd almost reached the grand entry hall when a shadow suddenly formed in front of her. Her head snapped up. For a horrible moment she thought it was Jack come to slash her throat, but this shadow's hands didn't clutch a knife. And as menacing as it appeared, it made no move to grab her.

"The kitchen's back that way, Cassie," Morgan said, blocking her path with his body.

She pressed a fist to her racing heart. "My God, Morgan," she said in a tight voice. "Don't do that. I thought you were Jack. Why aren't you still with those men?"

"You're lucky you aren't still with those men," he retorted, motioning her to turn around. "Rape is a common indulgence here, Cassie. Except it isn't called rape, so you're unlikely to find any justice as a victim."

"Look, I only want to see the party. Is that such a crime?"

His smile was a mere movement of lips. "Don't lie, Cassie. What you really want is to see Jack."

"Maybe I already have," she countered, watching his face in unintentional fascination. There must be a way to crack his butler's armor. "Those men didn't strike me as being above suspicion. Neither did Dr. Peach, for that matter. Or Sir Gerald."

"You've met Sir Gerald?"

"Unfortunately."

He took her by the arms. "Where?"

"In Lady Mary's room." She eyed him with growing mistrust and a deepening sense of confusion. "What's wrong with Sir Gerald?"

Morgan's expression told her nothing. "He likes women. That doesn't necessarily make him Jack," he added, forestalling the interruption. "It just makes him dangerous, especially to any female servants foolish enough to attract his attention."

"I didn't—" she began, but before she could continue Morgan was hauling her sideways, into a tiny alcove.

Cassie wasn't sure why they needed to hide, yet as unnerving as it was to be pressed against Morgan's firm body she remained silent. It wasn't until he slackened his grip on her mouth that she dared to wriggle away. "What's wrong?" she whispered.

He responded by pulling her back into his chest and setting his mouth close to her ear. "Be quiet."

The seconds crawled by. Cassie heard only the music from the party—and felt far too much of Morgan behind her. Finally her nerves couldn't take it anymore. "This is ridiculous," she said, giving her shoulders a yank. "I don't—"

It erupted out of nowhere, or maybe it lunged at her, she wasn't sure. But as she twisted out of Morgan's grasp someone hit her very hard.

Off balance, she stumbled backward, barely managing to catch herself on the lip of a wooden shelf. Stale breath poured over her from the depths of a thick shadow. She detected the low, eerie sound of laughter and saw a man's face emerge.

Except it looked more like the face of a corpse than a man. Its painted lips drew back in a leer, its eyes glittered in the sputtering candlelight. And then it launched itself at her again....

"THIS IS BLOODY WINE. I ordered cognac. What the hell is Morgan playing at tonight?"

A thoroughly intoxicated Sir Patrick Welland staggered through the ballroom door and into one of the serving boys. A loaded tray crashed to the carpet at Bartholomew's feet. Shoving the startled boy aside, Sir Patrick continued to bellow for Morgan.

"I say, old chap, what's the problem?" Sir Gerald emerged from the ballroom, followed by a lithely muscled man in lavish silk and lace whose chestnut brown hair was coming free of its ponytail.

"No problem, sir," Bartholomew answered while Sir Patrick plopped down onto a cushioned bench, grumbling drunkenly and flexing his white-gloved fingers.

Sir Gerald nudged his companion, a slightly effeminate actor who made London ladies swoon both on- and offstage. "Committee problems, I'll bet," he said out of the side of his mouth.

The actor, Christopher Crowley, grinned. "Sir Patrick does seem to be fighting a losing battle in that regard. As I recall, Morgan and Julian and I were staring at Baroness Roth's body long before Paddy here bothered to drag himself out of bed."

"Yes, well, Morgan's on top of almost everything around London," Sir Gerald acknowledged. Did he emphasize the word *almost?* Did he sound smug? Bartholomew wasn't good with nuances. Awkwardly efficient, he swept up the mess of broken crystal.

From his seat, Sir Patrick let out a snarl. He was a big man—not as tall as Procopius Rowe, or as flamboyant, but

Bartholomew wouldn't bet against him in a duel. Thick-chested and strong-limbed, he stood a good six feet tall. He had a large nose that suited his squarish face, curling brown hair and the kind of voice and bearing that commanded attention. At forty-eight years of age, he'd been in and out of His Majesty's army twice, with long stints abroad on both occasions. He liked to drink, had a particular fondness for young boys and married women, and enjoyed seeing his name in print. He also didn't give a damn that Baroness Roth was dead, despite his position on the parliamentary street-violence committee.

"What's going on out here?" Lady Mary emerged with dignified slowness from the ballroom and surveyed the broken glasses. "Lady Annabelle's asking for you, Christopher."

The actor made an unconcerned motion. "I'll get to her later. Let someone else entertain her for a while."

Lady Mary sighed. "Where's Morgan?"

"I was wondering that myself," Sir Gerald said.

Bartholomew continued to sweep up. "Problem with the staff, I believe, ma'am."

A leer parted Sir Gerald's pink mouth. "Problem with Grandmother's new maid, more likely. You should see this one, Chris. Bit skinny for my taste, but what a face she has, and tons of hair, bright as polished copper."

Lady Mary's lips compressed. "You mind your place with her, Gerald. You have your pick of women. This one's not for you. Bartholomew, go and fetch Morgan. I fear Sir Patrick may require a bed for the night."

"Yes, m'lady." He bowed clumsily.

"And when you've done that, fetch Mr. Crowley and myself a pair of hunting knives, two robes and a bottle of red wine," Sir Gerald added, his eyes sparkling.

Lady Mary's fingers tightened their grip on her cane. "What are you planning?" she asked, but he simply smiled at her.

"Nothing untoward, Grandmother. Party larks is all."

The old woman's eyes found Bartholomew's. "Fetch Morgan," she repeated.

And Bartholomew didn't think he imagined the quaver in her voice.

IT LOOKED LIKE A FACE with no blood in it, something cosmetically painted, made of wax or worse.

A short scream burst from Cassie's throat. She scrambled backward, her heart hammering in her chest, her mouth and throat dry.

From the shadow, long, skeletal fingers rose up and spread.

"I'm most dreadfully sorry," a man's low voice apologized. "I didn't mean to frighten. Morgan, is that you?"

"Yes, Mr. Athelbert, it is." He caught and steadied Cassie as he spoke. "Is the ballroom on fire, sir?"

"Not at all." The man, if you could call him a man, stepped into a pool of candlelight. Illuminated, he looked even more like a cadaver. Two bright spots of rouge shone in his cheekbones. His face was powdered white. "I became a snowflake for an instant," he explained theatrically. "Blown along by a gust of wind."

"Of course you did." Morgan's tone implied a lack of surprise and more than a few doubts about the man's mental state. "I assume you have a new poem in the works."

"I've titled it 'Blood Pudding.'" Bony white hands made a caption in the air. "In honor of the baroness. Both my late and lovely patron." His somber blue eyes shifted abruptly to Cassie's face. "Who's this?"

"I'm Lady Mary's personal maid," she said before Morgan could take over. "Tell me, do you often become a snowflake and run full tilt down darkened corridors, Mr. Athelbert?"

"Oh, no," he assured her quite sincerely. "I only do that when my creative half seizes control. It's an unpredictable thing, you understand, completely beyond my control. The way dreams are at night." His smile showed black-rimmed teeth and hollowed-out cheeks. "You'd make a fine snowflake, my girl. Red blood in the snow—the red being your hair, naturally. Perhaps Lady Mary will permit you to pose for me."

Pose for a poem? Wisely, Cassie confined her response to a dubious smile.

Spreading his arms, Athelbert appealed to Morgan. "Nearest water closet, please?"

"Down the corridor on the left, sir," Morgan said with a polite half bow.

Cassie watched as the man flew off, his dirty blond ponytail streaming along behind him. "What a ghoul," she said and glanced at Morgan's profile. "Is he always like that?"

"Most of the time."

"Sounds as if he's on something to me."

Morgan took her arm. "He is."

She didn't resist the pull he exerted. "And you're still looking for Jack?"

He arched a meaningful brow. "One brief encounter and you're convinced that Ignatious Athelbert is the man who murdered your friend?"

"Butchered her. And no, I'm not. But I'd certainly put him on the list and see what I could find out about him." Aware that he was leading her away from the ballroom, Cassie dug in her heels. "Oh, come on, Morgan," she pleaded. "Let me at least see what an eighteenth-century Christmas party looks like."

He paused, then released a heavy breath. "If I do, will you promise to behave yourself for the rest of the night?"

She grinned. "Of course."

He rolled his eyes. "Oh, God. All right, come on, then. We'll go around to the terrace. But whatever you do—" he held up a warning finger "—don't let anyone see you. Do you understand?"

Nodding, Cassie followed him. "There is one thing, though."

He glanced back, only half-interested. "And what's that?"

"It's about this Jack of yours—the man you believe is Jack the Ripper. You say he's a time traveler."

"Yes. . . ." Morgan drew the word out warily.

"In other words, he's changing the history I was taught in school. Is that right?"

"He could do. What's your point?"

"I'm not sure really. I guess what I want to know is, will what he's doing here be written up in twentieth-century history books when I get back, and if it is, will I have learned about it in history class like everyone else or will it be a separate and unique memory for me?"

Morgan sighed. "It's a complicated question, Cassie, but basically the answer is yes. What happens here becomes history from this point on. If it's significant, it'll be taught in schools, if it isn't, it won't matter."

"What about me?"

"You're here while events are unfolding. You're experiencing them. Your knowledge will be firsthand, not taught. Now come on." He stole a covert look around. "I have things to do."

"No. Wait." She tugged on his sleeve, holding him back. "There is one more thing."

He let his head fall forward. "Yes?"

"About Jack. Is he—I mean, he's here in 1790 and you really believe he's killed in other times, as well?"

"Yes."

Cassie's skin went cold. "There's no doubt in your mind that your Jack is that Jack. They weren't just copycat killings in my time or this one?"

Morgan stared at her but said nothing.

What was there to say, Cassie thought. A sick knot climbed from her stomach to her chest. She didn't want to believe it, but there it was. The Jack who'd killed Joelle was the same Jack who'd murdered five women in Whitechapel in 1888. They'd called him Jack the Ripper back then. And for all she knew, he might be partying under the same roof where she stood right now.

Chapter Five

December 10, 1790
2:00 a.m.

Morgan sat at the small desk in his room and struggled to catch up on his journal entries. The party continued upstairs, but he was not needed. Sir Gerald would be gloriously drunk by now. If he required more than his valet or the underbutler could provide, Morgan knew he'd ring loud and long.

As for Lady Mary, she'd retired hours ago, leaving Cassie free to seek a hot bath in the back rooms. Since the household staff still tended to look on water as if it were poison, the tub was usually free. For Cassie's benefit, Bartholomew had filled it cheerfully.

Stretching a hand across his brow, Morgan massaged his aching temples with his thumb and middle finger. He'd gotten nowhere in his search for Jack tonight. Much as he wanted to blame Cassie for that, it wasn't really her fault.

His suspects had all been upstairs at one point. He'd watched them as he served, but they'd given him nothing. As the night had worn on, they'd dispersed, until the only ones left were Sir Gerald and a snoring Sir Patrick Welland. Now only the drunkards remained, and he knew they would remain until well past dawn.

"All caught up, Mr. M.?" Bartholomew inquired cautiously from the door.

"No, I'm not." Morgan knew he sounded cross, but he didn't care. "Is Cassie asleep?"

"I don't think so." The little man shifted his weight. "I, uh, took her some more clothes."

Morgan's eyes hardened. "What?"

"Well, she can't wear the same dress every day...."

"She's not staying."

"But, sir..."

"No," Morgan said with emphasis. "As soon as I'm finished here, I'm going to make the necessary time calculations. Now go on upstairs and make sure Sir Ladykiller Gerald isn't trying to bang down her door. Then take some food out to the coachman."

Bartholomew hesitated, a sure sign he had something else on his mind.

Morgan stared straight ahead, resigned. "Yes, what is it, Bartholomew?"

"I was thinking about Jack, sir."

"And?"

"Well, what if he saw her tonight and decides to follow her back to her own time."

"Oh, God." His quill poised, Morgan turned impatiently in his seat. "You really are a clod sometimes, Bartholomew. Think about it. How could Jack possibly know she's from another time, let alone what time she's from?"

"He might have guessed. She's not like our women."

"That's assuming she met him."

"He could have done. And if he did, he could follow her particle trail or whatever it's called back to her century—couldn't he?"

The pounding in Morgan's temples increased. "*If*, Bartholomew. It's a small chance."

"But he could do it."

Morgan's hand hit the open journal. "Not if I set the field for five different times, he couldn't."

"But couldn't he—"

Morgan snapped his head around. "Oh, shut up. I'm aware of the risks, Bartholomew. It's extremely doubtful that Jack would bother to chase one woman through time. Now get up those bloody stairs and check on her before I decide to send you back to the Dark Ages."

"Yes, Mr. M." Bartholomew's injured tone wasn't intended to irritate, but in Morgan's current frame of mind it did.

He got cranky with too little sleep and too many setbacks. Learning about Abigail Dexter Booth's death tonight had been the last straw.

There was also the little matter of Bartholomew being right when he said that Jack might pursue Cassie back to the twentieth century. No matter how many false trails Morgan laid down, it wouldn't take a genius to latch on to the right one. If Jack did suspect that Cassie came from another time, logic would tell him it could only be from the one he'd just left.

With a sound that fell halfway between a grunt and a snarl, Morgan sat back. The woman was a royal pain. He wanted her gone. Bartholomew must have been crazy to think he could be attracted to someone as irritating as Cassie Lachlin. She was stubborn and pigheaded and too damned curious for her own good. That he also found her delectable, particularly when she told him off or went the other route and tried to charm him, was completely irrelevant. He had no time for women, and most specifically no time for the strong-willed Scottish-American Cassie Lachlins of the world.

His eyes rose to the closet rafters, where he kept his few personal possessions, including his time box. By tomorrow afternoon she'd be gone. For her safety—and his own peace of mind—he had to make sure of it.

THE SNOW FELL in gentle, glorious flakes. Her skin was still warm enough to melt those flakes where they landed.

The scent of blood filled his head. Hot at first, it grew colder as the fever passed.

Agitated fingers stroked her honey-blond hair. It had looked red at the party tonight—why didn't it look red now? The streets were poorly lit, that was it, and the lantern on her carriage was weak. But it should still look red....

Jerkily, he rubbed some of the spilled blood into the long strands. It must have been the candles in the ballroom at Amblewood House that created the illusion of fire. Yes,

Morgan always made sure there were plenty of candles burning. So, actually, this was Morgan's fault, this mistake.

Except it wasn't a mistake, because looking very closely he could see strands of burnished gold in the woman's hair. And burnished gold bordered on red.

Jack's breath came in rapid spurts. His fists clenched. Finish it, his mind commanded. Kill her completely. But don't let Mother see.

His furtive gaze swept the darkened lane. He remembered Mother well. Mother had loved her pretty red-haired daughter. Daughter came from Mother's womb. Son hated Daughter and Mother.

Jack's throat constricted. His mouth tasted sour, like bile. "I hate you," he swore at the memory. His knife worked furiously on the woman's body. "I've hated you since the day you were born."

Nothing alive stirred in the snow-filled alley. Sitting back on his heels, Jack cleaned his knife in a small, wet drift. A sense of being watched stole over him and he snatched his head around. But there were only the horses to see him, their breath steaming whitely in the cold night air.

He checked the carriage, anyway, just to be sure. Jaw slack, pulse slow but steady, the driver saw nothing. And yet the feeling persisted.

Returning, Jack packed up his bundle of tools and other possessions. His skin still tingled with excitement—and with fear. He'd been observed last time, he knew that for a fact. Someone had seen him kill the baroness, but he hadn't gotten a clear look at her face. He only knew she had red hair.

The tingling faded as the thrill wore off.

He regarded the dead woman at his feet through dispassionate eyes now. So a redhead had watched him murder a high-class whore. So what? He was going to kill all the ones with red hair, anyway. Sooner or later she'd wind up dead. Still, he would rather it was sooner than later.

Closing his eyes, he rocked back and forth on the snowy ground. Who was it that had spied on him? If only he could remember her face.

2:30 a.m.

TOO KEYED UP TO SLEEP, Cassie made her way down the rear staircase to the kitchen. She'd considered exchanging her green satin dress for the Irish linen peignoir set Bartholomew had brought, but decided on a simpler high-waisted dress of soft gray-green instead. Since hems dragged on the floor, she substituted her boots for satin slippers and, for the first time since coming here, felt more secure.

Flipping her hair over one shoulder, she paused at the foot of the stairs to listen. The kitchen sounded empty, which was more than could be said for the main floor. Parties must go on forever in this century.

Jack the Ripper. She shuddered just thinking his name. Was he really here in 1790? Had he murdered her friend in 1993?

Inching open the door, she slipped into the shadowy kitchen. Please let Morgan be asleep, she prayed. Because she had to get past his bedroom to get to the storeroom, where she'd carelessly left her backpack after her bath.

"You'd think that would be the last thing I'd forget," she murmured as she started across the floor.

"What!"

The outside door burst open behind her. Cassie spun swiftly. "What?" She echoed the frantic ejaculation of the man on the threshold, then demanded weakly, "Bartholomew is that you?"

"Yes, ma'am." He rushed over, hopping up and down like a terrified kangaroo. "There's been another killing."

"What? Where?"

"Down by the Thames. Near the docks."

Recovering her composure, Cassie shook him. "Which docks?"

"I don't know." He continued to hop about. "Near Blackfriar's Bridge, I think. It was the coachman who told me. He got it from a cabbie who drove someone from the committee over to fetch Sir Patrick. But Sir Patrick's not upstairs anymore." He pushed her hands away. "I've got to tell Mr. M.!"

"No, wait, Bartholomew..." But she was talking to the shadows. Already she could hear him running down the rear corridor.

"Mr. M., there's been another one!"

Cassie reached the door in time to note Morgan's reaction. He'd had his head down on his desk, resting on his folded arms. He'd either been asleep or close to it. Disoriented, he sat up. "Another what?" he asked, not sounding as if he knew where he was.

"Murder, sir. Another murder!"

"What?" The haze vanished. Morgan was on his feet in an instant, shaking the distressed Bartholomew. "Where did it happen?"

"I...I..."

"Near the docks, by Blackfriar's Bridge," Cassie supplied from the doorway.

"Who told you about it, Bartholomew?"

The little man swallowed. "A cabdriver. One of the men on the committee came to fetch Sir Patrick."

"Except Sir Patrick apparently isn't here anymore," Cassie added as Morgan reached for his discarded butler's coat.

He looked around, frowning. "He was here at midnight."

"So were a lot of other people," Cassie said, "including Sir Gerald and a man in a red-lined cape. I saw them leaving from Lady Mary's window."

"Together?" Morgan tugged a heavier coat over the first one.

"No." It was Bartholomew who answered. "They went out the door together at twelve-thirty, but they got in separate coaches. Then, about an hour ago, Sir Gerald's coach came back empty. I know 'cause Wilkie, the driver, came into the kitchen and wanted me to fix him something to eat. He said Sir Gerald sent him home so's Lady Mary wouldn't know he was still out if he didn't come back until morning, which Wilkie didn't think he planned to do."

Morgan's brow furrowed. "Yes," he said slowly. "I suppose there might be some sense in that jumble of words,

Bartholomew, but I haven't got time right now to figure out what it is. Am I to assume that Sir Gerald's not here?"

"No, sir. I mean, yes, sir. No one you suspect is here. They all went off ages ago."

Morgan set a tricorn hat on his dark curls. Cassie thought it made him look rather roguish, despite his ponytail. She caught his arm before he could get past her.

"I want to come with you," she said firmly.

"Fine. Take my cloak. Where's Wilkie?" he asked Bartholomew.

"With the cabdriver, sir."

"Tell him to bring Sir Gerald's coach around. And put my journal away after we leave." Tugging on a pair of gloves, Morgan regarded an astonished Cassie. "Is there some reason you're not moving?"

The note of sarcasm cut through her shock. She'd been anticipating a loud *No!* to her decision to accompany him, or at least an argument. She'd received neither.

Removing the black cloak from its peg, she ran after him. When she caught up, halfway through the garden, she couldn't resist a breathless "Why?"

Morgan glanced back, then around at the darkened bushes. "Because I don't know who Jack is, and knowing you, you'd follow me, anyway."

She opened her mouth, then closed it again, her eyes lifting to the unlit second-floor windows. "You're not sure about Sir Gerald, are you?" she asked as he signaled for the coach.

"Not really, no."

"So why do you work for him? Why a butler in the first place?"

"Because butlers are privy to information."

"Like murders in the middle of the night?"

"Yes, like that."

"But how could Sir Gerald be Jack? He has a grandmother. He can't be an impostor. People born *in* this time don't have the ability to travel *through* time."

"And people in your time do?"

"Well, not ordinarily, but..." An eloquent arch of his brows finished the point. "So what you're saying," she translated, "is that Sir Gerald could, in fact, be Jack, even though he was born in the 1700s."

"It's possible," Morgan agreed, waiting with mild impatience for the coach to draw closer. "Other time travelers have been here. Someone indigenous to this era could have gotten hold of a time box. It's happened before."

"That doesn't sound very promising."

"It isn't. Now come on, and whatever you do, when we get to the docks, stay close to me."

"I intend to." She frowned, halting as he handed her into the elegant coach. "Wait a minute—you can't think Jack will show up there."

"He might do. It depends on who he is. One thing's for sure, he's cunning and smart." Morgan's gaze shifted to the Thames. "He's also bloody mad."

NO MATTER HOW OFTEN he confronted it, Morgan never got used to the sight of death. Not like this. Lady Annabelle Mercer hadn't been murdered—she'd been viciously slaughtered.

Morgan stared with false detachment, aware of Cassie at his elbow, yet unable to look at her.

"It's just like Joelle and the other women in my time," she whispered, sounding slightly choked. "I don't believe this."

"Who the devil are you?" a man's loud voice intruded. "Morgan, who is this woman? What's she doing here?"

Sir Patrick Welland strode over, a pompous, still somewhat intoxicated picture in his party clothes and black silk-lined cloak. Evidently one of his men had located him. How and where, Morgan could determine later.

"She's a friend, sir," he replied politely.

"This is no place for a woman." Irritated, Sir Patrick raised his slurred voice. "Where's that fop of a poet? Has he come round yet?"

"He's starting to," Julian Stockwell replied from behind Morgan's shoulder. Like Sir Patrick, the *Times* reporter still wore his party clothes. He had his notebook out and his pencil poised. "So, Morgan," he said. "Here we are again, it seems." He glanced at Cassie but made no comment, only a brief notation in his book. "What do you make of this one?"

"Left-handed," Cassie murmured.

Her observation brought Julian's dark brows up. "Beg pardon?"

Morgan summoned a polite "She's referring to the murderer, sir. Obviously, from the angle of the incisions, he's left-handed."

"Observant little thing, aren't you? I'd have thought it would take a physician to make such a determination." Julian jotted down another quick note. Someone jostled his arm and he scowled. "Sir Patrick, can't you order these peasants back?" With his pencil, he pointed to the bloodied ground. "What's this nonsense again, Morgan? All her personal effects laid out like a place setting at a formal dinner. It was the same with the baroness, wasn't it?"

"Yes, sir," Morgan agreed. Without appearing to, he took stock of the murder scene. They were in an isolated alley, hidden from street view. Not that that made much difference in 1790 London. There were few lamps to be found in the best part of town, and virtually none down here.

Water from the Thames lapped against the pier, which was about a block distant. The brick walls around them contained no windows. The buildings were sooty and deserted, storehouses for the most part. Jack had chosen the site with care. No prying eyes to witness his butchery.

At the top of the lane stood a coach and four—Lady Annabelle's coach, Morgan knew. From inside he heard a dramatic moan. Thirty seconds later the poet, Ignatious Athelbert, was helped out.

Hand pressed to his head, he lowered himself to a seat on the coach step. "It was ghastly, I tell you. We were driving along and suddenly we stopped. I heard a thud like a falling body and then a horrible black shape filled the window. It yanked open the door and hit me here." Athelbert indicated his right temple. "I heard Lady Annabelle scream, and then nothing. Maybe the driver can tell you more...."

"The driver hasn't regained consciousness yet," a man in a red uniform said. Morgan recognized him as one of Sir Patrick's subordinates on the committee.

"Morgan, look." Cassie nudged his arm, nodding ahead of them. "I think your Sir Patrick's doing something to that brick wall."

"What?" Morgan brought his head swiftly around. With a succinct "Put your mind to that for me, Cassie," and a motion at the personal items near Lady Annabelle's body, he was off, crunching through the snow to the scorched wall at the end of the lane.

Sir Patrick, busy scrubbing something white off the blackened bricks, glanced around. "Urchins, bloody urchins," he muttered as Morgan approached.

"Sir?"

"Writing obscenities on anything that stands."

"So you don't think it might have been a clue then, sir?"

"Of course not." Sir Patrick gave the bricks a final swipe with a piece of burlap.

"What do you think, Morgan?" Julian Stockwell appeared at Morgan's side.

"I'm not sure I would have disturbed anything at the crime scene, if that's what you mean."

"Oh, that's good." Julian scribbled the quote in his notebook. Without raising his head, he inquired, "What did the writing on the wall say, Sir Patrick?"

"None of your damned business."

Julian's smile was cold. "May I quote you, as well, sir?"

"Excuse me, Sir Patrick," the committee member in red interrupted. "The crowd's getting rather large now, sir. Shall we fetch the wagon to take Lady Mercer away?"

"If I might suggest, sir," Morgan inserted with a politic incline of his head, "mightn't it be preferable to wait until the doctor arrives before moving her? Naturally, you'll have sent for him."

"Yes—yes, certainly." Sir Patrick gave his subordinate a shove. "Go and see what's keeping him, Morris. Dr. Peach. Twenty-two Briar Lane."

"Right on top of the situation, as usual." Julian shook his head and turned away. "The man's as bright as a snuffed candle."

No, the man was a little brighter than that, Morgan suspected, noting the agitated twitches in Sir Patrick's neck and shoulders. He'd wiped some message from that wall tonight, and whatever it was, he hadn't liked it at all.

A SILK PURSE, a fan and a perfume bottle were piled on one side of the body. A knotted handkerchief and an emerald choker had been set out with care on the other. Neither grouping made sense to Cassie. She studied the arrangements for ten minutes before Morgan came along and lifted her to her feet.

"Well?" he said, his eyes on the moaning Ignatious Athelbert.

"I have no idea, except I don't think the purse, fan and perfume are important."

A frown crossed his mouth. "Why not?"

"Because of the way they're lying there, as if someone had just tossed them aside. It's different here than it was with Joelle and the other women in my time. He made two rows of personal items with them."

"Meaning?"

"I don't know, Morgan. But I do remember that he put Joelle's cosmetic bag, wallet, comb and—well, her date book in the top row. The cameo pendant she used to wear was wrapped inside her handkerchief and placed below the other things. There might be some significance in the fact that there were two rows. Also, why did he wrap Joelle's cameo in her handkerchief? It must have been Jack who did it, because Joelle always, always wore her cameo pendant. She absolutely loved it." Cassie forced herself to look at Lady Annabelle's face. "It's only my opinion, but I think if there's a message involved here, it's more likely connected to the handkerchief and emerald choker than the other things." She paused. "I wonder why he didn't take the emeralds?"

"This wasn't a murder for gain, Cassie."

"Thank you, I had realized that. I'm just trying to understand Jack's thinking. Are they real?"

"Certainly," Morgan said. "Annabelle's father is a viscount."

"Very impressive. But my grandfather was an earl, and he never had any emeralds to give to his wife."

"Yes, well, things are a bit different in this time." Morgan urged her forward with a hand pressed to the small of her back, a surprisingly erotic touch, considering the circumstances. "Come on, I want to hear what Athelbert has to say."

"But I haven't figured out the meaning of the arrangement yet," Cassie objected. "I know it's important, Morgan. It has to be."

His brow furrowed in distaste. "For God's sake, Cassie, you've been kneeling beside a dead body for ten minutes. Isn't that long enough?"

She exhaled a patient breath. "I don't focus on the carnage when I look at her."

Morgan's frown deepened. For an irrational moment, Cassie was tempted to reach up and smooth the ridge that formed between his eyes. "What do you mean? How can you ignore it?"

Unprepared to explain her background, Cassie said vaguely, "It's a family trait. What was Sir Patrick doing?"

"Something he shouldn't have been." Morgan gave her another small push. "This way."

Cassie quit arguing and turned her attention to the poet.

"We left the party together," he was explaining to a member of the Parliamentary Committee on Street Violence. "She wanted to drift among the snowflakes before returning home." His thin, painted face grew pensive. "I told her we two were snowflakes of a sort, ephemeral beings in a world without end. Our time here is but that of a single powdery flake, unique as it were, yet all too short-lived."

Sir Patrick strode up. "What is this addle-brained gibberish, Athelbert?" he demanded. "Did you or did you not see the face of the man who attacked you?"

The poet nursed his right temple. "How can you ask me that when I sit here with a lump as large as a goose egg on my skull?"

Cassie leaned in from the side. There were enough lanterns that she had a fairly good view of his face. She saw a faint red mark on his forehead but no sign of a lump where he was rubbing.

Athelbert smiled wanly when he noticed her; Sir Patrick scowled and Cassie stepped back. Apparently it was not a woman's place to make observations, even when they might concern Jack the Ripper.

Shivering despite the warmth of her wool cloak, Cassie took a further step backward into Morgan's chest. He wasn't large or protective or even particularly sympathetic toward her, and yet she felt safe with him. What surprised her was that she wanted to be here. She wanted to stay and help catch Jack, and not strictly because of Joelle.

Good Lord, she'd just been zapped back two centuries in time and here she was ready to plunge into an all-out murder investigation. She must be more adaptable than she thought. Either that or the full shock of what had happened hadn't hit her yet.

Athelbert's melancholy voice rose above the murmuring crowd of onlookers. "Lovely, lovely snowflake, falling from the sky. Fall on Lady Annabelle. And so two beauties die..."

"Oh, God," Cassie heard Morgan murmur under his breath. She knew he was rolling his eyes. However, before she could glance back, her own eyes were drawn to another man, the reporter Julian Stockwell.

He stood on the edge of the crowd, his pencil flying over a page in his notebook. A moment later he tore the page out, took a furtive look around and removed a coin from his waistcoat. Then he handed both paper and coin to an urchin boy and nodded toward the street.

Cassie might not have thought twice about Julian's action. But then he smiled and began to chuckle, and the sound of his laughter slid through her veins like iced gelatin.

"Stupid fools," he whispered softly. His eyes traveled from Sir Patrick beside the coach to Lady Annabelle's butchered body. "Blind, stupid fools." And flipping his notebook closed, he melted into the crowd.

THEY STAYED FOR ANOTHER thirty minutes. Morgan made discreet inquiries while Cassie returned to her inspection of the dead woman. This time, though, instead of studying her possessions, she examined Lady Annabelle's body.

She did it clinically as her parents and sister had taught her. Focus on one thing. Don't think beyond that. The body is merely a repository for the soul. Remember that, Cassie.

It was a difficult procedure, even so. She kept seeing Joelle lying there—laughing, crying, arguing with her. How in God's name could anyone commit such atrocities on another human being?

Cassie's eyes moved doggedly over Lady Annabelle's ravaged body. Her left hand was gloved. Her right one was bare, and several of the fingernails were broken.

Careful not to draw attention to herself, Cassie leaned closer. She'd aroused suspicion with her angle-of-incision theory; she didn't need to compound that mistake by letting Sir Patrick catch her hovering over the dead woman's body.

First the hair, she decided. It was golden blond. Cassie didn't see any red, but Jack might have. In certain light, Cassie's own hair often appeared more brown than red. The same might be true for Lady Annabelle.

Taking a deep breath, Cassie forced herself to touch the woman's ungloved hand. There was something under her fingernails. Not blood, something thicker, not as dark.

Skin? She swallowed but didn't flinch. No, not skin; the texture was wrong for that. It felt more like...

"Putty," she murmured, testing a bit of it between her index finger and thumb. Then suddenly conscious of her action, she rubbed her hand in the snow.

Standing, she searched for Morgan. He was busy with Sir Patrick. Dr. Peach's coach was gliding to a halt at the top of the alley. She would have to improvise.

Not giving herself time to think about what she was doing, Cassie scraped away more of the putty and wiped it very carefully onto her own handkerchief. As long as she didn't smear it, there'd be enough to show Morgan when they returned to Amblewood House.

For an unguarded moment, Cassie stared down at Lady Annabelle's face. Her stomach twisted into a knot. She shouldn't do this, it only made things worse, but she couldn't help it. No doubt there had been hundreds of murderers in London over the years, but none as monstrous as Jack.

"An eye for an eye," she said softly to the night. "Even that's more mercy than you deserve."

She thought briefly about Julian Stockwell's odd behavior and Ignatious Athelbert's claim to have been knocked unconscious. She considered the putty under Lady Annabelle's fingernails, the knotted handkerchief, the emerald choker—and the message Sir Patrick had erased from the brick wall that struck an odd chord in her memory. Most of all, however, she considered Morgan, the enigmatic time-traveling butler who was determined to send her home.

Home. The word echoed hollowly in her head. Home where she belonged.

Raising her head, Cassie cast a surreptitious glance at Morgan's unrevealing profile. Did she belong at home, though? Or did she really belong someplace else entirely?

Chapter Six

"We shall be at the house of Lord and Lady Mercer all day," Lady Mary said to Cassie midmorning. "Blue hat or gray?"

"Blue," Cassie replied, while Desirée looked on in restless silence. Only Morgan's arrival with a tray of tea relaxed her somewhat.

Such a handsome butler. Desirée liked the way he moved. She liked his outward control. She also liked his sinewy body, but even more, she liked his mind, which never stopped working. She wasn't altogether sure she liked the way he was looking at Cassie, but that was none of her business, and a minor nibble in any event.

He'd done it again last night, the monster. She hadn't witnessed the murder this time, but she'd certainly seen the body afterward.

She started to shake inside, then told herself not to. She didn't dare cave in to fear. Maybe he would come after her eventually, but he hadn't yet, so possibly he didn't know she'd been there the night he'd murdered Baroness Roth.

"Oh, God, let that be true," she whispered, which earned her an inquiring look from Morgan as he turned to leave.

"Did you say something, ma'am?" he asked.

Ever the proper servant, she thought with a small sigh of regret. "I was just thinking that Lady Mary and I should be leaving," she lied, finishing her tea. "You were right, Cassie. The blue hat is perfect."

Lady Mary stood unaided. "Morgan, wait," she said.

He paused on the threshold. "Ma'am?"

"My grandson, did he come home last night?"
"Yes, ma'am."
"What time?"
"5:00 a.m."
"I thought as much." Her lips became a grim red slash. "I trust he's still in bed."
"He was the last time I checked ten minutes ago."
"Tell him I shall wish to see him this evening before we leave for Lord Griswald's ball."
Morgan gave a polite nod. "As you wish, my lady."
"Don't you 'my lady' me," she snapped, thumping her cane. "You know far more—" She caught herself midsentence and looked up sharply at Cassie's deliberately benign face. "And don't you play innocent with me either, missy. I know you both visited the murder scene last night."
Morgan's serene expression didn't falter. "Word travels fast in London, ma'am. Shall I have your carriage sent round?"
"We can take mine," Desirée offered. "It's already outside."
As she fussed with her curls, her eyes slid to Morgan. She wished she dared confide in him, or even in Cassie, but she couldn't bring herself to do it. Not yet. Not until she was sure....
Shaking the unpleasant thought away, she took Lady Mary's frail arm. "Be a dear, Morgan," she said, determinedly cheerful, "and tell Sir Gerald that I shall be happy to accompany him to the Griswalds' ball tonight. But only on the condition that Lady Mary travels with us, in both directions."

CASSIE CURSED LONG skirts and petticoats as she ran down the rear stairs. Pushing past Mrs. Dickson and her helpers, she darted out the back door into the garden.
"Now, see here," she heard the cook bellow in her wake. "Mr. M., what's going on?"
"I'll explain later. Which way?"
"Through the garden door."
Snowflakes drifted downward from a dove-gray sky. The garden was a Christmas card, covered in virgin white. There

were no cars or snowplows to muddy up the streets. It was all sleighs and carriages jingling past—and Morgan close behind, gaining on her.

Bunching her cloak tightly in one hand and her skirts in the other, Cassie ran through a rose arbor into another area of the garden, but he caught her before she could find a place to hide. Holding fast to her shoulders, he spun her around to face him.

"What have you done with it?" he demanded, which wasn't the question she'd been expecting.

Suspicion crowded in. "What have I done with *what?*"

"My time box. It's gone, and you took it."

"Took it!" She twisted ineffectually in his grasp. "I don't even know what it looks like. Let me go, Morgan."

"So you can run off and hide? Not a chance." He stabbed a finger in her face. She resisted the urge to bite it. "You're going back."

"I'm not."

"So you did take it, then."

"No, I didn't."

"So why did you run the moment Lady Mary was off?"

"Because I knew you'd try to send me home, and I didn't want to go. And Lady Mary doesn't want me to go," she added with a pointed glare. "Anyway, who was it who found the putty under Lady Annabelle's fingernails? And who saw Julian Stockwell give a note and a penny to a peasant, then call Sir Patrick a fool and disappear. Who noticed that the lump on Athelbert's temple wasn't big enough—"

"Yes, yes, all right." Morgan held up a surrendering hand. "You did all those things, Cassie, and I'm grateful."

"You don't sound it." She squirmed again. "Let me go."

"No."

"Damn you, Morgan, why can't you be reasonable?"

At close range she could feel the heat of his barely controlled temper. "You're the one who's not being reasonable," he retorted.

The small shake he gave her to emphasize his point only succeeded in making her more aware of him. Cassie loved a man with a temper. Not the abusive kind, but the kind that when it burst out did so with unrestrained passion. Gaelic passion, her grandfather called it—anything from breaking dishes on a wall, to making love on a stone floor.

"I want to stay," she repeated stubbornly.

He gritted his teeth. "You don't belong in this time."

"That's just an excuse, Morgan. You don't want me here because you think I'll hamper your investigation."

He gave her another shake. "I don't want you here," he growled, "because I'm afraid Jack will come after you."

Cassie opened her mouth to argue, then realized what he'd said and closed it. "You mean you're worried about me?"

"Does that surprise you?"

"Frankly, yes."

"You're too kind," he said with polite sarcasm that swiftly gave way to aggravation. "Now, where is it?"

She sighed. "Think about it, Morgan. Would I run if I had it?"

He darted a quick look over his shoulder. She heard the snarl that formed in his throat. "Bartholomew, you little..." A false smile crossed his lips and he released her instantly. "Sorry. My mistake. I should have known."

Cassie didn't trust him. "Don't you dare hurt Bartholomew," she warned.

His equanimity restored, Morgan straightened his vest and cravat. "I wouldn't dream of it." He glanced around, completely ingenuous. "You haven't seen him at all, have you?"

"No, and if I had I wouldn't tell you. For God's sake, Morgan, will you listen to reason for once? I can help you. I know self-defense, and I wouldn't wander off alone." At his unmoved expression, she released an exasperated breath. "Look, don't you have any friends? People you care about and don't want to see hurt? That's what Joelle Terry was to me, a friend, and he killed her. You tell me he's Jack the Ripper and that he's done the same thing to other women in other centuries. I see a woman who's been slaughtered lying in an alley, and I'm not supposed to care about that?" She went to stand directly in front of him, fists clenched at her sides. "Well, I do care, and I'm not going back, and when I find that creep I'm going to cut off his— Well, I'm going to make sure he pays for what he's done." This time it was Cassie who shook a finger under Morgan's nose. "And if you do anything to Bartholomew for taking your time box, I swear I'll... I'll..."

"Have me horsewhipped?" he suggested, straight-faced.

Or kiss you, she reflected irritably. Dragging her eyes from his mouth, she regarded his chest. "It's a thought."

When she looked up, she saw that there was snow clinging to his hair and lashes. God, but he suited this time.

"Well?" she demanded after a long pause.

"I can't watch you and search for Jack at the same time," he said flatly.

"I'm not asking you to. I can take care of myself. Women from my time are considerably less passive than they are here."

"Jack managed to kill several women from your time."

"His victims could just as easily have been men, Morgan. I could murder you if I set my mind to it."

He studied her through doubtful, half-closed eyes. "You really are pigheaded, aren't you?"

"Is that a yes?"

"It's a conditional maybe." Assuming the offensive, he advanced on her until she was forced to either step back or be knocked over. "You don't know what you're getting into, Cassie. Jack is dangerous—in fact, he's deadly. He's evil, he's unpredictable, and more experienced people than you and I have died at his hands."

Unable to prevent the nervous fluttering in her stomach, Cassie nevertheless lifted her chin. "I'm not stupid. I know he's deadly. I also know he can't go on killing people at will. So where do we start, and when? With Sir Gerald this morning?"

Morgan looked briefly away. "No, with the theater this afternoon. There's an actor in a play at the Haymarket whose dressing room I want to search."

"That sounds—"

The warning finger came up. "Say it sounds like fun and you'll be back in the twentieth century before you can finish the word."

She wondered what he would do if she kissed him. It was a tempting thought—he had such a wonderful mouth—but extremely ill-advised. If he'd send her back for a poor choice of words, he would undoubtedly do so much faster for an errant kiss.

"I was going to say it sounds intriguing," she told him, trying not to sound smug. He wouldn't appreciate that, either.

Some of her satisfaction must have transmitted itself to him even so, because he stopped advancing. Releasing a heavy breath, he closed his eyes. "I'm going to regret this," he said to himself.

"No, you won't." Cassie took his hand before he could renege. "Come on, let's go inside and you can tell me all about your suspects, including the actor whose room we're going to search. What play is he in, by the way?"

"*Macbeth.*"

She halted on the garden path. A strange sense of breathlessness gripped her, like an icy hand momentarily closing about her throat. "'Out, out, brief candle!'" she quoted tremulously. "It's eerily appropriate, isn't it?"

Morgan's gaze traveled over the rooftops of snowy London. "'Life's but a walking shadow,'" he continued the quote, "'a poor player,/That struts and frets his hour upon the stage,/And then is heard no more.'"

"NOW REMEMBER, CASSIE," Morgan warned. "Keep your head down, your cowl up, and let me do the talking."

Her breath hissed out in the chill air. "For the twentieth time, I get the message. You know these people. You can handle them. And if I mess this up for you, you'll throw me bodily into the time corridor with Bartholomew close behind."

"Exactly. Now be quiet and stay close."

Taking her hand in his gloved one, Morgan pulled her along behind him to the rear door of the Haymarket, an unlicensed theater that nevertheless boasted an impressive list of patrons. Ironically, the more notable the patrons the more contempt Christopher Crowley had for them. However, he had sufficient wisdom not to let that fact be known.

Except, of course, when the knowing could do him no harm.

More than once, Morgan had heard him refer to Sir Gerald as a self-centered jackass and Lady Mary as a domineering old shrew. He played the fop in public just enough to be fashionable, yet never quite to the extent that it put his female admirers off. He'd known Abigail Dexter Booth, Baroness Roth and Lady Annabelle Mercer intimately. In fact, if the rumor down servants' way was to be believed, he'd been born to a woman of noble blood. A bastard son, disowned at birth, with no claim to either his mother's wealth or her social standing.

Unfortunately, those things didn't make him Jack. Because of that, Morgan had sent Bartholomew out to follow up on two other suspect leads, one concerning Sir Gerald, the second Dr. Peach. With luck, he'd have an answer to both of his questions by tonight.

"Afternoon, Mr. M." A fat beagle of a man with a ruddy face and a fringe of dirty white hair greeted him inside the stage door. "What brings you round this cold winter day?"

Morgan put on his diplomatic butler's smile. "Good afternoon, Coggins. I've come with a message for Mr. Tudbury. A rather personal message, if you take my meaning."

Coggins's beady eyes lit on Cassie, well concealed in her cloak and cowl. "'Course you have," he chortled. "Not a bad bit of sidelining, eh, Mr. M.?" Giving a lewd wink he flapped a fat hand in the direction of the dressing rooms. "Go on in, then. Tudbury's is the second door on the left."

Morgan dipped his head politely. "Thank you, Coggins. Come along, Gretel."

Cassie didn't utter a word until they were out of Coggins's range, then she shoved back her cowl and demanded, "Gretel? As in Hansel and?"

"Quiet." Tugging her hood back in place, he took a covert look down the corridor, knocked, then pulled her through one of the doors.

"Mr. Tudbury, my foot," she muttered, once he'd established that there was no one about. "I wouldn't put it past you to deliver me as promised."

Morgan moved through the fluttering shadows. "Haven't you ever heard of a ruse, Cassie?"

"Many times, but you might have warned me that in this case I was going to be part of one. Who's Mr. Tudbury when he's not devouring young women?"

"He's a three-hundred-pound Romeo and an actor who owes me a favor. Now, stop asking questions and start looking through Crowley's dressing table. He does his own makeup. The kit should be around here somewhere."

"From the number of candles burning, I'd say that Mr. Crowley is also around here somewhere. What if he... No, that's negative thinking." She squared her shoulders. "Is it just actor's putty we're looking for?"

"Or blood," Morgan replied as he went through a box of scripts and costumes. "Although I suspect Jack disposes of any soiled clothing before leaving the murder scene."

"You mean he burns them?"

"He could do. He always ensures there are no witnesses about."

Cassie, pawing through a drawer, hesitated. "Was Athelbert wearing a cloak last night? Or gloves?"

"You mean you didn't notice?" Morgan retorted with a hint of mockery. "The answer is no, he wasn't."

She made a face at him.

Morgan watched her for a minute, then shook himself and resumed his own search. Unless they were subordinate to him, he wasn't accustomed to working with people. He'd spent the past fifteen years of his life in the company of individuals much like those from this century, unwilling to embrace the new or the unexplained. He'd never had a problem with that attitude; on the contrary, it made his job a great deal easier.

If only he could dismiss Cassie as readily, but she was resilient, not the brooding perfectionist he tended to be, and open to almost everything, as far as he could tell. That combination made her infinitely more difficult to cope with. She was pretty, smart and mentally tough. God, he thought, digging irritably through a wooden truck, his mother would probably love her.

That didn't mean he had to.

Morgan was a master at shutting out his emotions. In his line of work, he had to be. The last thing he needed was for some troublemaking female from the twentieth century to come along and take potshots at his emotional equilibrium. It would be business between them, he'd promised himself before coming here, and nothing more. And if her hair, her eyes, her mouth and body tempted, he would simply exert his not insubstantial control and fix his mind on more important matters.

"Rice powder," he heard Cassie say doubtfully. "And rouge." She tested it with her finger. "This stuff's horrible. Lead-based, too. I'm surprised people had any skin left after a few years of wearing this."

"They didn't." Frowning, Morgan nudged back his tricorn hat. "It's not here. He must have taken it with him."

"Well, then all we have to do is wait until he comes back and—" She suddenly stopped, snatching her head around. "Somebody's coming."

More than one somebody, Morgan realized. Locating the nearest door, he yanked it open. "In here," he ordered, and stuffed Cassie into a small room crammed with shelves overflowing with folded costumes and other theatrical paraphernalia. Wedging himself in beside her, he left the door cracked so that he could see out.

"Come along, my dear Mistress Brede." With a flourish, Christopher Crowley ushered a woman into his dressing room. "I'll even leave the door open as propriety demands."

Morgan recognized the wicked answering cackle instantly. Jane Brede had been Sir Gerald's guest many times, both at parties and for more intimate evenings alone. Her coy manner was nothing more than a facade to placate her stuffy rich brother. She had an annoying tendency to pout, a curly mane of burnished red hair and a coquettish "yes" poised on her lips to the sexual advance of any man under ninety who didn't reside in a cemetery—provided he came bearing gifts.

"Well, I really don't know," she hedged now, already eyeing the wine bottle chilling on the actor's dressing table. "I suppose I could share a small glass with you, but that door must stay open— Oops. Clumsy me." Her shrill giggle reached the anteroom. "I've accidentally closed the door. Still, I'm sure I can trust you to be a gentleman, Mr. Crowley. Oh, yes, a bit more wine, if you please. It's terribly cold out today, don't you think so? I've been so busy rushing about, visiting friends and neighbors and answering all those horrid people with their questions about poor Lady Annabelle. And, of course, placating Dr. Peach, who insists I really must slow down because women are much too fragile to run about all day making chitchat with their brother's chums who aren't really chums at all, you know, but rather men of standing in the community. Although few people of any social standing would include government officials as part of the community. Personally, I say the arts should be welcomed, but members of the commons, well... Oh, please, yes, this wine is quite delicious. Makes a girl dizzy and ever so warm, what with all these layers of clothing we're forced to wear."

Morgan felt Cassie's head pressed against the back of his shoulder. "This is disgusting," she whispered.

He shifted position for a better view, and because Cassie's closeness strained his control to the limit. "Jane Brede is famous for her endless prattle," he said dryly. "To say nothing of her damned witch's cackle."

"I meant this room, Morgan, not Jane Brede."

"What's wrong with this room?" Peering out, he saw that Crowley had maneuvered Jane onto the sofa. His fingers played idly with the ends of her dark red hair.

"It smells awful."

"Of course it does. There are clothes in here. Now shut up and let me listen."

She punched him, waited, then whispered, "Well? What are they doing now?"

"Oh, Mr. Crowley, really," Jane cackled again. "You do have a way with words." An astute observation, Morgan reflected, since Crowley hadn't been able to get one in edgewise. "How can a woman refuse you anything, I wonder?"

The actor smiled. "Then you'll agree to accompany me to the Merrydales' Christmas party?"

"Oh, no, I couldn't do that," she protested, pressing a hand to her throat. "I mean, I should love to, but I promised Sir Gerald that I would accompany him."

"Promised?" Crowley poured more wine.

"Well, implied." She ran a gloved finger around the top of her glass. "He's very fond of me, you understand. Why, only last month he gave me this perfectly exquisite bracelet. Diamonds and rubies, to match the fire in my hair, he said."

Crowley waved a dismissing hand. "A mere trinket. Sir Gerald is forever giving women presents. But can he give them what they really want?"

"Oh dear," Morgan murmured with a discerning sigh.

Cassie's fingers, wrapped about his arm, tightened. "They wouldn't, would they?"

"They might. Do you want to change places so you can get a better view?"

"Don't be a pig. I was looking at the Florentine table next to the door. There's a black case on it that wasn't there before."

"Yes, I know. The problem is getting to it."

"That's not the only problem. For God's sake, Morgan, close the door. I'd rather suffocate than watch them make out."

"Don't worry," he said, taking another quick look. "I recognize the expression on her face. She'll want a present first."

"Is that the voice of experience talking?"

"Certainly not," he snapped.

"Not your type, huh?" Cassie teased. "Or is it that you've risen above annoying distractions like sex in your time." She moved against him. He wasn't sure if the contact was deliberate or not. "But you must think about it once in a while, Morgan. Men can't have changed that much."

It was deliberate. Morgan eased himself away. His only defense was stoicism, and that wouldn't last long if she moved another inch to her right.

"Look, Cassie," he said in a tolerant if somewhat impatient whisper. "This is hardly the place for a confrontation. Save it until we get back to the manor."

She sighed. "God, but you're logical. I hate it. All right, what are they doing now?"

Crisis over, Morgan hoped. He glanced out. "Crowley's plying her with more wine. He's taken off her hat."

"Very smooth for a fop."

"He's not a fop, Cassie. It's an act."

"Yes, well, it's an awfully good one. Not that he's quite pretty enough to pull it off, mind you."

Morgan frowned over at her. "What does that mean?"

"Well, he's handsome enough, but he's too—I don't know—well-built and virile to have a lace handkerchief draped over one finger. It's such a stupid charade, anyway. Do women here really go for that?"

"A lot of them do. Wait a minute." He looked out again, holding Cassie back when she would have pushed past him. "They're standing."

"We'll see," Jane said. "That's the best I can promise, Mr. Crowley." She tilted her head suggestively, causing her red curls to tumble over her fur-trimmed collar. "Of course, I could always accompany Sir Gerald to the party, then manage to lose him in the crowd for a while. That way I needn't go back on my word, and we could be together."

"Or you could just do it right now on the floor," Cassie muttered, "and take money for payment instead of jewels."

Morgan's leather-gloved hand clamped itself over her mouth as Crowley's head turned.

"Did you hear something?" Crowley asked Jane.

Busy admiring her ruby bracelet, she shook her head. "Only my expectant heart."

"Oh, God." Morgan rolled his eyes, but maintained his grip on Cassie.

"I'm sure I heard a noise," Crowley insisted.

The fop act had disappeared. Morgan tensed as the actor started for the wardrobe.

"It was in here," he said, and opened the door.

Blending into the costume-laden shelves was the best Morgan could manage. Cassie stopped clawing at his hand and plastered herself against him as Crowley's eyes scanned the shadowy interior. "Smells a bit like flowers," he noted. "Orchids, I think. Or wild roses."

"What?" That got Jane's attention. "Lady Dorothy wears an orchid perfume. You haven't been seeing her, have you?" She joined him at the door, her foot tapping a petulant tattoo while Crowley flicked through the costumes.

His response was a dismissive "Must have been a rat," followed by a theatrically charming "Good Lord, no, my dear. How could I possibly prefer Lady Dorothy to you? Now, about tomorrow night. You will at least agree to come to the theater and watch me perform."

Her cackle filled the stuffy room. "Now, that I will promise, Mr. Crowley. Er, did you find anything?"

The actor's roving hand brushed against Morgan's coat but didn't linger. "I'm afraid not," he said finally, "Oh well, I don't like rats, anyway. I had my fill of them last night, I fear."

"Not at Amblewood House, surely," Jane protested.

"No, no, this was—separate. Red wine and knives. Larks in the dark, my dear, nothing that need concern you."

"If you say so," Jane agreed vaguely. "Walk me out?"

Crowley bowed. "It would be my pleasure, Mistress Brede."

Morgan waited until they were gone before releasing Cassie. Once free, she kicked open the door, turned on the threshold and, planting her palms on his chest, shoved him mightily back inside.

"You creep," she accused, her dark eyes glittering. "I couldn't breathe."

He recovered his balance readily, as well as his composure. "Get the kit, Cassie," he said.

Teeth gnashed, she marched over and unfastened the black make-up case. "Putty," she said, tossing him a small capped pot.

"Is there any more?"

Calmer now, she went through the jars and bottles. "No, that's it. Does the color match?"

He removed the handkerchief she'd given him from his coat pocket. "It's close."

"But you can't be sure?"

"What you found on Lady Annabelle was probably mixed with rouge and powder. The texture's the same, though, so it was putty under her fingernails."

"Not necessarily from Christopher Crowley's face, though," Cassie finished. "Wonderful. So what do we do now?" She brightened suddenly. "I know. Why don't I—"

"No." Morgan took her firmly by the hand, cutting her off mid-idea. "Close the kit and let's go."

"But—"

"No," he repeated with greater emphasis. "Now let's get out of here before he comes back."

She grumbled but didn't argue. Forty minutes later they were back at Amblewood House, entering the steamy kitchen by way of the garden door.

Before Mrs. Dickson could snarl at Cassie, Bartholomew darted over to meet them.

"I thought you'd never get back," he panted. Pulling a folded piece of parchment from inside his grubby trouser pocket, he handed it to Morgan. "This came while you were out. Someone stuck it under the door. Mrs. Dickson found it." He pointed. "It's got a funny seal, Mr. M. I can't tell what it's supposed to be, can you?"

Morgan regarded the parchment and the red dab of wax that secured it. He could feel Cassie peering over his shoulder.

"It's not a scarlet pimpernel, that's for sure," she said softly.

"What is it, then?" Bartholomew asked.

"It's the jack of spades," Morgan told him. "Jack's sent me a message."

FROM THE WINDOW of his room, Jack pictured the words he'd written slashed across the London night sky. He envisioned them written in her blood, although he'd actually used black ink. They read:

> My dear butler: For months now I've known about you. I've observed you from a discreet distance. Although you've yet to discover my identity, I feel it my duty to congratulate you. You're better than your

predecessor, old Kroat, and heads above those button-pushing bounty hunters who are foolish enough to think that their computers can capture me.

What they, unlike you, fail to understand is that logic doesn't apply in my case. I am an ephemeral presence, and I select both my time and my victims with care.

Three dead already, Morgan. You did, I assume, note the manner of the last death closely. As I'm sure you've come to realize, I was in a fit of rage when I killed her. I am still in that fit, I fear.

She was near me today, very near. The whore who will die next is a woman of good breding. It is strictly because I have a grudging admiration for your talents, that I've decided to give you a clue, to serve notice in the matter, as it were.

She dies tomorrow. She dies horribly tomorrow. Alas, who knows, maybe this time she will die for good. Forever. For the sake of all those who have died in her place.

I remain,
Jack

Chapter Seven

He was a clever fiend, Cassie thought. Cruel and evil and brazen, too. Writing taunting notes to Morgan. Why not wave a red flag and be done with it?

"He's angry, isn't he, Bartholomew?" she asked much later over the kitchen table. "He hasn't said a word since we got back. Except to Sir Gerald before he left for the Griswalds' party."

"It's best not to cross him when he gets like this," Bartholomew advised. "All he wanted to know from me was, did I find out if Sir Gerald ever gave Lady Annabelle an emerald necklace, and was Dr. Peach on good terms with his sister before she died."

"Well?" Cassie prompted. "Did Sir Gerald and was Dr. Peach?"

"Yes, and no." Morgan came up silently behind Cassie, who didn't even jump. "Sir Gerald and Lady Mary are bringing guests back to the house after the party. See that there's food, wine and coffee set out for them. Tell Mrs. Dickson to start preparing it now."

"Right you are, Mr. M."

The half grunt, half snarl Morgan emitted warned Cassie that his mood hadn't improved. Not that she'd expected it to. Whatever Bartholomew's new information entailed, it evidently hadn't shortened his suspect list.

"I still think Christopher Crowley's your best bet," she said when he didn't speak. "After all, he was with Jane Brede this afternoon, and the word *breeding* in Jack's message was misspelled. On purpose, I'd say, because if it was

Crowley who sent this message, he couldn't have known that you and I were hiding in his dressing room, therefore, he couldn't have known that we knew that he was 'near' Jane Brede today. Plus he made that reference to red wine and knives, which could be a symbolic reference to blood and death."

Morgan's response was another preoccupied grunt. He began to pace back and forth, tapping his thumbnail against his bottom tooth. It seemed a promising sign to Cassie, enough so that she pushed the evening *Times* across the servants' table.

"Did you read Julian Stockwell's account of Lady Annabelle's murder? He says—"

"Yes, yes, I saw it." Morgan made an impatient gesture and continued pacing.

"Well, for a man who called Sir Patrick Welland a fool, he was certainly kind in his column. There's no mention of the writing Sir Patrick erased from the wall, or of the fact that he was drunk, or of the very pertinent fact that the committee member who found him was actually found *by* him in the vicinity of Blackfriar's Bridge."

Morgan's eyes sharpened. "Who told you that?"

"One of the upstairs maids. Wilkie the coachman told her. You did know all that, didn't you?"

"Of course I did."

"Well?" she said expectantly. "What was Sir Patrick doing down by Blackfriar's Bridge at three o'clock in the morning?"

"Patronizing his favorite tavern, I should think." Morgan's brow furrowed. "Or his favorite brothel."

"You don't think his being in the area is just a little convenient?"

"Of course I do," he snapped, straightening as if she'd just insulted him.

Cassie bit back her amusement. She loved the way he did that, took every question she asked as a personal affront. Must be the perfectionist's curse, she decided; never having been burdened with the quality, she could only assume it would be a curse. Certainly, where Jack was concerned, Morgan tended to be touchy.

He resumed his pacing, ticking off items on his fingers as he went. "Sir Gerald gave Lady Annabelle a gift of an emerald choker. We found that choker next to a knotted handkerchief beside Lady Annabelle's body. Sir Patrick erased a message on a wall, *and* he was down on the docks at the time of the murder, *and* he was rumored to have been having an affair with the first victim. Ignatious Athelbert, minus his gloves and cape, was inside Lady Annabelle's carriage right before she died. He claims to have been knocked out, but there was no evidence of a lump to support that claim, and the driver couldn't corroborate his story. For the second time, Julian Stockwell arrived at the murder scene before I did. He gave a note to a peasant boy which he wrote with—which hand?"

"His right," Cassie supplied. "But I'm sure that in my time, and in the late 1800s when Jack the Ripper was on a rampage in Whitechapel, the consensus was that the incisions had been made by a person using his left hand."

"Well, possibly," Morgan conceded, "but as far as I know, only Sir Patrick is left-handed. But let's leave that for now." He returned to his list. "Actors use putty to cover facial flaws, and the putty you discovered under Lady Annabelle's fingernails was a close match for the putty in Christopher Crowley's makeup kit. Also, Dr. Peach didn't get along with his late sister, which means he probably didn't perform her abortion."

Cassie's head came up. "Her *what?*"

Morgan made a dismissing motion. "She had an abortion three months before she died."

"When did she die?"

"Seven years ago."

"So does her having had an abortion signify something?"

"It might."

"Could you be a bit more specific, Morgan?"

"Because of the way Jack cuts up his victims," he replied.

Cassie shivered. "You mean, because he removes their sex organs?"

"Yes."

"But he never rapes them, does he?" she mused, pressing a reflexive hand to her stomach. "So it must be a perversion, a sickness he's trying to work out through violence. And the red hair—Desirée was right about that. Well, sort of. I didn't see any red in Lady Annabelle's hair, but sometimes the light can play tricks, especially candlelight. Don't you think so?"

He nodded, staring through her in a way she couldn't begin to interpret. She would have said he seemed mesmerized, but no doubt that was just wishful thinking. More likely he was off on some new mental tangent. The man's mind never let up.

And yet, in his own way he was extremely attractive, despite the waspish tongue, bouts of temper, moody lapses and his general impatience. When he wanted to, he could be completely charming. Too bad he exerted so little of that charm around her.

From the street beyond the garden, Cassie caught the sound of voices, male and female, singing "Adeste Fideles." She could picture the women in their cloaks and bonnets, their breath white in the frosty night air.

"Holding carol books and sprigs of mistletoe," she said finishing her perfect picture. "Too bad Christmas can't be that simple anymore."

"What?" Morgan was pacing again, deep in thought. She wondered if he ever remembered to eat. She'd never seen him do it.

"There are carolers outside," she explained and stood with a determined motion. "Can't you hear them?"

He made an acknowledging sound in his throat.

"Morgan, stop and listen to them."

Another abstracted grunt.

Resolutely, Cassie walked around the table. She planted herself in front of him, setting her hand on his chest when he would have walked through her. "Will you stop for one minute and listen?"

"I can't."

"Yes, you can," she said, then smiled as an idea came to her. "I know, let's dance."

"Let's what?"

"Dance. You remember, Morgan. Everyone was doing it last night. Surely they haven't outlawed dancing in your time."

"What?" His eyes narrowed mistrustfully. To Cassie's delight, he seemed discomfited, as if he wasn't sure how to deal with her request. He backed up a step, putting some space between them. "You can't dance to a Christmas carol," he said.

Definitely uneasy, she realized, and pounced on the lapse, advancing slowly. "Why not?" she asked.

"Because it isn't music."

Cassie saw his eyes slide sideways. He was searching for an escape. He wouldn't find one. She was feeling very determined tonight. She wanted to touch him, to understand what it was about Anthony Lazarus Morgan that caused her to react to him the way she did.

"Voices are music," she pointed out.

"No, they're not," he snapped.

"Yes, they are." She paused. "Are you afraid of me, Morgan?"

That earned her the desired response. "Certainly not," he retorted and stopped his retreat.

"Then dance with me. Come on." Taking his hand, she placed it on her waist. "And the other one."

"Cassie..."

"Stop arguing. Honest to God, you'd think I was asking you to walk naked through the streets of London." Not a bad idea, since he almost certainly had a fabulous body under those butler's clothes, but right now she would settle for a dance.

As she urged him reluctantly out from behind the table, she recalled the words the straw-haired maid had spoken yesterday. "Mr. M. only does it with ladies."

Possibly true, and if it were, Cassie bet he did it with total dispassion. So maybe his reluctance with her was an uncommon thing. Maybe he was attracted to her and didn't like it.

Or maybe he was a snob and really only *did* do it with ladies.

Five seconds later and one tiny brush of their bodies dispelled the last notion, or at least part of it. He wasn't unmoved by her. And Cassie knew a moment's panic of her own when she discovered just how strongly she was reacting to him.

There had been a hint of it in the actor's change room this afternoon. He'd smelled so wonderfully clean. And his hair...she loved the texture of his dark curls and his skin, and the hardness of his body.

Her breath caught tightly in her chest as the voices outside swelled. Maybe this wasn't such a terrific idea after all.

Torn between a desire to press herself tightly against Morgan and the totally opposite desire to shove his hands away and run back to her side of the table, Cassie submitted as she often did to the less wise of the two.

"You see?" She even managed a teasing smile. "It's not so bad, is it?"

"Umm..."

She knew he was searching for something to say, for some graceful way out. As delightful as that was, his obvious discomfort puzzled Cassie a little. She could picture him all too readily going through the motions of sex, with absolute correctness and a credible amount of passion. No emotional involvement, just another duty performed with his customary calm efficiency.

Her thigh brushed his again. He wasn't a great deal taller than her; their bodies were a perfect fit. Too perfect, she thought, panicking a little.

His hand on her waist burned through the satin of her peach-colored dress. His warm breath grazed her neck and collarbone. The only thing that saved her was Morgan's obvious desire to put as much distance between them as he could.

"I really don't think this is a good idea, Cassie," he said with a glance at the stairs. "Mrs. Dickson will be down in a minute, and you know what she's like."

He was floundering, making excuses. If Cassie hadn't been so shaken herself, she might have questioned why he bothered. As it was she simply stood there staring at him and evaluated her sanity.

What on earth had she been trying to prove? Whatever it was, it had backfired miserably.

She watched his face mutely, waiting for his self-control to reassert itself. To her surprise, instead of distancing himself, he closed his eyes and murmured a fateful "Oh, damn."

Before Cassie could react, he'd inclined his head. She felt his mouth close over hers in a kiss that was unlike anything she could have anticipated. The impact jolted inside and out.

She didn't know how to respond, so she left that to her instincts. Her hands found his shoulders and slid across them. The back of his velvet waistcoat was made of satin, the material smooth and sleek. She could feel the heat of his skin beneath it. His mouth was hot and devouring, practiced, yet at the same time hesitant, as if he was doing this against his better judgment.

The taste of him only made her insanity worse. She didn't know where he came from, or how he lived. Maybe he had a wife and six kids tucked away in some future year. Maybe fidelity meant nothing in the centuries to come. It meant little enough in the 1990s.

Where logic told her to protest, curiosity and desire drove her on. The feel of him, so hard against her, did delicious things to her metabolism. For all his previous reluctance, he was a fantastic kisser. And he touched her in all the right places, a stroke of his hand across her breast, a gentle sucking on her lips, a slight shift of his hips against hers.

But it was only a healthy physical response. His mind was still completely resistant to her.

Even so, Cassie wouldn't have pushed him away. It took the sound of footsteps on the kitchen stairs to accomplish that.

Morgan heard it first. Dragging his mouth free, he stepped back as if burned and immediately tugged his waistcoat into place as Bartholomew, oblivious to the scene he'd interrupted, ambled around the partition.

"Mrs. Dickson'll be right down, Mr. M.," he said. Then he stopped dead, looking swiftly from Morgan to Cassie and back again. Backpedaling, he hastily mumbled, "Uh, I'll just go and tell her not to hurry, shall I?"

"Don't bother, Bartholomew." Morgan's voice contained a note of infinite weariness, in tandem with his reflexive unease. "I have things to do. You and Cassie fix yourselves something to eat before Mrs. Dickson gets here."

"Back in the saddle again," Cassie murmured. She watched with a mixture of regret and lingering astonishment as he took his coat from the back of the chair and headed for the stairs. A sigh escaped her. "He's a complete enigma, Bartholomew."

"Is that like a mystery?"

"Exactly like a mystery." She pushed the layers of brown-red hair from her face with an impatient palm. "One minute he's snapping at me, the next he's charming Lady Mary all over the place, then he turns around and becomes Mr. Proper and Efficient Butler whose composure an earthquake couldn't shake. Who is he, Bartholomew? Is he nice or nasty or a combination of the two?"

Bartholomew's elfin features lit up. "I don't know about that, miss, but I do know one thing for sure."

"And that is?"

"He likes you." His smile widened. "He likes you a lot."

"SIR, I THINK PERHAPS you should return to the parlor," Morgan said firmly.

He was standing in a candle-lit corridor between Cassie and the flamboyant member of parliament, Procopius Rowe. Holding up a politely determined hand, he faced the man with no apparent fear, despite the fact that the M.P. was quite drunk.

"Falling-down drunk" was how Cassie had termed it when he'd lurched around a corner and crashed into her very hard. Before she could recover her balance, he'd proceeded to back her up against the wall. If Morgan hadn't magically appeared behind him, Cassie would have had no choice but to bring her knee up into the M.P.'s groin. Unless of course he'd succeeded in overpowering her first. He was a very, very large man, inches taller than Morgan and a great deal brawnier.

"Sir," Morgan repeated, steadfast in his resolve. "I assure you that Lady Mary would be most displeased if you were to harm her personal maid."

Undeterred, Procopius grinned. With his long red hair and full beard, he reminded Cassie of a Viking. All he needed was the horned hat and sword.

"I'm not going to hurt her, Morgan. I only want to take her into the library for a while."

"I don't think that would be wise, sir."

"Why not?" he thundered. "Has she got the pox?"

"Now wait a minute," Cassie protested, indignant. Morgan held her off with his other hand. His eyes remained fixed on Procopius's. "No, sir, she doesn't. What she has is a nasty tendency to bite."

The M.P. rubbed his large hands together in anticipation. "All the better, then."

Morgan sighed. "Sir," he repeated, "this is Lady Mary's home, and Cassie is Lady Mary's maid."

"And I'm Lady Mary's guest." That righteous declaration cost the M.P. what remained of his already meager balance. With an ungainly lurch, he staggered back into the wall and sent one of the Italian sculptures crashing to the floor.

Folding his hands in front of him, Morgan watched the fine porcelain shatter. "I could fetch some coffee, sir, if you'd like."

Procopius stared fuzzily at the smashed statue. "Blast the Griswalds' wine. Was that expensive?"

Morgan summoned a polite smile, nothing more than a faint curving of his lips. "I believe so, sir." Turning, he offered an easy "Run along downstairs," to Cassie, then started toward the intoxicated man. "The coffee is this way, Mr. Rowe."

"What? Oh, yes." The M.P. staggered upright, gave the statue a final look and Cassie a cheerful wink. "Next time, eh, my pretty?" Then he laughed with gusto and said to Morgan, "Bites, you say?"

"So I'm told, sir. I believe it's the Scottish blood."

Procopius Rowe's boisterous laughter echoed along the corridor long after he and Morgan had disappeared. Cassie made a face in their wake and started off in the other direction.

"You have to watch him, you know." Ignatious Athelbert's voice floating solemnly out of the shadows ahead of Cassie startled her. His covert stance beside a darkened niche suggested the air of a man who'd been eavesdropping for quite some time. Evidently this was a heavily trafficked passageway. "He's a lusty man, that one. Cassie, isn't it?"

"Yes, sir."

"Well, Cassie." He offered her a faltering smile. "Perhaps you would accompany me to the library. I'm quite harmless, I assure you. We could—talk."

He'd painted his lips and cheeks a bright shade of pink tonight. The color reminded Cassie of bubble gum. It was the only color on his face. He looked more like an undertaker than a poet, she thought—sickly and sallow-skinned. Even his dirty blond hair had no life in it.

"I believe Lady Mary wishes to see me," she lied, linking her fingers together. Compared to the overbearing Mr. Rowe, Ignatious Athelbert would be easy for someone with her training to handle. Of course, she'd lose her job if she karate-kicked a guest, but better that than be molested. "If you'd excuse me, sir," she murmured.

The poet's hand closed on her wrist before she could escape. She shivered at the touch of his cold, moist fingers but didn't flinch.

"You don't understand him," he whispered.

He sounded slightly desperate to her. His eyes, a washed-out shade of blue, glittered when he regarded her. There was a sheen of perspiration on his face and no bruise at all on his temple. And, she noticed, a tremor crawling slowly down her spine, he was using his left hand to emphasize his words.

"He murdered Lady Annabelle," Athelbert confided in a nervous and fearful tone. His eyes darted about the hall. "He came like a shadow, Death in the form of a man, creeping up from the sewers of my mind. And suddenly there he was before my eyes."

Cassie tugged discreetly on her wrist. "You mean you saw him? You saw his face?"

"No, no," he denied in mounting agitation. "There was no face to be seen."

"Then what . . . ?"

"In my mind."

He leaned closer, and instinctively Cassie recoiled. His face was wet with perspiration, his eyes overly bright as they peered into hers. His left hand made a wild scrubbing motion in the air.

"He hit me, as I said. But the mind can function even in darkness. The eyes can see. I saw him in a dream, if you will. Yes, a dream." Eyes misting, he stared at a point far above her head. His hand stilled. "She was so beautiful, Lady Annabelle—the beautiful lark met her death after dark. I knew he would kill her, I saw it in my mind before I passed out. I mean, before I lost consciousness. We have this gift in my family, the power to see beyond what exists in the physical world."

"You mean you're psychic."

"We see things," he repeated, blinking rapidly. "My mother, my sister . . . me."

His pupils were dilated, although that wasn't affecting his grip in any way. He squeezed hard enough to hurt.

"You must take care," he said, his voice dropping to a conspiratorial level. "My mind portended death for Lady Annabelle last night. It was only a flash, a fleeting premonition of doom, and at the time I didn't understand what it meant. But tonight, as I watched you with Procopius, I saw the same thing again. For you. A shadow fell across your pretty face. Death's shadow." Long, cold fingers grazed her cheek, then curled into her hair. "The precious flame of life burns for but a moment of time, then, like the lovely snowflake, is no more. Death is a monster of the mind, Cassie Lachlin, a seeping, spreading poison. As it came for Lady Annabelle and the others, so it will eventually come for you."

FROM HIS HIDING PLACE, Jack heard every word the poet spoke. He saw the look of fear and determination on Cassie's features. He saw her gorgeous red-brown hair, shiny like silk and full of deep, glorious waves.

Was she the one? a distant part of his mind wondered.

No, no, this was a servant.

But she had red hair. All the red-haired females must die. It was the only way.

Control, though. He must exercise control in this as in all things. She must not be alerted to his intention. First the other whore must die. Then he would see.

For the moment, he needed to remain hidden, from them and from himself. Let the poet warn her. It would do no good.

Hide, he thought. Don't let her know. And watch out for Mother, too. Don't let her find you. You know what will happen if she does....

Chapter Eight

December 11, 1790

"Say what you like, Morgan, I still think Desirée's afraid because she knows something, or at least suspects it."

They'd just exited Lady Mary's fancy carriage, which apparently Morgan borrowed at will. Wilkie the driver saluted him, said, "Back in a tick, Mr. M.," then gave the reins a sharp slap.

"Well?" Cassie demanded as they made their way into the alley toward the darkened stage door.

"Well, you might be right, but there's nothing I can do about it now."

"You could have talked to her last night."

He cast her an ironic look over his shoulder as he tested the door. "If you'll recall, I was busy with Procopius Rowe last night. Not to mention Sir Gerald. I hardly had time to go looking for Desirée. Damn, it's locked." He pulled a slender metal pick from his coat pocket, glanced quickly about the alley, then asked, "What did she say to you?"

"Well, first she told Mr. Athelbert to get lost—and by the way, that man is definitely on something. After he gave me that creepy warning in the hallway, he pretended to go on to the privy. But I knew he was following me so I headed for the parlor. That's when Desirée came by and noticed him. I could see right away that she was upset. Or scared."

"Of Athelbert?"

"Possibly, although he did slink off when he saw her. Still, she was awfully edgy. She didn't say anything specific, just talked about the Griswalds' party and how queenly Lady Mary looked, but it was only lip service. Oh, and then there was Lady Mary herself," Cassie recalled, tapping his arm. "She was unusually quiet getting ready for bed last night. And yet tonight, when Dr. Peach came by to check her heart, she seemed perfectly fine. She even asked him for a sleeping draft."

Morgan's lips curved. "That's probably because she suspected I was going to slip a similar draft to Sir Gerald." He gave the pick a gentle twist. "Got it. What time is it?"

"Almost eleven."

"Good, we made it before the final curtain."

Once inside the door, Cassie hugged the shadows behind Morgan. They neatly avoided prop men, actors and various other theater personnel. Onstage, Lady Macbeth's mad lament rose up. "'What's done cannot be undone. To bed, to bed to bed.'"

"'But screw your courage to the sticking-place,'" Cassie quoted softly, "'And we'll not fail.' Morgan, where are we going?"

"To Sir Gerald's and Lady Mary's private box. We'll be able to see the whole theater from there. Be quiet on the stairs."

Long skirts were a cumbersome nuisance, Cassie decided as they climbed. She would sell her soul for her jeans and suede jacket. She'd sell even more than that for a bacon double cheeseburger, fries and a Coke.

Christopher Crowley's voice billowed upward from the stage when they reached the Peregrines' plush private box. Once inside, Morgan let his gaze sweep the shadowed audience.

"There she is," he said, pulling Cassie with him to a darkened corner. "Third row back. Jane Brede, in the company of Mr. and Mrs. Gilbert Addinsell."

She wished he wouldn't stand so close. It was quite unnerving. "Why the sarcastic tone?" she asked.

Morgan stole a look around the edge of the tasseled curtain. "Because the Addinsells are famous for their boring personalities. Jane will probably ditch them before the applause has died down."

"Is that a problem? We planned to follow her, anyway, with or without her escorts. Besides, you figured she would bring her own carriage no matter whom she sat with."

"Yes, well, I'd also hoped that prig of a brother of hers would insist on accompanying her, but I don't see any sign of him."

"Morgan, if Jack plans to make Jane Brede his next victim, no one is going to stop him.... And did you really slip Sir Gerald a sleeping powder?"

"What?" He glanced back, frowning slightly. "Of course I did."

She leaned over his shoulder to whisper, "Are you sure he drank it?"

He looked back again, the frown on his lips fully formed now. "What do you mean?"

"Oh, nothing." Feeling more in control now, Cassie rested her back against the papered wall. "It's just that Lady Mary mentioned something yesterday about being tempted to dump Dr. Peach's prescriptions in the nearest potted plant. She said it was a trick she'd picked up from her grandson when he was younger."

"Well, that's reassuring."

Cassie noted his sardonic tone but chose not to take it personally. "Morgan, if it turns out that Sir Gerald dumped his drink tonight, that would mean he knew what you were doing when you slipped him the drug. He might fire you."

"He won't fire me, Cassie," Morgan said with a tolerant sigh. "He'll think Lady Mary told me to drug him."

Cassie's mistrust of Sir Gerald deepened. "Why would she do that? Because *she* suspects him, too?"

Morgan motioned with his hand for her to keep silent. His eyes roamed the stage. "Suspects him, yes, but of mischief, not murder. Sir Gerald's mother preferred her daughter Emily to him, so Sir Gerald used to misbehave to get her attention. I gather he never outgrew that behavior."

"Where are his mother and sister now?"

"His mother's dead. I don't know about Emily. No one talks about her. There's a rumor that she wasn't really Lord Peregrine's daughter, but as I say, her name is seldom mentioned."

A possible illegitimate sister for Sir Gerald. Cassie wondered briefly if Emily had red hair, then dismissed the unfounded notion as the actor playing Macduff began his closing address.

Her eyes scanned the audience. "Morgan, look," she said, poking him. "There's Desirée and Athelbert. And Dr. Peach."

"Together?"

"No. Well," she amended, "Desirée and Athelbert might be together, but Dr. Peach seems to be alone."

Morgan's gloved fingers closed on her arm before she could determine the doctor's status. "Jane's leaving," he said shortly. "Come on."

He was not an easy man to follow in a crowd, Cassie discovered. He moved like a tracker, and somehow bodies always seemed to part for him. He reached the front entrance a good thirty seconds ahead of her.

Finally, however, the human tide carried her through the doors.

"Cassie, hello. What are you doing at the theater?"

Desirée swept forward before Cassie could conceal herself in the crowd. A swarm of carriages filled the street, all jingling and creaking as their owners climbed in. A large man in a hurry brushed rudely past, jostling her. It gave her a moment to think, but even that wasn't enough.

"I, uh..."

"Snuck away?" Desirée supplied when Cassie's mind went blank. Her brown eyes sparkled. "Don't worry, I won't tell. It was a good play, don't you think?"

"Mr. Crowley plays a convincing Macbeth," Cassie agreed. She saw Ignatious Athelbert approaching and tensed. Why didn't Morgan ever get caught by these people? "Good evening, Mr. Athelbert," she said.

He gave no indication that he'd heard her. His glazed eyes surveyed the assorted carriages.

"I don't see your coach, Mrs. Deveau," he said to Desirée.

She kept her response civil. "It's here, Mr. Athelbert. However, as I explained to you when you insisted on partnering me inside, I am not a woman who fears to attend social functions unescorted."

"Ah, but such behavior is most unseemly, my dear." Dr. Peach joined them in his poor-fitting wig and huge black coat. His plump red cheeks still said Santa Claus to Cassie, but his blue eyes seemed less than jolly. In fact, they were downright disapproving, and not just of Desirée.

"Do you make a habit of attending the Haymarket?" he inquired reproachfully of Cassie.

His tone rankled. She forced a smile, but couldn't quite restrain her temper. "Why, is it illegal for servants to patronize theaters?"

"Technically, no. However—"

"Good evening, Dr. Peach," Morgan interrupted, both his tone and his manner pleasant. "You're looking very well this cold December night."

The doctor's expression lost a measure of its criticism. "Ah, Morgan. Good evening to you. I trust you're with this young woman."

"Yes, sir, I am," he replied easily. "Good evening, Mrs. Deveau."

"There it is," Athelbert sang out, flinging an exaggerated arm toward the street. "Your coach, my lady."

Desirée ignored his theatrical bow and lifted her skirts. "If you'll excuse me," she said, then sent Morgan a meaningful look. "Perhaps you would see that Mr. Athelbert finds a cab to take him home. I don't think he's quite himself tonight."

Morgan gave his head a polite bow. "Certainly, ma'am. Will you be requiring a cab, as well, Dr. Peach?"

"No, no, my coach is waiting." Hands on his walking stick, the doctor turned to Cassie. "Lady Mary was resting comfortably when you left, I trust?"

"Very much so—sir."

A young boy pushed roughly past her to hand the doctor a note while Morgan deposited the dreamy poet in his cab. "Gent down the way said I should give you this, sir," the boy panted.

"Gent? Oh, yes, of course." Dr. Peach skimmed the note, then signaled for his carriage. "I've an emergency, it seems. See that Lady Mary doesn't overdo, Morgan."

"I will, sir. And good night."

As soon as the doctor heaved his massive body into the coach, Cassie stuck out her tongue at him. "Good night to you, too, you pompous jerk."

"He's a man, Cassie," Morgan said.

"Which translates to the same thing in this century. Where's Jane?"

He nodded through the crowd. "Over there with Crowley."

Cassie strained for a clear view. "I don't see him."

"He's in the shadows."

"Trying to coax her back into his warm dressing room?"

"Maybe. But it won't work if he doesn't come up with a present."

"And they called Joelle a hooker," Cassie said in disgust.

Five minutes passed, then ten. The theater emptied, most of the patrons departing swiftly. Darkness prevailed on the snowy street, darkness and the earsplitting squawk of Jane Brede's laughter.

"No, I really mustn't," she insisted, drawing back. "My carriage is waiting, as you see, and my brother will be expecting me."

"Not bloody likely," Morgan muttered, easing Cassie into the shelter of the old theater.

"I thought you said her brother was a prig."

"He is, but he's not a stupid one."

Uncomfortable in his grasp, Cassie squirmed free. "Well, anyway," she noted, "Jane's leaving. And it looks as if Mr. Crowley's going back inside."

Morgan nodded in agreement. With a hand on her arm, he held her in the shadows until Jane's horses had clopped past, then he motioned for Wilkie, a silent specter across the wide street.

It was beginning to snow again. Cassie could feel the carriage wheels slipping as they plodded along behind the other coach.

"Not too close, Wilkie," Morgan called up. Then, a few minutes later, he added impatiently, "I said not too close, but don't fall back so far that we lose her."

Wilkie leaned down. His cap and eyebrows were covered with wet snow. "Sorry, Mr. M., but I've got a lame horse here. We'll have to stop so's I can have a look."

Swearing under his breath, Morgan tugged on his leather gloves. "Cowl up," he told Cassie.

"We're not going to follow on foot," she protested, knowing that's exactly what they were going to do.

He glanced at her feet. "You wore your boots, didn't you?"

"Well, yes, but..." She hadn't expected him to notice. "Even so," she said reasonably. "We'll never be able to keep up with horses."

"Fine, you stay with Wilkie."

"That's not what I—Morgan!" But he was gone. With an irritated grunt, Cassie hopped from the carriage. "You try wearing a long full skirt and a million petticoats and see how much you like to run," she muttered crankily.

To see much of anything at night in 1790 London was difficult at the best of times. With the snow blowing in her face and only the odd oil lamp to break the darkness, seeing more than a yard or two in front of her was next to impossible. Cassie barely managed to keep Morgan in sight. Jane Brede's carriage was a lost cause.

One thing she was sure of, this was no upper-class neighborhood. The air felt damp despite the snow. That meant the river must be close by. Jack usually murdered in the vicinity of the river, Cassie recalled with a shiver. At least, he did in this century.

"Morgan." Cupping her mouth with her hands, she shouted his name into the wind. He'd never hear her. All she could do was keep going and hope that the moving shadow ahead of her was him and not a figment of her freezing imagination.

"I hate you, Anthony Lazarus Morgan," she swore as she ran. "It's cold, it's dark and I have no idea where I am."

She would have gone right on cursing him if she hadn't in the process of turning a sharp corner, collided full force with a solid black wall. The impact knocked her breath from her lungs and left her gasping for air as she stumbled backward.

It wasn't a wall she'd hit, she realized with a start. It was a man!

Strong hands gripped her arms while panic gripped her mind. She twisted in his grasp and would have planted her foot in his stomach if something hadn't suddenly clicked in her head. The smell of his hair and skin. Only one man in this time understood the value of soap and water.

"Morgan," she growled, tempted to kick him, anyway. "You bas—"

She never finished the word. Her neck snapped painfully as he whirled her around and grabbed her hand. "That's Jane's carriage up there," he said. "Come on."

Cassie forgot her annoyance and squinted through the driving snow. "Where? I don't see anything."

She heard something, though—the snap of a whip behind her, followed by the pounding of horses' hooves and then a great whoosh of breath.

"Morgan, look out!"

Using all her strength, Cassie shoved him sideways out of the line of the charging horses.

No lanterns swung on the sides of the carriage they pulled. Cassie caught a glimpse of a large black blur careening past and felt a rush of air on her cheeks. Then it was gone, or at least the immediate danger was gone. The resounding clatter of wood, chains and thundering hooves hung like an evil miasma in the cold night air.

On his knees in the snow, Morgan said through his teeth, "It's Jack." His eyes were trained on the swiftly vanishing rear of the coach. "Here." From his coat he produced a gun, a .44 Magnum of all things!

"You do know how to use this don't you?" Morgan demanded.

Cassie shook herself. "Of course I do. It's just— Never mind."

"Cover me, then," he said.

He was off and running before Cassie could collect either her skirts or her wits. She caught sight of the black coach a moment later. It had lurched around a corner and now stood motionless at the side of the road opposite Jane's.

Cassie still couldn't pinpoint her location, but this was definitely some dark, dismal part of London, possibly an area where people lived above their shops.

If the brick-and-stone buildings were in fact shops, they were cluttered ones, tall and narrow, old even at this point in time, and extremely run-down. This wasn't the Mayfair or Belgravia area of her time. Billingsgate, maybe, nearer London Bridge. Why on earth would Jane Brede come here?

It was a pointless question. Jane *was* here. Her halted carriage proved as much.

Morgan was far ahead of Cassie by now, but still not close enough to intercept the figure that darted across the street to Jane's coach. One blow to the driver's jaw and he went down. The figure then slid into a snowbank, and yanked open the carriage door.

Jane's initial peal of laughter turned to a bloodcurdling scream. Cassie heard Morgan shout for her to use the gun. Skidding to a stop, she took aim. She raised the Magnum two-handed, held it steady, then squeezed the trigger.

The figure ducked at the last second; he must have. Cassie knew her own ability was considerable even in these conditions. The bullet whizzed through the snowy air where Jack's shoulder had been and on through the night.

Jane screamed again as the horses reared in their harnesses. The scream became a gurgle, then suddenly a wild screech, as Morgan drew nearer. Cassie saw Jack hesitate, then release the woman. Tossing her squirming body in the snow, he spun and ran.

She thought about firing again, but realized that Jack had flung Jane down directly in front of the panicked horses. Another loud bang and they'd trample her for sure.

So she ran instead, slipping and sliding to where the woman lay sobbing in the snow. Morgan had the horses by their bridles and was settling them. Jack had already darted off down a nearby lane.

Cassie's mind worked rapidly as she dragged Jane Brede out of harm's way. Jack hadn't gone for his carriage, although he might have reached it before Morgan caught him. That implied to her that tracing the carriage and horses would do them no good in terms of identifying him.

And he'd been spry, she recalled. Well, as spry as you could be in this kind of weather. That might let Dr. Peach off as a suspect. The doctor used a walking stick and weighed at least three hundred pounds. On the other hand, some of that bulk might be padding.

"Are you all right?" Morgan asked Jane, who'd wrapped her fingers like talons around Cassie's arms.

"I think so," she said in a squeaky voice. "Oh, Morgan, it was awful. He was all black and he had something on his face, a mask or something. He looked like a jester."

"Jack of spades," Morgan said, then stabbed a determined finger at Cassie. "You stay here." He looked around in the snow. "Where's my gun?"

"No, Morgan, wait," Cassie protested. "You can't go after him. What if he's waiting for you?"

She had hold of his coat, but he shook free, dropping the Magnum deep into his coat pocket. "Stay with Jane" was all he said, then he vanished into the blowing snow.

The wind howled in Cassie's ears. He'd get killed; she knew it. One shouldn't rush blindly into things. She had rushed into the cellar of Amblewood House and look what had happened to her.

With great difficulty, Cassie extricated herself from Jane's clinging hands. "Can you drive your coach?" she asked.

Jane blinked, wet-eyed. "Drive?"

"Yes, drive. Can you do it?"

"I—think so. But you can't leave me."

Cassie set her frantic hands away, hauled her to her feet and shoved her toward the carriage. "Keep a tight rein on the horses, but get out of here," she ordered. "Go to the nearest place you know." She hesitated, then asked, "Do you know anyone who lives down here?"

"Mr. Crowley," the frightened woman answered. "And Mr. Athelbert. The Crimptons who make my brother's shoes, and Mr. Stockwell, the *London Times* reporter."

"Go to the Crimptons'," Cassie decided, pushing the reluctant woman up into the seat beside her groggy driver. "And see that he gets to a doctor."

"But—"

"Go." Cassie gave the lead horse's backside a smack as she hopped down.

Trusting that Jane Brede's fear of Jack would overcome her fear of handling the unwieldy coach, she started for the alley. Not that she knew where to run exactly. She did know it wasn't the brightest idea she'd ever had. But she couldn't let Morgan go after Jack alone. What if Jack ambushed him, stabbed him, had a gun of his own tucked away somewhere?

Cassie stumbled on, legs trembling, heart racing. She didn't pass a soul, either in the alley or on the streets. Dark, ugly buildings pressed in on her. If candles burned in the upper windows, she couldn't see them.

But she could smell the water. The Thames hadn't frozen over yet; she must almost be at the river.

Snow crunched under her boots. Large flakes blew in her eyes, obscuring her vision. No, not quite obscuring it. Something moved to her left, a black silhouette streaking through the curtain of white snow.

It wasn't Morgan—the gait was wrong, too jerky. It was, however, running straight toward her. That meant whoever it was had spotted her. And Morgan had taken back his gun.

A momentary sense of panic enveloped her. She shoved it ruthlessly down. Veering, she switched direction, almost lost her footing, regained it and ran on.

Think, she commanded herself, fighting a breathlessness born of exhaustion and terror. She might be able to flip him. If it was Jack he would undoubtedly grab her from behind. That was the usual method. Grab the victim, throw her down, slit her throat, then cut her up. No rape, just murder and mutilation.

Why? Cassie's frantic brain wondered as she plunged on. Why in his most recent murders had he decided to prey on women with red hair? Why prostitutes in other centuries and noblewomen now?

Oh, damn, why hadn't she listened to Morgan?

A sob crawled into her throat, threatening to choke her. He was behind her now, very close behind. She heard the harsh panting of his breath above the wind.

Fingers clutched at the black cloak that blew out in her wake. She slipped again on the snow.

"Stop," her pursuer cried. Any other words were whipped from his mouth.

She felt the fingers grope for her cloak again. This time they caught and held. With the clasp securely fastened, his merciless yank almost gave her whiplash. Her head snapped back; her feet flew out from under her. She landed on her bottom so unexpectedly that he had to jump to avoid stepping on her.

Considerate of him, Cassie thought desperately, scrambling up. She aimed a kick at him, but he rolled away. Then, out of nowhere, another pair of hands seized her.

"Are you crazy, lady?" a man's voice growled in her ear. He smelled of soot and sweat and shag tobacco. "You all right, Artie?"

"Bloody hell, she's a wildcat," the first man gasped. "Kicked me good, she did, as I was going over her head."

Irish.

Cassie wriggled and twisted and stomped on her captor's foot with the heel of her boot. The man's response was to shake her so hard that she saw spots. Still, she managed to work herself around so she could view his face.

It was black—not naturally, but with grime. He was short and wiry, as skinny as a weasel—and she'd never seen him before in her life.

"I don't know you," she declared, knocking his hands away with her elbows. "Who are you?"

The man treated her to a mocking, yellow-toothed smile. "Well now, I don't know you, either, do I, but I sure would like to."

Free of his hands, Cassie immediately edged sideways. "You're not Jack," she said mistrustfully.

"Ah, he'd be your husband, would he?"

"Who?"

"Jack."

Cassie shuddered. "Hardly." Her mistrust deepened. "Who are you, and why was Artie here chasing me?"

"Well, Artie thought he was doing a good deed, 'cause that's the way Artie is." The man inched closer. "Me, though, I say women of breeding who run about the docks after dark must be looking to make a few quid on the side."

"Knock it off, Derek," the Irishman ordered. "Don't you mind him, miss. We'd just finished a job on Grimpole's chimneys when we saw you go running by. You were heading straight for the river."

"I was?"

"Yes, ma'am, you were. We saw someone behind you for a minute and reckoned you were being chased. He disappeared when he saw Derek and me, but you just kept right on running for the Thames."

Scrunching the sides of her cloak together, Cassie managed a faint smile. "Thank you for stopping me," she said, "but I don't think I'd have fallen into the Thames."

"Don't you, now," Artie replied gently. "Well, I wouldn't be too sure of that if I were you."

He pointed at Cassie's feet, and she followed his outstretched finger down. The icy water of the river spread out below her like a huge, wet grave not six inches from where she stood.

JACK STOOD MOTIONLESS at the upper end of the dock. "You were lucky tonight, my pretty redhead," he whispered to her through the swirling snow. "And Jane was lucky, as well. I don't like that, not one little bit."

He closed his eyes, wrapping his black coat tightly about him while he regained his breath and his control.

He blamed Morgan for his failure tonight, but everything else was her fault. Hers because she was what Mother had really wanted. A lovely little daughter to dress up and parade about.

And yet Mother hadn't been especially nice to her, either. No indeed, Mother had hurt her quite badly, as he recalled. Sometimes he used to sneak in and watch the horror unfold, but mostly he'd preferred not to be there.

Because Mother could be mean when she wanted to be. He knew that from experience. Before her daughter had been born, Mother had lavished all her attention, some of it good but most of it bad, on her son. So if he was honest, Jack would have to say he hadn't minded her being there in the beginning. Let Mother's little girl be abused for a change instead of him, he'd thought. It was only fair.

A gust of wind hit him full in the face, reviving him. He saw red hair in his mind and then a flash of her smiling face. She was taunting him. She'd been taunting him from birth. She would taunt him after death. But it would be all right. Once all the red-haired women were dead, there'd be nothing left to remind him of her.

Smiling, he let his head fall back, let the snow touch his cold cheeks, let himself dream of that glorious day. When all the red-haired women were dead.

Chapter Nine

December 12, 1790
2:00 a.m.

"I had him," Morgan said through gritted teeth. "I was that close, and then I lost him."

Frustrated, he paced the floor in his bedroom, tapping the side of one hand against the fingers of his other. Cassie, wrapped in a blanket in front of the fire, sipped hot tea and watched him in thoughtful silence. Bartholomew sat on a low stool near the window and regarded them both. He tried very hard not to grin, because Mr. M. wouldn't like that, and his temper was on the verge of snapping.

Not that Cassie seemed worried about it. Wary, yes, but not worried. It didn't matter, of course. Mr. M. would never hit her.

"He sent her a note," Morgan mumbled to himself, his brow furrowed in concentration.

Bartholomew leaned forward. "Who sent a note, sir?" he asked.

Morgan sent him an irritated look. "Well, how should I know? Jack, obviously, whoever he is. Anyway, the handwriting matches."

Bartholomew appealed to Cassie, who explained, "The handwriting on the note Jack sent to Morgan is the same as the writing on a note that Jane Brede received at the theater tonight. We went to the Crimptons' flat and talked to her. She told us that a young peasant boy gave her the note between the first and second acts of *Macbeth.* The writer—she doesn't know who that was—asked her to come to Poldart Street after the play."

"So that's why she didn't go to Mr. Crowley's dressing room," Bartholomew said. "But then, doesn't that mean Mr. Crowley isn't Jack?"

"No, it doesn't," Morgan retorted shortly. "Christopher Crowley is famous for playing games. The note said, 'Come to Poldart Street and meet one who admires your charm so sweet. Say naught to anyone who asks, and you shall receive a treat.'"

"Bad poetry," Cassie said, "but Mr. Crowley certainly could have sent the note, Bartholomew. Jane said he did something similar once before, sent a message during one of his performances to a woman asking her to come to a certain Kensington coffeehouse. After the play he pretended to try and seduce her into coming back to his dressing room, knowing full well she'd be too intrigued by a note from a mysterious admirer to resist going to the coffeehouse. She went and, voilà, enter Mr. Crowley with wine, flowers and charm to spare.... And stop glowering at me, Morgan. I know you're angry, but you went running off after Jack. Why shouldn't I have gone running off after you?"

"You could've been killed."

"So could you."

"I had a gun."

"Jack might have had two guns, for all you knew."

"That's not the point, Cassie. You should have gone with Jane. What if he'd circled back to his carriage?"

"But he didn't, did he? And you said later that the carriage belonged to a Scottish couple you know—" she emphasized the word *Scottish* deliberately "—who are out of town for the holidays. So we're practically positive the horses and carriage were stolen. All we have to do is confirm that with the couple's groom later today. And what gives you the right to tell me what I can and can't do? I'm not some passive pedestal-sitting female who wants her decisions made for her, or even accepts that they will be."

"No, you're not," Morgan retorted dryly, tapping his fingers on the desk. "You're an annoyance and a distraction, and I should have sent you back the moment I realized where you came from."

A delighted grin lit Bartholomew's sparrow features. He'd never seen Morgan so testy, and he'd seen Morgan a lot of ways in three years. Cassie must be something very special to be affecting him like this. Morgan hadn't been much more than mildly aggravated when he'd made Bartholomew return his time box.

"Where is it, Bartholomew?" he'd said in a resigned voice yesterday afternoon.

"I don't know," Bartholomew had replied, straight-faced.

Morgan had sighed. "You do know, don't you? All right, hand it over or I'll put you on privy duty."

Bartholomew had relinquished the box with a twinge of reluctance. Cleaning out potties was the worst job at the manor. But he didn't want Cassie to leave, either.

Well, she was still here, and intact despite almost plunging into the Thames, an incident that Morgan would use against her for a long time.

"You'd have drowned if you'd gone into the water. You know that, don't you?" he was saying now as he paced. "I don't know why I let you stay, I really don't."

Tossing off her blanket, Cassie went to stand in front of him. It was something you didn't see the women here doing very often, Bartholomew thought. Only Lady Mary challenged men, and only because she was old and she'd had a weak husband.

A weak husband and a shrew of a daughter, as Bartholomew recalled. A shrew in sheep's clothing, though. Beautiful, vain and, as Morgan would say, mad as a bloody hatter.

Luckily, Morgan had never met her, but he knew about her even so. Sir Gerald told Morgan everything about his mother and his sister—as well as his sex life, which was rumored to be neither modest nor typical.

Setting aside those uncomfortable thoughts, Bartholomew listened to the argument between Cassie and Morgan, although he only heard it with half an ear. Something was happening out in the kitchen, a racket that shouldn't be there at two o'clock in the morning.

"Mr. M.?" he said when it persisted.

"What?" Morgan snapped.

"Someone's banging on the door, sir. Shall I answer it?"

"No, I'll get it." He waved a dismissing hand. "It's probably that idiot lord of the manor, lost between his carriage and the front door. And don't say I told you so," he warned Cassie from the threshold. "He drank the bloody draft—it just didn't take effect."

When he was gone, an exasperated Cassie appealed to Bartholomew. "Is that man ever not disagreeable?"

Bartholomew grinned. "You're catching him at a bad time is all. He gets cross when people get murdered."

"Well, so do I, but you don't see me taking it out on everyone around me." She pointed at his hand. "What's that?"

"What? Oh, the evening paper. Mr. Stockwell wrote another article on Lady Annabelle. Said the parliament should consider appointing a new committee if this is the best Sir Patrick's lot can do."

"Really?" Cassie reached for the folded *Times*. "That's not what he said yesterday."

"Well, he sometimes changes his opinions when he does a second piece like this."

Cassie scanned the column. "I wonder why?"

"Mr. M. says he enjoys being contro—something."

"Controversial."

"Yeah, that's it. Mr. M. doesn't trust him, either. Says its too convenient how Mr. Stockwell showed up so soon after the baroness died and then again when Lady Annabelle was murdered."

"What about the first woman?" Cassie asked.

"Mrs. Booth? I didn't know about her until Mr. M. told me yesterday. They kept her death quiet on account of Sir Patrick's father who's such a prig."

"His father, Jane Brede's brother—sounds like an epidemic."

"Beg pardon, miss?"

"Nothing. So what exactly does Sir Patrick's father have to do with the hushing up of Abigail Dexter Booth's death?"

"He didn't want another scandal marring the family's good name," Morgan answered as he reentered the room. He seemed engrossed in an unfolded piece of parchment. His thumbnail rested on his bottom tooth, which was a bad sign, Bartholomew knew. "Not that Sir Patrick could do any more damage than his mother did," Morgan continued distantly, "but the old lord's a religious fanatic. He thinks the devil possessed his wife, then when she died, moved into his son." A ridge formed between his eyes. "Where's Clophardy Alley, Bartholomew?"

"That's in Whitechapel, sir," Bartholomew said proudly. "Near the cemetery."

Morgan tapped his thumbnail lightly on his tooth. "Same writing," he murmured. Then he said to Cassie, "Get your cloak."

"What? Why?"

For an answer, he handed her the parchment. She read the message out loud.

"'Your interference accomplished nothing. Look to Clophardy Alley if you don't believe me. They're all the same in the end. Highbred or not, they're whores, in their hearts and in their souls.

"'There she lies now, where she belongs. But remember this, Morgan, it could have been any of them. It could have been the one who was with you tonight....'"

CLOPHARDY ALLEY WASN'T near the cemetery, it was in it, and it was a ghastly place, replete with bottomless black shadows and stark headstones.

"It reminds me of the place where the Ghost of Christmas Future brought Scrooge," Cassie whispered to Bartholomew.

Nervous and silent, he walked beside her. A few feet ahead of them, Morgan lit the way with an oil-burning lantern. "I don't know any Scrooge," Bartholomew said, pressing closer to her, "but I do know I don't like this place.

All I can hear is us walking. It's like the rest of the city's dead."

"Well, everyone here certainly is," Morgan remarked, his tone ironic though somewhat abstract. "I don't see any unburied bodies."

After the earlier events of that night, Cassie made a point of staying right on his heels. "I still think it's a setup. Three in the morning, a dark, deserted place—it's a perfect setting."

She saw Morgan's ponytail move from side to side. "It doesn't fit Jack's personality."

"Which is?"

"He loses control. When the urge to kill comes over him, he needs to satisfy it. He couldn't have Jane, so he murdered another woman in her place."

"Agreed, but that doesn't mean he won't also try to murder us."

"Have it your way," Morgan said, not looking back. "Keep that gun up, Bartholomew, or else give it to Cassie."

"Yes, Mr. M." Bartholomew immediately relinquished possession of the unwieldy weapon.

"There's a lot of trampled snow over there, Mr. M.," Bartholomew said, pointing left.

The storm had subsided. Only the odd snowflake floated through the cold night air. The temperature had dipped well below freezing. It would be like sleeping in a meat locker on the third floor tonight, Cassie reflected gloomily.

Morgan lit the way to the patch of ground Bartholomew had indicated. There were smears of blood on the snow, though surely not as much as Jack usually left.

Shining the lantern around, Morgan shook his head. "It looks more like a small animal was attacked here."

Cassie raised her eyes to the bare-limbed trees. Icicles clung to the tips of the branches, frosted with snow and now caught in the glow of Morgan's lantern. It was a beautiful sight, so much so that she forgot for a minute that she was standing in a graveyard. Her mind conjured pictures of plum pudding and Christmas crackers, turkey and pine trees . . . and Morgan.

"Damn," she whispered, shutting her eyes. Why couldn't she stop thinking about him? Why did his mouth absolutely fascinate her? Why did almost everything about him fascinate her?

She should have known better than to walk backward with her eyes closed. Before she realized what was happening, her heel caught in a snowy rut, her foot snagged in the hem of her long dress, and for the second time that night, she wound up on her backside, wondering for the umpteenth time how the women of this era coped with such ponderous clothing.

It surprised her that Morgan was the one who reached her first.

"You really are a klutz in that outfit, aren't you?" he said with no small amount of sarcasm.

So much for chivalry. She slapped his hand away and started to climb to her feet. Then, looking down at her own hand, which had embedded itself in a snowdrift, she stopped.

"You're lucky that gun didn't discharge," Morgan continued. "They're not the most reliable weapons."

She kept staring. "Morgan."

"Well, come on then." Giving Bartholomew the lantern, he reached impatiently down for her. "You can't sit there all night."

"Morgan!"

"Oh, God." He rolled his eyes. "What is it now? Did you sprain something?"

Cassie stared at her palm in mute horror. "It's blood," she whispered dizzily around the lump in her throat. "I put my hand in a puddle of blood."

"What?"

Bartholomew began to hop about. "She's right, Mr. M." He jabbed a finger. "Under the snow. It's all red. And there's part of a—"

"Yes, yes," Morgan snapped, cutting him off. Yanking up Cassie's cowl, he lifted her off the snowdrift and turned her head firmly sideways. "Don't look. Don't think about it. Here." He pulled a handkerchief from his inside pocket and wiped off her hand. "Take this and go stand over by the trees. Bartholomew, go with her."

"What? No." Cassie came out of her trance. "I'm fine," she said shakily. At least, she would be once she got the blood off her hand. "I've seen dead bodies before." Bending, she scrubbed her palm in a clean patch of snow. "I told you that when Lady Annabelle was—" Her eyes widened suddenly, and she spun to stare at the white mound in revulsion. "My God, I fell on—it!"

"Her," Bartholomew corrected, then clamped his mouth shut at Morgan's dangerous sideways look.

The blood wasn't warm, Cassie thought sickly, but it wasn't frozen, either. Good Lord, Jack had sent the note to Morgan before he even . . .

She took a deep breath, but couldn't bring herself to dig as Morgan did. Bartholomew worked gingerly, uncovering the feet where Cassie knelt with her head bowed.

"She's a prostitute," Morgan said at last, sitting back on his heels. "Ruby Fox. She works out of a tavern in the area where Jane Brede was attacked."

Her stomach settling, Cassie asked, "Did he—cut her up?"

Morgan nodded, rubbing his temples between his thumb and forefinger, as if he had a phenomenal headache. "We'll have to contact Sir Patrick. Bartholomew, go and fetch a policeman. Tell him to find someone on the committee. Dill and Lambert live near here. They can find Sir Patrick."

"Yes, sir."

Cassie started to stand, then almost tripped over her hem again. Her fingers clutched at Morgan's coat. "Look!" she exclaimed. "Over there. Someone's running through the headstones."

"What?" He swung around, extending the lantern.

Cassie bumped into him from behind in her eagerness to see. "He's heading for the street. He's wearing a black cloak or coat, and he has—" She concentrated her vision, squinting into the shadows far ahead where the figure had vanished. Her fingers dug in deeply. "Morgan, he had red hair!"

DESIRÉE RAN AS FAST as she could away from the cemetery, away from the dread that gripped her. She'd risked her life by following him here tonight. He was vicious, insane and capable of committing any atrocity.

Her hood fell back once but she yanked it up. Had Morgan or Cassie or the little gnome with them spotted her? Had the man who called himself Jack seen her?

Oh, God, why had she done this?

"A graveyard, guv, in the middle of winter?" she'd overheard the prostitute with filthy red hair ask earlier. "Cost you an extra sixpence if I hafta do it in the snow."

The man at her side had smiled, a ghastly serene smile with no teeth. "Call me Jack," he'd said, and the prostitute had shrugged.

"Jack it is." She looked around at the crooked headstones. "So where d'you wanna do it, then?"

"Oh, here would be fine," Jack had said politely, setting his lantern down.

Desirée slipped on a patch of ice but ran on.

The prostitute hadn't had a chance to scream. With his arm, Jack had hauled her up against him, her back crushed to his chest. Then he'd raised the knife he kept hidden in his sleeve and slit her throat.

He'd talked while he did it, grunted and muttered and giggled like a raving lunatic. What would he do if he discovered she'd been watching?

Desirée knew the answer to that, and the knowledge spurred her on. He was lurking in the vicinity; she knew it. Maybe he would go after Morgan, but she doubted it.

Morgan. Banking down her hysteria, Desirée forced her reckless feet to slow before she broke a leg. There was no one behind her when she looked. She could think—she must think—about Morgan, who was surely not a mere butler, and Cassie, who just as surely was not a ladies' maid.

Think, yes, but she didn't dare risk confiding in them, Desirée realized mournfully. He would find out. He hadn't attacked her tonight; he'd gone instead for Jane Brede, and later for the prostitute. It was hoping for a great deal, but maybe he didn't realize that she'd witnessed his barbarous acts.

Yes, silence was the wisest choice for the moment. She'd lost her chance to do anything of worth tonight, of course, but there would be another time. God help her, if what she'd seen so far was any indication, there would be many times, many victims.

"But I won't—I *can't*—be one of them," she whispered, and the fierceness of that vow momentarily bolstered her courage.

Nevertheless, she looked backward several times before she reached the street and clung to the darkest possible shadows when she did. And she could only pray that he wouldn't be hiding in one of them.

TODDY CLAPPER'S Coffeehouse was a dark and dirty place, suited to rats and outcasts and typhoid. It sat on a street corner near the lower end of the cemetery, had very little light and a number of regulars who liked it that way.

Morgan knew many of these people quite well. He'd made a point of knowing them. But they weren't likely to talk to him when he was in the company of men like Sir Patrick Welland, Julian Stockwell and Christopher Crowley.

"Look, this is none of my business," the actor protested as the five men, Bartholomew included, took a table near the window. "I didn't attack Jane Brede, and I didn't kill the whore in the cemetery. I live miles from here. Not to mention," he added with a meaningful arch of his brows, "that I was in bed when Sir Patrick's goons came banging on my door."

"Why is your clothing all rumpled, then?" Sir Patrick demanded in his usual loutish fashion. "And your face paint is smeared. I don't know many people who sleep in their face paint."

Several shadowed heads turned at Sir Patrick's indiscreet observations. Morgan saw one little man listening with interest—Bertie, the church mouse who swept up after funerals and Sunday services. He spent a lot of time in and around the cemetery.

Giving Bartholomew a kick with his foot, Morgan nodded at the tiny man. "Make sure he stays put."

"Right you are, Mr. M." Obediently, Bartholomew worked his chair around so he would have the best possible view of the shop.

"I'm rumpled and smeared," Christopher said, giving his lace handkerchief a wave, "Because you dragged me away from Gertie just when things were getting good. I never said I was alone in bed."

"The dead woman was Ruby Fox and she worked out of the same tavern as your Gertie," Julian Stockwell told him, head bent over his notebook.

"So you were acquainted with Ruby Fox, too, were you, Julian?" Sir Patrick asked.

Julian's dark head came up. If looks could kill, Morgan thought, observing it all in silence. "Yes, I was," the reporter answered coldly. "Is that a crime?"

Crowley sniffed. "If my being with Gertie is a crime, then your knowing the dead woman would seem to me to be an even bigger one."

"Tell us, Mr. Crowley," Morgan inserted with deliberate innocence, "were you with Gertie all evening after your performance?"

"No...yes." The actor's hazel eyes slid to Sir Patrick, then back to Morgan. "I have no sense of time, you know that, Morgan. And neither does Gertie," he added hastily.

He had no sense of anything, if you asked Morgan, and not much talent, either. Cassie was right—Christopher Crowley was the wrong sort of man to be playing the part of the fop. He was too muscular, his features, though handsome, too rough around the edges to suit his adopted effeminate style.

"Don't trust him," Cassie had said while Morgan was practically shoveling her into a cab. "And don't trust Sir Patrick or his shadow, either."

His shadow being Julian Stockwell, who had arrived at the cemetery, in Sir Patrick's company, in Sir Patrick's coach, no explanation offered.

It had taken till dawn for the committee agents to round up their leader and bring him to the scene. It had only taken Julian Stockwell ten seconds to identify the corpse. "No arrangement of possessions this time," he'd noted as he

THE HARLEQUIN READER SERVICE®: HERE'S HOW IT WORKS

Accepting free books puts you under no obligation to buy anything. You may keep the books and gift and return the shipping statement marked "cancel". If you do not cancel, about a month later we'll send you 4 additional novels, and bill you just $2.44 each plus 25¢ delivery and applicable sales tax, if any.* That's the complete price, and—compared to cover prices of $2.99 each—quite a bargain! You may cancel at any time, but if you choose to continue, every month we'll send you 4 more books, which you may either purchase at the discount price . . . or return at our expense and cancel your subscription.

*Terms and prices subject to change without notice. Sales tax applicable in N.Y.

If offer card is missing, write to: Harlequin Reader Service, 3010 Walden Ave., P.O. Box 1867, Buffalo, NY 14269-1867

BUSINESS REPLY MAIL

FIRST CLASS MAIL PERMIT NO. 717 BUFFALO, NY

POSTAGE WILL BE PAID BY ADDRESSEE

HARLEQUIN READER SERVICE
3010 WALDEN AVE
PO BOX 1867
BUFFALO NY 14240-9952

wrote. "But the rest of it's the same. Chopped up, throat slashed, organs removed."

"Buried in the snow," Cassie had reminded him. "That's not the same as the other victims."

"Good point." He'd written it down. "The incisions look identical, though. Made by someone who's left-handed, isn't that what you said last time?"

"Did I?" she'd murmured, and glanced at the pencil he held.

In his right hand, Morgan reflected now, sitting back. He looked over at Bartholomew, saw that he was doing his job watching Bertie, and returned his attention to the conversation.

"Bloody hell, I broke my pencil." Julian scowled at the tip. "Who owns this sewer, Morgan?"

"Toddy Clapper," Sir Patrick answered. "He's over behind the bar." At Morgan's veiled sideways glance, he hastened to add, "I know a number of these coffeehouses by repute. Part of the job. But that's not the point, is it?" he blustered. "And while we're on the subject, Morgan, what brought you to the cemetery in the middle of the night?"

"A note, sir," Morgan replied, curving his lips politely.

"From whom?" Sir Patrick thundered. "The murderer? Why didn't you tell me this before, Morgan? It's evidence, and I'm the head of the bloody parliamentary committee. Where is this note of yours?"

"Right here, sir." Morgan produced the parchment from his pocket. No flicker of recognition crossed either Christopher Crowley's or Julian Stockwell's face.

"What's that?" Julian inquired of the broken red seal.

"Looks like a jester," Crowley said as he flopped back in his chair.

"It's the jack of spades," Morgan told them, still watching both men.

Sir Patrick muttered while he read. "Damned peculiar," he grunted between lines. "Highbred...whores. Sounds like a loon to me. Why did he send this to you, Morgan?"

"I have no idea, sir," Morgan lied. Then, at Bartholomew's agitated gestures, he gave the edge of the table a tap with his fingers. "If you'll excuse me, gentlemen. Back in a minute."

Sir Patrick offered a disinterested growl while Julian went in search of a new pencil. Christopher Crowley, slumped over his coffee cup, unfastened his long chestnut hair and fidgeted with a raisin bun. His actions were those of a sullen artist—not a bad acting job considering that his left hand was balled into a fist in his lap.

Morgan was in the doorway when he spotted Julian scribbling in his notebook over near the counter. The reporter tore off a piece of the parchment and handed it, along with a penny, to a young beggar boy, directing him out the rear door with an imperative wave of his hand.

Morgan hesitated, but opted for his original destination and went outside.

"Where did he go?" he demanded of Bartholomew, who motioned to the side of the building.

"I couldn't stop him, Mr. M. Said he had to sweep out the church before the bishop showed up. Should I stay here, sir?"

Morgan nodded, tugging on his gloves with his teeth. "Stop hopping about, and keep watch for me. If anyone leaves, most notably Julian Stockwell, come and fetch me right away."

The murky lane between Toddy Clapper's Coffeehouse and the coffin maker's next door was beginning to shimmer with the first frosty light of dawn. Bertie crouched beside a pile of rubbish, waiting for him.

Careful not to let his coat drag in the foul-smelling refuse, Morgan sat down on an overturned crate. His eyes swept the area. Nothing stirred except Bertie's twitchy fingers. "Do you have something for me?" he asked, and Bertie smiled, revealing a gaping hole where his front teeth should be.

"Might," he said. "How much you got?"

"A penny," Morgan said.

"Tuppence," the little man bartered.

"All right. What is it?"

"Well, I heard you talking to those fancy blokes in the cemetery earlier, and how you said you'd seen a red-haired chap running away in the dark."

"Yes," Morgan said slowly.

"Well, I saw a red-haired bloke, too. 'Course, this was before you came, maybe around two in the morning. He was all dressed in black with a hat like yours and a long cloak he kept wrapped tight around him. A big man he was, too, Mr. Morgan. Near seven feet tall, I'd say."

"Or six feet?" Morgan suggested.

"No, he was bigger than that. Oh, he was a giant of a man. His hair was untied, and he had a great full beard."

Morgan's eyes narrowed. "Are you sure about this, Bertie?"

"Yes, sir, Mr. M. I saw him plain, striding off smartly to Wickle's Tavern. Kept his collar full up except when the wind blew it back. That's how I saw him so clear. Came right past the old church and went into Wickle's Tavern."

"Did he come out again at all?"

"I didn't see him, but he probably did." Bertie winked conspiratorially. "You know how it is there, sir. 'Here's your hat, what's your hurry.' Mr. Wickle, he believes in fast in, fast out."

"I'm sure he does," Morgan said in a considering undertone. "Is that everything you know?"

"That's the lot, sir." Palm up, Bertie extended his hand. Lost in thought, Morgan put tuppence in it. "Anything else I can do, Mr. M.?" the sweeper asked, closing his grimy fist.

Morgan tapped his tooth. "No.... Yes, tell Bartholomew to check Wickle's Tavern for a tall red-haired man with a beard."

"Will do, and thanks, guv."

An abstracted sound in his throat was Morgan's only response as Bertie scurried off into the frosty shadows.

Procopius Rowe—it had to be. Beards weren't commonplace these days, and while the M.P. didn't live there, he was known to frequent Whitechapel and areas like it. Had he murdered Ruby Fox, though? And what about that note Julian had sent off?

Streaks of pale gray light filtered into the lane. Morgan heard the jingle of a passing sleigh ahead of him. Then he heard a more fateful crunch of frozen snow behind him.

On his feet in an instant, he was still only half-turned when the blow slammed hard against his skull. He saw nothing except a black shape, heard nothing except a whoosh of breath as a blinding pain filled his head. And his mind slipped silently into darkness.

Chapter Ten

"You understand now, do you, missy?" Lady Mary shook an arthritic finger at Cassie from the settee in her sitting room. "You're not to let that fusspot of a doctor see you. You go around to the kitchen door, and you ask for Mrs. Fitch. No one else but her. She'll give you the tonic I want."

"Yes, ma'am." Cassie would have smiled at the mock severity in Lady Mary's tone if she hadn't been so tired, and so worried about Morgan.

He hadn't returned to Amblewood House yet, and it was after nine in the morning. The place was in a major state of chaos. It also wouldn't be long, Cassie suspected, before Sir Gerald, who'd returned home just past dawn, would be awake and demanding Morgan's immediate presence.

Lady Mary climbed to her feet like a frail little bird and came to stare sternly up into Cassie's weary face. "Shadows under your eyes, pale cheeks, hair neat but unpinned and the simplest dress you could find on your back." Her cane tapped Cassie's foot. "You've been up to something, haven't you?"

"Not really, ma'am," she began, but Lady Mary fixed her with an imperious stare.

"I don't tolerate liars in my employ," she said in what Cassie called her Queen Victoria voice. The cane thumped on the carpet. "You were up to something last night with Morgan, weren't you?"

"Yes, ma'am, I was," Cassie admitted, still half-tempted to smile. She pushed back her unruly hair. "But please don't ask me what."

"Why not?"

"Because it isn't my place to explain."

"It is if I decide it is," Lady Mary declared. She eyed Cassie's pale blue dress with its tiny white flowers, its empire waist and soft bands of ribbon around the short puffed sleeves. "You're quite a comely creature," she remarked. Her bright eyes came up sharply. "How old are you?"

"Thirty," Cassie answered automatically, then substituted a hasty "I mean, twenty."

The old woman moved closer. "You mean thirty—and don't lie," she warned as Cassie opened her mouth to do just that. "I've been watching you, young Cassie. Your hair is soft and shiny, your skin fresh and unblemished. Oh, you use cosmetics, I'll grant you, but they're not like the ones my grandson and his friends favor. Now, I may be old, and America may be a great distance from England, but you don't look or sound like any colonial I've ever met."

"It's been mentioned," Cassie murmured, linking her fingers in front of her.

"By whom?"

"Julian Stockwell."

"That reporter for the *Times?*" Lady Mary snorted. "Too pretty for my taste."

"Yes, he is very striking-looking," Cassie agreed. "All that long black hair and those blue eyes—I could see him playing the fop, but I still don't understand why Christopher Crowley does it."

"Christopher Crowley is an ingratiating fortune hunter who despises people of wealth and title for the simple reason that he can't get his hands on either."

Cassie trailed Lady Mary to her vanity stool. "So the rumors are true, then? Mr. Crowley is the illegitimate son of a wealthy noblewoman?"

Lady Mary merely smiled into her mirror. "Perhaps it's true," she said. "I'm not one to spread gossip. And we've strayed from the topic, in any case."

Cassie feigned ignorance. "We have?"

The old woman's cane hit the floor with a cranky thump. "You and Morgan puzzle me. He fits in here, you do not. On the other hand, Morgan is cunning and devious and only pretends to like us—with the exception of me, of course." Her bewigged head lifted in triumph. "He likes me, I think."

"And Bartholomew," Cassie said.

"And you," Lady Mary finished, staring half-lidded at Cassie in the mirror. One gnarled finger drew an invisible picture on the tabletop. "I find you a curious creature, Cassandra Lachlin. You and Morgan both. I'll have to ponder this some more. You and Morgan, hmm. Off you go in the meantime. Fetch my potion and bring it directly back to me. Perhaps by then I'll have reasoned this riddle out."

Cassie doubted it but didn't argue—because she'd just noticed something about Lady Mary's invisible table drawing. It had been done left-handed. And yet she'd seen Lady Mary wield a writing quill expertly in her right hand. What if Lady Mary was ambidextrous? What, Cassie reflected on a darker note, if Jack was?

She glanced at the threatening sky and wished again that Morgan would return.

"MR. MORGAN, WAKE UP." Bartholomew shook him, gently at first, then more urgently. "Please wake up, Mr. M.," he pleaded.

"What?" Groggily Morgan lifted his throbbing head. Eyes closed, he turned, distantly aware of the numbing cold that penetrated right to his bones. "Where am I? What happened?"

"You're in the lane." Bartholomew attempted to lift him from the ground. "Behind the big rubbish pile."

"God," Morgan mumbled, pushing himself upright. "What was I drinking last night? I feel like— No, wait. I wasn't drinking. Someone hit me."

"And took your wallet," Bartholomew revealed.

"What!" Outrage temporarily blotted out the pain. Morgan checked his pockets. His wallet was missing, and his watch. "What time is it?" he asked, still thickheaded.

"The clock just chimed the half hour, sir. It's nine-thirty." Kneeling down, Bartholomew gave him a frightened look. "I couldn't find you," he explained. "So I went back into Clapper's, but you weren't there, either, and all the other blokes had gone. I didn't know what to do, so I waited. Then when you didn't come, I started to look again."

A pile of snow and bricks sufficed for a seat. Morgan worked his way onto it with a testy "Yes, yes, all right," followed by a less sharp "Thank you, Bartholomew." He massaged his aching temples. "Did you learn anything from Wickle, the tavern owner?"

"Only that there was a man with red hair and a beard in there last night around two-thirty. They wouldn't say his name."

"Was there any blood on him?"

"No one would say. And no one'll say who he was with, either. But he ordered a bath, which is unusual."

"Yes, it is," Morgan agreed slowly. "Is he a regular there?"

"I think he might be, 'cause when I told Mr. Wickle it was you who wanted the information, he looked like he felt bad."

"But he still wouldn't give you anything."

"No, sir, no one would."

"So this man must be someone important, then," Morgan mused.

"Like Mr. Rowe?"

"Possibly. But let me talk to Mr. Wickle."

Bartholomew helped him stand. "But wait," he said as Morgan began straightening his clothes. "Shouldn't you be getting back to the manor? They'll have missed you by now."

"Don't worry about it, Bartholomew." Morgan dismissed the matter with an unconcerned wave. "I'll make up some brilliant excuse later. In the meantime, go back to the house and make sure Cassie got home safely. And try to keep her out of trouble, will you? Not that anyone could," he added in a sardonic undertone.

"I'll try, Mr. M.," Bartholomew said more cheerfully.

Morgan slid him a dry, sideways look from under his lashes but let the subject drop. Someone had knocked him out today and stolen his wallet. It might or might not have been Jack. The note he'd received, however, had definitely been Jack's. It had told of one death and foretold another. Cassie's.

His head still pounding, Morgan set his sights on Wickle's Tavern. He had no intention of dying in this or any other century, but if Jack wanted Cassie, he'd have to go through Morgan to get to her. And while that was always possible, Morgan didn't plan to let it be easy.

CASSIE SPOTTED Sir Gerald and Ignatious Athelbert as she passed the parlor. The sight of Sir Gerald out of bed at such an early hour surprised her, but that was only a mild shock compared to the state the poet was in. His sunken eyes were red-rimmed and purple-shadowed, his lips were white and cracked, his dirty blond hair askew, his clothes streaked with mud and God knew what else.

Sir Gerald appeared not to notice. Ostentatiously dressed as always, he hailed her from the tea trolley. "Ah, Cassie. Come in, come in. Just the bird I wanted to see."

Bird? "I was on my way out, sir," she said in a suitably deferential tone. "Your grandmother wants me to run an errand for her."

"Yes, yes, fine," he said, a smile lighting his slender features. "But first I want you to tell old Ignatious here that he looks an absolute horror."

"You look an absolute horror, Mr. Athelbert," Cassie complied. Her gaze rose to Sir Gerald's ingenuous face. "May I go now, sir?"

He moved closer with a suggestive "Are you sure you want to? My bed's very comfortable, you know. And I love red hair."

"I think my hair's more brown than red, sir," Cassie pointed out, easing backward. Her hand located the edge of the tea trolley. "Uh, shouldn't you see to Mr. Athelbert before he slides out of his seat?"

"What? Oh, that." Sir Gerald laughed and continued to close in. "He's just had a rough night is all. A good sleep on the carpet and he'll be right as ninepence." His painted brows went up. "Do you like champagne?"

"No." Were his eyes beginning to glitter, Cassie wondered uneasily, or was that a trick of the light?

He took another step toward her. "Sherry then. That's a ladies' drink, isn't it, Carol?"

"Cassie." She skirted the trolley. "I don't drink sherry, either, Sir Gerald."

"Of course you do—I've seen you."

"I beg your pardon?"

"Last night in the garden. You and me." He stopped suddenly, looked away and blinked. "Or was that someone else?"

"I think it must have been." Fumbling for the bell cord behind her, Cassie gave it a desperate tug.

Sir Gerald's lips puckered in a frown. "Yes, perhaps it was, at that. Oh well, it doesn't matter, does it?" His face cleared, the smile returning full force. "What were we talking about?"

"The Garden of Eden," Athelbert said from the sofa where he was sprawled. "Temptation, sin." His haunted features grew dreamy for a moment. "No snowflakes," he said sadly. "No poppies."

"So that's it," Cassie murmured with a comprehending glance.

"Did I mention that my bed is exactly the same as the Prince Regent's?" Sir Gerald asked. The glitter became a sparkle as his gaze swept her from head to toe. "Very soft and cloudlike. White silk sheets."

"Like snow," Cassie said, giving the cord another pull.

Sir Gerald was about to touch her cheek when he stopped again. She saw his brow knit. "Speaking of snow," he said, frowning, "where's Morgan?"

Although she had no idea how snow and Morgan were connected, Cassie took the opportunity to slip away from the wall.

Sir Gerald scratched his head. "You know, come to think of it, I haven't seen him all bloody morning. Jenkins," he shouted just as a man appeared in the doorway.

"You rang, sir?" the valet said quietly.

"Did I? Yes, I guess I must have done. Well, it doesn't matter. Where's Morgan? I want to see him immediately."

"I'm afraid that won't be possible, sir."

Sir Gerald seemed miffed. He'd completely forgotten about her, Cassie realized. What a very odd man he was.

"Why not?" he demanded with a great display of righteous indignation. "Is he in the kitchen? Is he sick, injured, dead?"

Cassie started around the sofa—and had to stifle a scream as the poet's clammy fingers brushed across the back of her hand.

"Death comes stalking," he told her, his bloodshot eyes unnaturally wide. "Stalking, stalking. Look to the arrangements left behind." A pathetic giggle bubbled from his lips. "Pretty maids all in a row." His face darkened. "In a row of graves, that is. Do you understand? He comes out at night, stalking, stalking. He stalks his victims well. That's what my little dream voice said to me last night. He stalks them well and kills them dead." His long fingernails scratched weakly at Cassie's cloak. "Look to the arrangements..."

"SAID THE SPIDER to the fly," Cassie said as she ran up the back stairs to Dr. Peach's kitchen door. Ignatious Athelbert was a nut, she decided. She only hoped that's all he was. "Good morning," she said brightly to the woman who answered her knock. "Lady Mary Peregrine sent me to collect some tonic from Mrs. Fitch."

Frazzled, the woman, a laundress who'd been walking past the door, let her in. "I've got to get these clothes in to soak," she clucked to one of the maids. "Nothing worse than blood, grease and rust for making stains. Mrs. Fitch will be down presently," she said over her shoulder to Cassie.

Nodding, Cassie remarked, "Dr. Peach must have had a bad night. That's a lot of blood on his shirt."

"More still on his trousers, and they were brand-new."

"Sheets, too," a large, lumbering woman announced, coming down the rear stairs with an armload of laundry. "The old goat must've gone to bed with his soiled clothes on. Blood everywhere. You'd think he murdered someone with this mess."

Yes, one might certainly think that, Cassie thought. Her fingers itched to steal a pillowcase for blood typing, but she knew Morgan wouldn't be set up for it. With the exception of his time box and his Magnum, he seemed singularly lacking in sophisticated equipment. Maybe there was a time law about it. Bartholomew had alluded to what he called the rules of time while he'd been filling her bath yesterday, though he claimed to know very little about the subject.

"You ask Mr. M. your time questions, miss," he'd said with a wide smile. "He'll tell you what you want to know." His eyes had twinkled. "'Course, it wouldn't hurt to put some brandy in his tea first...."

"Mellow him out," Cassie murmured to the memory. She shifted her weight from foot to foot at the kitchen door. The second laundress had dumped her sheets in a pile about five feet away and was currently viewing them with disgust.

"What happened last night?" Cassie risked asking.

She scowled. "His nibs claims there was some toff who got himself hurt in a duel. I say any toff who's spilled this much blood must be dead as a doornail by now."

"What time did the doctor get in, do you know?"

"Wouldn't surprise me if it was nearing dawn." The woman's voice dropped to a conspiratorial level. "You wouldn't think it to look at him, but he's quite the carouser."

"Really?"

"Oh, yes. Ever since Emmalina died."

"And she was...?"

"His sister."

"Ah, so Emmalina didn't like parties."

"Oh, good Lord, girl, she loved them. It was the doctor back in those days who was so stuffy. He was such a prig as you've never heard tell."

"I don't know, I've heard tell of quite a few lately," Cassie said. "Was it Emmalina's death that changed Dr. Peach?"

The woman shrugged. "It could've been, I suppose. Stranger things have happened, and death does have a way of affecting people." Ponderous footsteps on the staircase brought her head around. "Ah, here she is. Mrs. Fitch," she called. "Lady Mary's maid's come to see you about a batch of tonic."

As hard as she tried, Cassie couldn't get close enough to the sheets to swipe anything. She was, however, able to see the bloodstains quite clearly. The laundress was right. Anyone who bled that much would be dead by now. As dead as the red-haired prostitute, Ruby Fox.

GLASSY, OBSESSED EYES fixed on the evening newspaper.

Throat-slashing Murderer Slays Lady of the Night, the headline read.

Jack's lips moved as he scanned the rest of the article.

> Sir Patrick Welland, head of the Parliamentary Committee for the Investigation into Street Crime in London, is at present unable to connect the murder of one Ruby Fox, late of Wickle's Tavern, Whitechapel, to the murders of other more notable women which have taken place in the city in recent days. Death stalks all women in London it seems, from the high to the low. But do not blame Sir Patrick, good people, for his inability to solve this most puzzling of crimes. For who among us could do more than he? Who would dare to try? Not this reporter, certainly....

There was more, but Jack's eyes blurred on the small newsprint.

Lady of the night. Who would dare to try and stop the killing? Who except Morgan and that interfering female he'd recruited from somewhere.

Seated in a high-backed chair, Jack was sure he felt a pair of eyes boring into him. He responded by clenching the sides of the newspaper tightly in his fists.

It was nothing, he told himself. He was killing women in his own backyard, so to speak. That made him nervous and tense. He'd become jumpy because of it, convinced that every shadow contained a pair of spying eyes.

He walked around the room, anyway, and checked the windows. As he'd expected, no one lurked outside. Unless of course Mother's ghost was watching him. Mother or her so-adored red-haired daughter.

"I hate you," he said quietly to both of them. "But I hate *you* most of all," he said to the redheaded female who'd been born when he was seven years old. "Mother wanted you—she never wanted me. She was cruel to me, then you came along and she was cruel to you. Fair is fair, is it not? You took all the attention away from me, both bad and good. You toughed it out. You called me weak. Well, my dear, now it's payback time." The corners of his mouth lifted in a grim parody of a smile. "Goodbye, red-haired slut. Watch out, Morgan's pretty new friend. I'm still here, and whether you know it or not, I've seen you."

"DOES IT HURT?" Cassie asked Morgan.

He twisted around in his seat at the servants' table to glare at her. "Yes, it bloody hurts. Now, stop poking me and finish explaining about Athelbert and the doctor."

"I've already told you everything," she said, with surprising patience considering his snappish mood. "Mr. Athelbert believes that clever Jack is too adept at choosing his victims to be caught."

"Is that what he said?"

"Not exactly, no." She pressed a cold cloth to the bump on his head. "He said that Jack stalks his victims well. He also made a point of saying that we should look to the arrangements left behind."

Morgan frowned, and glanced back again. "You mean the arrangements of the victims' possessions?"

"Which are," Cassie recalled, "a knotted handkerchief and an emerald choker in Lady Annabelle's case, a cameo inside a folded handkerchief in Joelle's case, and I don't know about the other women."

"I wrote it down in my journal," Morgan told her. "I'll look through my notes tonight when I get back."

"Back?" She leaned over him from behind, close enough to set her cheek against his. She didn't, but the silky hair that brushed across his face was almost as disturbing. "Are we going somewhere?"

He didn't quite jerk sideways, but Morgan didn't want to touch her. No, that wasn't true. He wanted to; his instincts simply knew better than to let him give in to temptation.

Regarding her in profile, he summoned a deliberately high-handed "I am. You're staying here with Bartholomew."

"Why?" She came around to face him, resting her hip on the side of the table and folding her arms across her chest. In spite of himself, Morgan breathed a sigh of relief. "You're going to stake out Procopius Rowe's house, aren't you?"

A ridge formed between his eyes. "How could you possibly know that?" As if he couldn't guess.

She challenged him with a meaningful widening of her eyes. "Well, it's true, isn't it?"

"It might be."

"It's dangerous," she said flatly. "You'll need someone there with you."

"It's necessary," he retorted. "And if I need someone, which I don't, I'll take Bartholomew."

Her smile was a little too confident. "No you won't. He's not here."

"What?"

"Don't sound so outraged, Morgan. It isn't a personal affront. Sir Gerald sent him off to help out at some charity thing that's going on tonight in Westminster. Noblesse oblige, I think he called it, and since you weren't here—"

"Yes, yes, all right." Morgan raised a hand to cut her off. "He's not here. That still doesn't mean I'm going to let you come along."

Sighing, Cassie reached for a bottle behind her on the table. "God, but you can be stubborn, to say nothing of grouchy."

"You'd be grouchy, too, if you'd been hit over the head in an alley and had your wallet with a hundred pounds in it stolen." He leaned back in his chair, tapping his tooth with his thumb. "Now, be quiet and let me think. And no more talk about coming with me tonight."

"Whatever you say," she agreed, then smiled and held up a steaming china cup. "Care for some tea?"

"FOR HEAVEN'S SAKE, Cassie, keep your head down and stay out of the light," Morgan reproached. "If he sees you he'll know you're a woman in a minute."

Crouched next to Morgan beneath a sleazy tavern windowsill, Cassie held her temper. "I'm bundled up like a Christmas package, Morgan. If *I* saw me I wouldn't know I was a woman. Where are we, anyway, and what's Mr. Procopius Rowe doing in there?"

"We're in Stepney, in the heart of the East End, and he's dancing with a woman."

"Sounds like an Irish jig," Cassie noted, tugging down the tricorn hat Morgan had given her.

That he'd given in and let her come with him tonight to follow Rowe was, she knew, entirely due to the brandy she'd added to his tea. It had made him affable for a good thirty minutes, long enough that she'd been able to con him into letting her accompany him, but sadly not long enough for her to maneuver him into an uncompromising situation.

The man must be made of iron, she decided, recalling her disappointment. There she'd been, all hot and bothered in the kitchen, and what had he done? Stiffened up and pulled away. So either Lady Mary and Bartholomew were crazy and he wasn't interested in her, or she'd been right before and sex had become passé by his century, whatever one that was.

Regardless, at 8:00 p.m. precisely, they'd positioned themselves outside Procopius Rowe's narrow Kensington house. At 8:27 p.m., the M.P. had emerged through a side door, head down and dressed as a peasant. Only his red beard had given him away. He'd walked briskly through the snow for four blocks, hailed a cab and come directly to Stepney. Now he sat inside one of the slimiest waterfront taverns Cassie had ever seen. Even Sherlock Holmes would have been appalled.

Feeling reasonably secure in her boy disguise, which consisted of a long black cloak, a hat on top of her hair, which was tied back in a ponytail, a pair of Morgan's breeches and her own boots, Cassie risked a peek over the dirty sill. The M.P. was, in fact, dancing a jig, with a woman who looked more like a man in her dress than Cassie did in her breeches and boots.

"What a dump," she whispered, wrinkling her nose in distaste. "No health inspectors around to close it down, huh?"

"Not yet." Morgan pushed on her head. "Stay down. I'm going inside."

"Not without me, you aren't."

"For God's sake, Cassie," he said in exasperation, "most of these men are sailors, eighteenth-century sailors. They're as willing to sleep with a boy as a woman."

"I'll be careful," she promised. "If they ask, I'll tell them I'm with you."

"Oh God." He sighed, but pulled her to her feet even so, shoving her firmly behind him as they started for the rear door. "Not a word," he warned, and she nodded her promise.

It was all noise and dirt inside, mingled with the smell of sweaty bodies, brine and beer. The music was bad, the lighting worse, and the women, many of them toothless and wearing rags, reminded Cassie of dried apple carvings with garish makeup.

Plank floorboards sagged beneath a dozen boisterous pairs of dancing feet. There was a stage on one wall, but nothing appeared to be happening there. Well, nothing except that an ancient prostitute was in the process of lifting a sailor's wallet.

"Wah-hey, what's this, then?" A meaty hand caught Cassie from behind and spun her around. "Never seen you here before, boy."

Morgan had his fingers on her upper arms before Cassie could react. "The boy's mute," he told the large man holding her. "He also has syphilis."

Cassie shot him a nasty look, but didn't contradict him.

"That so?" The man seemed unconcerned. "So who are you, then?"

"A palace emissary," Morgan replied smoothly. "My charge is rather precocious. The prince felt he should visit a London tavern before returning to France."

"A Frenchie, eh?" The man's lip curled.

"Half-French," Morgan lied, his tone pleasant. "His mother's a blend of Welsh and Scottish."

"And he has the pox, you say?"

"Yes, well, it's rather more like a scourge at this point." His smile completely false, Morgan shooed Cassie away. "Come along, Arthur. You don't want to infect these men."

Cassie waited until they were alone at a corner table before snarling, "You bastard. Syphilis! Why not consumption?"

"Nine out of ten people here have consumption, Cassie," he replied absently. His eyes scanned the nearby tables. "It would scarcely be a deterrent."

A glass smashed on the floor, causing Cassie to look around sharply and the music to stop. "Bloody slut!" Procopius Rowe declared in a loud voice. "Go on. Go with him, then. I've had better for tuppence on the docks."

"Ah." Morgan set his hands on the edge of the table. His eyes were fastened on the belligerent M.P. in his peasant outfit. "I think it's time we left."

Cassie wasn't stupid. She recognized trouble when she saw it. And this situation had the potential to become lethal.

The man who had challenged Procopius Rowe was heavyset and every bit as drunk as his adversary. A blond woman in a torn red dress stood between them, her eyes glittering with fury.

"Well, you're a pair, aren't you," she said, but a stick of a man shoved her aside and stabbed a finger in the M.P.'s face.

"You can take your tuppence, mate, and get stuffed. This bloke's a regular of the house, and—"

Procopius Rowe's fist slammed into the man's teeth before he could finish. Like a flung preying mantis, he sailed backward and hit the floor with an unceremonious thump.

"Go," Morgan snapped at Cassie, who, despite her fascination, had the good sense to scramble obediently out of her chair.

It was as she'd expected. The punch thrown by the M.P. set off an immediate chain reaction. Within thirty seconds, pandemonium reigned. Bodies reeled and sagged and stumbled into tables. Beer glasses went flying and fists struck out at anything that moved.

Morgan shoved Cassie toward the door, then got caught by a staggering sailor who landed a hard right to his jaw.

"No, you don't." Furious, Cassie launched herself at the man. She didn't expect to collide with his broad back, but when it happened, she made the most of it and aimed a kick at his knees. They buckled, and he stumbled forward into Procopius Rowe, knocking him off balance and over the side of a chair.

The women were fighting, too, Cassie realized as she stole around trying to locate Morgan. They climbed up onto the chairs, jumped on the men's backs, then clawed and bit them from behind.

One of the women yanked Cassie's ponytail. Cassie retaliated by kicking her backside. "Morgan!" she shouted, then ducked as the barrel-chested sailor who'd accosted her earlier lumbered past, off balance. "Syphilis," she muttered, and gave him a mighty two-handed shove. "You've probably got it yourself, creep."

Above the ruckus, she heard Procopius Rowe's booming laughter. He was on his hands and knees across the room, with blood trickling from his mouth, as he watched a man accidentally backhand the woman who'd caused the brawl. Actually, whether that was a woman was still a questionable point in Cassie's mind. But it didn't matter—finding Morgan was her only real concern.

She lost sight of the M.P. after that, except for a disconcerting moment when she was in the center of the room and looked toward the window. He seemed to be staring straight at her.

Concealing herself quickly, Cassie continued to hunt for Morgan. Since the safest place seemed to be next to the wall, she stationed herself there, inching along the cracked plaster and ducking occasionally whenever a stray fist or bottle flew past.

Fights in 1790 were like mini-riots, she thought. She was almost dragged into the fray several times. Finally she spied an open doorway and made her way toward it.

"Where are you, Morgan?" she whispered through clenched teeth.

A dark shadow enveloped her. Had she reached the door already? Her searching eyes told her no. So did the gloved hand that snaked out of the darkness to seize her throat from behind.

"Pretty," a rusty, unidentifiable male voice crooned in her ear. "Come with me, eh, pretty lady?"

She couldn't utter a sound, didn't have a prayer of screaming. His gloved fingers squeezed hard, cutting off her voice as well as her oxygen supply. A knife gleamed dully in her peripheral vision.

"Yes, pretty one," he said with a gravelly chuckle. "It's me." His lips grazed her ear. She recoiled instinctively, but he held her fast. "Did you think I wouldn't want you? Did you think I wouldn't recognize you in those clothes? Silly girl, it's a feeble disguise, and not nearly as effective as mine."

He felt large to her, weighty. Her elbows sank in when she jammed them into his belly. But was it flesh or clever padding?

Her mind, numb with terror and dizzy from lack of air, couldn't tell. She also couldn't guess at his height. Not right then.

A strangled cry broke at last from her aching throat. She was going to pass out. All that her scratching and kicking earned her was a harsher grip and the sound of heavy breathing in her ear.

It didn't help to dig in her heels or butt him or try to flip him. He knew the tricks and refused to fall for them.

The knife blade hovered on her left. His left, too, she realized with a start. He held her with his right arm, the knife in his left hand.

She knew he was dragging her toward the open door. He'd almost reached it when a body rammed him, knocking him sideways. His grip slackened just enough for Cassie to tear his fingers away and stumble forward.

She gulped air as if it were water. Her muscles had turned to jelly. It took all her strength to remain on her feet. By the time she remembered to look behind her, he was gone. Only two female prostitutes remained, and they were tearing at each other's hair.

"Cassie!"

Morgan appeared in front of her, dishevelled and bruised, yet remarkably composed. His irritated gaze swept the tavern. "I lost him." Then he looked down at her, and his fingers tightened on her arms. "Are you all right?"

"No," she croaked. Pushing at her hair, she pointed through the tumbling bodies. "He was here. Jack. He had a knife. He grabbed me, but I couldn't see him."

"What!"

There might have been a glimmer of fear and concern in his outburst, but she couldn't be sure with all the noise.

He cast a final quick look over his shoulder, then gave her a gentle push and said, "Come on. Let's get out of here."

And while Cassie was only too happy to oblige, she couldn't quite block the sound of Jack's taunting first question. "Did you think I wouldn't want you?"

A shudder tore through Cassie's body. It was a nightmare, the worst she'd ever had. Jack the Ripper wanted her dead.

JACK FLEW DOWN the snowy streets on a horse stolen from behind the tavern. He saw red in his mind, the red haze of fury.

That made two who'd eluded him now. It was two too many, and substitutes did not satisfy his blood lust.

He forced his brain to function. He wouldn't kill tonight, he promised himself. He would plot instead. He would fuel his hatred with promises and laugh at the fools who believed he was only what he claimed to be.

Because it was all so very clever. Who would ever guess that he, Jack, had in fact been born in this time? Oh, what an advantage he had over Morgan.

"It wouldn't occur to you, would it, Mr. Elegant Butler?" he mocked as his stolen horse raced through the night. "That's the problem with you futuristic bastards. You think everyone before your time is an idiot. Well, I'll show you. I'll show them. And I'll show you, too, Mother—you and that slut of a daughter of yours."

His hatred boiling now, Jack drove the horse recklessly onward. He would kill Morgan's friend, and Jane Brede as well; that was understood. But there was another one, he'd discovered, a quiet, dangerous one. Maybe she should die first.

Jaw clenched, Jack lowered his head against the buffeting wind. And wondered if one lifetime would be sufficient to kill all the red-haired women.

Chapter Eleven

December 13, 1790

Cassie recovered well, better than he did, Morgan thought broodingly. Sitting back, he contemplated his open journal. He didn't want to think that Jack might have killed her last night. His mind refused to accept what could have been. Protests or no, he should damned well send her back.

But...

"I won't go," she'd warned him when he'd walked past the storeroom that morning.

She must have glimpsed the prospect in his eyes. He only hoped she hadn't glimpsed anything else. Wasn't it just like a bloody twentieth-century woman to stand there wearing nothing except a towel and expect to have a perfectly normal conversation with a man?

"So you decided not to send her home, then," Bartholomew assumed, coming into Morgan's room.

"For the moment." Closing his journal, Morgan stood and started to pace. It was the best way he knew to relax.

Bartholomew walked to and fro with him. "I don't understand, Mr. M. I thought—"

"Well, don't," Morgan snapped, halting. He jabbed a finger at the ceiling. "I swear, Bartholomew, that woman is more trouble than fifty women from this time. Don't ever let anyone tell you they don't use feminine wiles in her century."

Bartholomew blinked, not understanding. "Are, uh, you going to take the tea up to Lady Mary and her guests?" he asked.

"What?" The frown that had appeared between Morgan's brows dissipated slightly. "Oh, yes, I am." Waving an absent hand, he reached for his coat. "Tell Mrs. Dickson to set out lemon scones."

"Yes, sir." In the doorway, Bartholomew hesitated. "But won't it be awkward for you?"

Morgan's frown deepened. "Why should it be awkward?"

"Well, I heard that Mrs. Parsons is one of Lady Mary's guests."

"Yes, yes, I know." Morgan dusted the matter off as easily as he used the clothes brush to dust off his cuffs. "Believe me, Millicent Parsons is the least of my problems right now."

"If you say so, sir."

A grunt was Morgan's only response.

Pulling the ponytail from under his collar, he straightened his coat. Who cared about Mrs. Parsons. Cassie, who was destroying his stoicism piece by bloody piece, was also upstairs; Sir Gerald, who was trying Morgan's patience to the limit, demanding to know where he'd been yesterday, was probably there, too; and Jack was God knew where. Upstairs, in a pub, Morgan couldn't begin to guess. He only knew that Jack had almost killed Cassie. And he was determined not to let that happen again.

DESIRÉE SAT IN a Hepplewhite chair next to the parlor window, a lace handkerchief twisting nervously in her fingers. It was growing dark, threatening to snow. Christopher Crowley sat across the room; Cassie stood at the back. Lady Mary and three of her elderly friends were huddled like hens about the sofa, and two men Desirée recognized as lords wandered around the room, chatting about the artwork and occasionally glancing out the window for Sir Gerald's carriage.

Restless, Desirée motioned to Cassie, who immediately joined her. "Did Sir Gerald say when he would be back?" she asked.

"Not to me," Cassie revealed. "You could ask Morgan, though."

On cue, Morgan entered, carrying a tray of tea and heavenly smelling scones. God, but he looked calm and unruffled. He glanced first at Cassie, then over at Lady Mary's group. One of the women, a dowager in her early sixties, stared back at him.

"Ah, Morgan, there you are. Have you seen my grandson this afternoon?" Lady Mary inquired, saving Desirée the trouble. "His friends are all here waiting. My friends are waiting. Mr. Crowley is even waiting, and he has a performance to give at the theater, if I'm not mistaken."

The actor, reclining foppishly in his chair, grinned at her with just a hint of disdain. Desirée smiled and added a tactful "We're all here at Sir Gerald's request, Morgan. I was told it had something to do with raising funds to restore a castle on the Cam. Sir Gerald said it was of vital historical importance, this castle."

"It used to belong to an earl who had his entire family beheaded during the reign of Henry VIII," Christopher Crowley put in. "He was a rather bloodthirsty chap. Lopped off the heads of his mother, father, sister, grandmother and three wives. It's also believed that he was involved in some kind of evil sorcery, that he dismembered those he'd executed, and that he collected their blood in bottles and drank it mixed with wine at parties."

"Well, that's disgusting," Cassie said, openly sarcastic.

"A lot of things are disgusting, Cassie," Morgan remarked, bending over so Lady Mary could pour the tea.

"I wonder why Sir Gerald would want to save the home of such a horrid man," mused the dowager who kept sneaking narrowed looks at Morgan. "One would think such a place would have evil sewn into its very foundations. Thank you, Anthony," she added when he offered her a scone.

Cassie's wary glaze slid to the woman's face. Desirée opted to close her eyes and rub her forehead with her lace-gloved fingers. She had no time for curiosity, and even less time to wait for the tardy Sir Gerald.

"I'm afraid I shall have to leave," she apologized to Lady Mary.

"Yes, of course, dear," the old woman murmured. Her shrewd gaze was fastened on Morgan. He neither seemed to care nor notice. He moved around the room with his customary aloof efficiency.

Immune to it all, Desirée reflected, standing. If only he knew half as much as she did. If only...

Ah, but if-onlys were pointless where Jack was concerned. Still, she couldn't help wishing that the jumpiness she'd been experiencing today would go away. And the throbbing headache.

"Desirée!"

Outside, Christopher Crowley hailed her as she prepared to step into her carriage. She waited for him to approach, forcing a smile. "Can I help, Mr. Crowley?"

He bowed with theatrical flair. "If I may be so bold, you could offer me a ride to the theater. It's dark and getting very late."

Desirée glanced at her driver, then nodded her reluctant agreement. "The Haymarket, Tolbert," she said. Her cold fingers tightened for a moment on his capable wrist. "And, Tolbert," she beseeched huskily, fighting to keep the desperation from her voice, "please hurry."

ANOTHER NOTE AWAITED when Cassie at last made her way down to the kitchen. Mrs. Dickson snarled at her in passing, but since it was almost ten o'clock she didn't bother with any nasty comments. Slamming the door at the top of the stairs, she marched away for the night.

That left Morgan, a dying fire and five candles burning in the shadowy room.

"'You won't thwart me this time, you interfering butler,'" Cassie read aloud. "'Not this time or the next or the next. I shall give no more helpful clues. This note is a promise only. My next victim dies tonight. A murder, Morgan, in the park. Death comes for her, after dark.'"

"Shut up, Cassie." Morgan preempted any comment in a muffled voice. He sat on a stool with his back to the fire, his arms folded on the table, his face buried in the white sleeves of his forearms. "He could be talking about any of a hundred parks."

"I didn't say a word," Cassie retorted, setting the note back down beside him.

"You were thinking it."

"What I was thinking," she said, "is that, one, Jack tends to use bad poetry in his notes, which could mean that the writer is Ignatious Athelbert trying to mislead us, and two, I believe the arrangement of the victims' possessions might, in fact, be the key to establishing Jack's identity."

She'd also been wondering about the now departed Mrs. Parsons, who'd been looking at him so strangely upstairs, but those questions could wait.

Morgan raised his head a little, interested if not completely convinced. "Go on."

"Well." Positioning herself behind him, Cassie gave in to temptation and let her fingers massage the tight muscles of his neck. That he didn't smack her hands away seemed an encouraging sign, so she elaborated. "The way I see it, the significant arrangements always appear to involve a handkerchief and some kind of a jewel, right?"

His deepening frown indicated a growing interest. She continued to massage his shoulders and neck.

"All of the baroness's jewels, rubies and diamonds were knotted inside her handkerchief," he told her. "What are you getting at?"

"Only that I don't think we'll be able to decipher the more complicated arrangements. By that I mean the things Jack left next to the bodies of his victims in 1888 and other times you've documented. But the simpler ones, like Joelle's cameo and Baroness Roth's rubies and Lady Annabelle's emeralds, those clues we might stand a chance of understanding."

He wasn't looking at her but he was listening. "Anything specific?"

Cassie slid her fingers along his ponytail, sighed to herself, then said, "Two of the handkerchiefs were knotted, weren't they?"

"So?"

"*Knot* with a *K* could translate to the other *not.* You know—homonyms."

That half grunt, half snarl she'd heard so often told her what he thought of that idea. "*Not* emeralds, *not* rubies and diamonds—what kinds of clues are those?"

"Ones worth thinking about," Cassie retorted.

She hesitated, then let her fingers slide across his shoulders. He had a taut, wiry build, all sinew and bone underneath his clothes. If he would just lower his guard for five minutes and forget about being a cosmic cop, maybe something wonderful could happen between them.

"There was no knot in your friend's handkerchief," Morgan recalled, while Cassie retied the bow in his hair. Was that a hint of discomfort in his voice? She worked the ribbon slowly, marveling at how such an effeminate thing could actually make him sexier.

"Yes, I know," she said. "Joelle's cameo was folded inside her handkerchief." She touched his dark curls. "Something hidden, maybe?" she speculated.

He grunted again, but didn't dismiss the idea outright.

Cassie gave him a few seconds to think, then nudged him from behind. "Well?"

"Yes, all right, it's possible," he allowed with a trace of impatience. Shifting slightly, he eased himself forward, away from her.

"Oh, God." Cassie sighed. "Are we going to go through this again?"

"Go through what?"

"Don't be obtuse. Look, Morgan, are you sure you're not afraid of me?"

He twisted around, defensive as she'd expected. "Certainly not."

"And you like me?"

"Yes, I like you."

Snappishly stated, but she believed him. "Then what," she said in mild exasperation, "is your problem?"

She felt him sigh. "It's nothing personal, Cassie, and it has nothing to do with fear. I just don't want to get invol—" Despite his tolerant expression, he seemed at ease with the denial—and more than a little irritated when a flurry of feet on the stairs interrupted him midword. She saw his eyes roll as something small and flustered raced across the floor. "Yes, Bartholomew, what is it?" he asked without looking.

Urgent hand signals accompanied the little man's breathless "She's upstairs. One of the maids let her in."

Morgan's head came around. "Who's upstairs?"

Bartholomew tugged on his sleeve and Cassie's wrist. "Mrs. Deveau. She was attacked. It was Jack, Mr. M. He tried to kill her!"

"IT WAS AWFUL," Desirée was whispering to the housekeeper when Morgan reached the parlor. Cassie had gone upstairs to fetch Lady Mary, who'd retired for the night. Sir Gerald, he knew, hadn't yet returned to the manor, which was odd since he'd invited the guests to his house in the first place.

"Oh, Morgan, thank God you're here," a wet, disheveled Desirée breathed when she saw him.

Mrs. Salton placed a wool rug around her shoulders. "Hot coffee and brandy," Morgan instructed, and the housekeeper marched off stiff-lipped in her drab robe and cap. Wresting his mind from the disturbing interlude with Cassie, he set it on the situation at hand. "What happened?" he asked, then did a double take as he spied Christopher Crowley, a bruised and bloody mess sprawled on the sofa.

Desirée's voice, cracking with shock, brought his attention back to her. "He came out of nowhere. I felt the carriage lurch and thought Tolbert, my driver, had lost a wheel. The carriage felt lopsided. I could see we were wedged into a snowbank and that one of the wheels had rammed into something, so I called to Tolbert. When he didn't answer, Mr. Crowley started to get out. And there he stood at the door, a man all dressed in black. He had a hood over his face with holes cut out where his eyes should have been. He pulled Mr. Crowley out of the coach and struck him. Then, before I could escape, he dragged me out, too. I don't know how I did it, but I got away from him."

"You kicked him between the legs," the actor inserted dryly from the depths of the brocade sofa. "I saw you do it, and he saw that I'd seen and gave me another crack on my skull with the butt of his gun. Wham!" Christopher brought his hand around in a vicious arc. "It was the last thing I saw until Mrs. Deveau revived me."

"Hullo, what's going on here?" Sir Gerald interjected from the open parlor door. A huge smile spread across his narrow, powdered features. "It looks like you two ran afoul of a band of highwaymen."

"One highwayman, sir," Morgan said, walking over to remove Sir Gerald's royal blue cape. "They were assaulted after leaving here earlier this evening."

"Really?" An astonished Sir Gerald stared in awe at the unkempt pair. He swung a finger from Desirée to the actor, his smile broadening into delight. "So you two left together, then?"

Morgan held on to his temper and his composure. "Sir, that's hardly the point."

"Isn't it?"

"No."

"Oh. Well, what happened, then? I mean, why is Christopher covered with blood?"

The rustle of a silk robe alerted them to Lady Mary's presence. She entered slowly, her eyes hard on her grandson's face. Cassie followed at a respectful distance, her more cautious eyes trained on the old woman's cane.

"He's covered with blood, Gerald," his grandmother said, "because he was foolish enough to accept the invitation you issued to join us for port after tea."

"Oh, yes, well, about that..."

"We'll discuss your behavior later," she promised, and hobbled across the room. "Desirée, my dear, you look dreadful. And your dress is torn."

Desirée's fingers moved to her collarbone. Her fichu was badly ripped, the skin beneath scarred. Morgan noticed the marks instantly. They were old wounds, though, as if she'd been burned a long time ago.

"It doesn't matter," she insisted, pulling the edges of the fabric together. "Please, it's imperative that someone be sent to attend to my driver. He hadn't regained consciousness when Mr. Crowley and I ran for shelter."

Lady Mary patted her hand. "Of course, my dear. Morgan, see that someone is dispatched, will you? Also send for Dr. Peach at once."

He offered a small bow and a polite "Certainly, ma'am," then nodded for Bartholomew, hovering in the shadows of the entry hall, to carry the instructions out.

Meanwhile Sir Gerald strode into the center of the room. "This is all a bit puzzling to me, Morgan. What's going on, for heaven's sake?"

"We were bloody attacked," Christopher Crowley snarled. "How much clearer can anyone make it?"

"Don't be rude," Desirée admonished gently, still fidgeting with her torn dress. Her other hand rose to smooth her dark red curls. "It was all perfectly monstrous."

"Especially the hitting part," the actor put in. He raised an arm and brought it slowly down in a striking motion. "Have you ever seen the butt of a gun coming toward your skull? I can tell you it's not a pleasant sight." He splayed the fingers of his left hand across his eyes. "The night was black and so were his clothes. It was as if a shadow leapt from the wall, intent on killing us."

At Morgan's side, Cassie spoke up. "How did you escape?" she asked.

He had to resist the strong urge to grip her arms, shake her hard and hiss, *You see now how dangerous it is for you here? It could have been you again tonight instead of Desirée. I can't live with that possibility.* He did nothing, however, merely folded his hands in front of him and took in as much information as he could.

"I'm not sure how exactly." Fingers pressed to her forehead, Desirée rubbed a bruise forming beneath her makeup. "I ran, and he chased me. But I must have run in a circle because suddenly I was back at my coach. It was very dark, and I did my best to move quietly. Mr. Crowley revived, and we slipped away. But it was slow-going. Many times we had to stop and rest. Your home was the closest, so we came here. I hope you don't mind, Lady Mary."

"Of course not, child. Ah, good. Here's some coffee. Give it to Morgan, Mrs. Salton, then go and watch for Dr. Peach."

"Can I help?" Cassie asked, and Morgan swallowed a snarl as Sir Gerald's eyes lit up in anticipation.

The bewigged baronet rubbed his hands together. "Well, now that you mention it, you could—"

"No, she couldn't, sir," Morgan cut him off in a firm tone.

Sir Gerald seemed put out for a moment, then he shrugged. "Oh, all right." Rebounding, he said, "Serve that damned coffee, will you, Morgan? And put an extra shot of brandy in Desirée's cup. She looks as though she's seen the dead."

"Or almost became one of the dead herself," Cassie murmured.

Morgan thrust a plate of biscuits at her. "Pass these around, then go downstairs and wait for me in my room. I'll deal with Lady Mary."

"But—"

"Just do it," he said tightly. His eyes flicked to Sir Gerald. "If you want a reason, look at his stockings."

She glanced obediently down, then stiffened. Her hand moved instinctively to her throat. "Red," she whispered. "Bloodstains. There are bloodstains on Sir Gerald's stockings!"

"I WANT TO TALK to you Morgan," Lady Mary said two hours later, as he was preparing to leave her parlor. "I've sent three servants along with Wilkie. They'll see both Mrs. Deveau and Mr. Crowley home safely. As for my grandson, I'm confident he'll go straight to his bed. I shall also save until tomorrow the choice words I have to say to Dr. Peach about this roistering habit he's developed of late. He was positively flushed red with exertion when he arrived, and not, I suspect, because he was rushing to our aid."

Morgan bowed his head. "No, ma'am."

"Now you stop that, this minute," she barked, stabbing her cane at him. "No more of this 'yes ma'am, no ma'am' nonsense. And don't waste any of your charm on me, either. I'm onto your tricks, Morgan."

His lips curved into a polite smile. "And what tricks would those be, Lady Mary?"

She ignored the question, pointing a bony finger at his cheek. "You have a bruise there. Where did you get it?"

"In a fight."

"Horse feathers."

"It's true, ma'am." He began collecting the empty coffee cups. "I got into a brawl in a tavern near the river."

"Brawl, my foot." She snorted. "Was Cassie with you?"

The question brought his head up and stopped his hand midreach. "Ma'am?"

"Aha! So it's true?"

"I didn't say that."

"You didn't have to. You blanched for a moment, Morgan. I saw fear in those unreadable dark eyes of yours."

Morgan forced himself to resume his task. "That's impossible," he said equitably.

The old woman rose and hobbled toward him. "You're in love with her, aren't you?"

If he'd been holding it, Morgan would have dropped the tray. As it was, he managed a halfway incredulous "Good Lord, not at all. It's a ridiculous suggestion."

"I don't think so." She sounded smug. "I think you're capable of a great deal of love. You simply don't wish to admit it."

Morgan felt his irritation rising. He forced a small smile and said calmly, "I can't believe you kept me here to talk about something as inconsequential as my emotions, Lady Mary."

"Emotions aren't inconsequential things, Morgan. And Cassie has very strong feelings for you, although she won't admit it any more than you will. You're a pair, you two. But a pair of what, I wonder?" Shrewd gray eyes peered up into his face. "Nothing," she said at length. "That mask you wear is excellent. It hardly ever slips in front of us. However, you're far from unfeeling, Morgan, much as you'd like us to believe that. You were also no more born to be a butler than I was. How do you know Millicent Parsons?"

He'd been waiting for that question. "Through you, of course, ma'am," he said graciously.

Her cane thumped his foot. "You *ma'am* me once more and I'll squash worse than your shoe. Where do you come from, Morgan?"

"Essex," he answered without a flicker.

"Where does Cassie come from?"

"Concord," said an amused voice from the door. Morgan slid his eyes sideways in a veiled warning which Cassie blatantly ignored. She strolled across the threshold. "It's in New Hampshire, Lady Mary."

"Which is where?"

"In America. New England."

"So that part was true, then?"

"Yes," Morgan said.

"That part," Cassie agreed innocently. "Our state was admitted to the Union in 1788."

"Two years ago." Lady Mary's expression maintained a suspicious edge.

After a pause and a look of pure black thunder from Morgan, Cassie said, "Well, two and a half actually. But that isn't why I barged in."

Morgan returned to loading the tray. Keeping his tone even, he inquired, "Why did you barge in, Cassie?"

She made a face at him which Lady Mary didn't see. "I came to tell you that one of the scullery maids saw Sir Gerald leaving on horseback."

"What?" Morgan straightened sharply. "When?"

"Twenty minutes ago. And don't shout, she only told me about it two minutes ago. I thought you—I mean, Lady Mary—should know."

"Oh, Lord." Lady Mary sighed. "That boy's going to be the death of me. Ring for that maid, will you, Cassie?"

"Yes ma'am." Cassie tugged on the bell chord, then on Morgan's coat when Lady Mary looked away.

He inclined his head to her. "Is there more?"

"There might be. The maid's not sure Sir Gerald took it, but apparently there's a knife missing from the scullery. A butcher's knife."

"Oh, great." Morgan rolled his eyes. "What else can go— Wait a minute," he interrupted himself. His searching eyes paralleled his searching mind. "When Christopher Crowley was here, he showed us how he was hit, didn't he?"

Cassie regarded him uncertainly. "Yes."

Taking her by the arm, he pulled her aside. "Don't you see, Cassie? Ignatious Athelbert was struck on the right side of his head. Crowley was hit on the left, and he used his right hand to demonstrate the blow."

"So if Mr. Crowley's reenactment was accurate," Cassie translated, "that means whoever attacked Desirée's coach tonight was probably right-handed."

"Exactly," Morgan said. He arched a meaningful brow. "Yet through the centuries, without exception, Jack the Ripper has always killed his victims with his left hand."

Chapter Twelve

December 14, 1790

"No one has an alibi for the time of the attack on Desirée's coach," Morgan announced in disgust.

It was morning, it was cold, and Bartholomew was half-dead from being up all night watching for Sir Gerald, who hadn't returned until thirty minutes ago. That he'd returned wearing clean stockings hadn't improved Morgan's mood one bit. Neither had Lady Mary's insistence that Morgan was in love with Cassie.

"No knife on Sir Gerald when he got back," Morgan mumbled as he paced in his overcoat and hat before the kitchen fire. "And no explanation from him because he was so bloody ratted that I practically had to carry him upstairs and undress him. Peach, Stockwell, Athelbert, Rowe, Welland—all unaccounted for. Putty and jewels and bad poetry. Probably a master of disguise, too. Damn."

Elbows propped on the counter, Bartholomew asked, "Are you sure Sir Patrick's butler told you the truth when he said he heard funny banging noises in Sir Patrick's room after tea, Mr. M.? Sir Patrick beats his servants, you know. Maybe his butler wants to get him in trouble."

"His butler's not that smart," Morgan said, absently tapping his tooth. "Sir Patrick could easily have left his room by the bedroom window, the same way Dr. Peach could have left his surgery by the side door without any of his staff knowing about it. No, the only one with a credible alibi is Christopher Crowley. He's got both Desirée and her driver to vouch for him." Frowning, he glanced up. "Where's Cassie?"

"Still asleep, sir," Bartholomew said, his eyelids drooping. "It isn't even six in the morning, and Lady Mary and Sir Gerald both like to stay in bed late on Sundays."

"A knotted handkerchief and an emerald choker." Morgan reverted to his former topic. "A cameo inside a folded handkerchief. He's trying to tell us something, Bartholomew. But what?"

"I'm not with you, sir."

Morgan waved him off. "Of course not. Don't worry about it. Just go upstairs and make sure Cassie's not under siege from Sir Gerald."

Bartholomew slid from the stool, hesitated, then ventured tentatively, "Are you in love with her, sir?"

Morgan rounded on him. "Of course not," he said indignantly. Then he narrowed his eyes. "Were you eavesdropping last night?"

"No," Bartholomew lied.

"You were, weren't you?"

Abashed, Bartholomew looked at his feet. "Yes."

Morgan stared straight ahead, at a point high on the wall. "Why?"

"Well—" Bartholomew licked his lips "—I had this dream, you see, and you and Cassie both got killed in it."

Head lowered, Morgan tapped the counter with tolerant fingers. "It was only a dream, Bartholomew," he said evenly. "I'm not going to die, and neither is Cassie."

"But what if Jack catches her again?"

He knew he didn't misread the vicious light that blazed in Morgan's eyes. "If he does, Bartholomew, then he'd better bloody watch out. Because I'll catch him, and I'll take him forward to a time where acts of torture and brutality have been perfected, and death—when it comes—is a blessing."

IT SNOWED AGAIN that day. Cassie was surprised the drifts hadn't reached the third floor by now, but since it tended to thaw in the afternoons, the Currier and Ives picture seldom varied.

There was no thaw this frosty afternoon and nothing for her to do with Lady Mary across town at her niece's home for Sunday dinner.

Decorating the manor, she'd learned, was left to the servants at Amblewood House. Unfortunately, none of the servants were interested in Christmas beyond the fact that it meant more guests and therefore more work.

"Bunch of old Scrooges," Cassie said. She watched from her window as large pine boughs and bunches of holly were wrestled through the side entrance, then turned to regard her makeshift Christmas tree, which was really only a branch reminiscent of a miniature pine. A few bells and beads, acorns, ribbons and bright red bows, and she'd be all set.

She'd scavenged most of those things this morning. Now, with Sir Gerald away for dinner, she could take a quick look through his suite for a gold button or two—and whatever else might be worth discovering.

She hadn't seen Morgan all day. He must be avoiding her. Otherwise he would have been upstairs first thing that morning, snapping at her for the things she'd almost said to Lady Mary last night.

"I don't care," she told herself as she slipped into Sir Gerald's sitting room. "Cranky butler, who needs him? Until it's time to go home, that is."

And Cassie did miss her home, she had to admit. She missed microwave convenience, electric lights, ibuprofen, Italian pizzas, Elton John, her cat Pippin and, most of all, Oreo cookies.

Still, she wasn't prepared to leave just yet. Partly because of Jack, but there was another reason creeping in. And its name was Morgan.

"Damn you," she whispered in aggravation. "Why couldn't you be like the caricature butlers in movies, Anthony Lazarus Morgan?"

"Because I'm not really a butler, and this isn't a movie."

Morgan's voice came from Sir Gerald's bedroom door. Cassie whirled to face him. He stood with a stack of shirts in his hand and stared at her with limited forbearance.

"What are you doing here, Cassie?" he asked.

She took a deep breath. "Looking for clues—and shiny buttons."

"What?"

"For my Christmas tree—well, bough. Never mind. I've been wondering about that putty we found under Lady Annabelle's fingernails."

"What about it?"

She widened her eyes to emphasize her point. "Sir Gerald wears makeup. It could have been his putty and not Christopher Crowley's." She rested an indolent hip on a small Chippendale writing desk. "Or have you already thought of that and searched his dresser drawers?"

Turning, Morgan walked into the bedroom, leaving Cassie to stare at his elegant back. "Sir Gerald keeps his makeup in his bureau," he said over his shoulder. "I have, in fact, searched. He does use putty, and it's a close match."

She crossed to the armoire and peered inside. "A closet lothario with blood on his stockings, huh?"

"Well, something red, anyway," Morgan agreed in an undertone. He glanced through the bureau drawers as he put the shirts away. "Here you go," he said, and tossed something to her. "Two silver buttons. Oh, and a pin."

Cassie caught them neatly. "You're in a good mood today," she noted with growing distrust.

"It isn't a good mood," he corrected. "It's that I happen to like Sundays."

She frowned. "Why?"

"Because they're slow, Cassie. I don't have to clean up after a dim-witted baronet, answer his nine million stupid questions or dress him because his valet Jenkins is busy brushing out his wig—and doesn't know a bloody thing about eighteenth-century fashion, in any case," he added under his breath. Straightening, he gave his waistcoat a perfunctory tug and said, "Right, now that we've got that settled, let's go down to the kitchen and have some coffee, shall we?"

"Is that what you call it?" Her amused gaze flicked to the pin in her hand. "I thought it was boiled mud.... Oh, my God," she exclaimed. "Morgan, it's Masonic."

An uncomprehending frown furrowed his brow. "What is?"

"The pin." She ran over and gave it to him. "It's a Freemason's pin. My grandfather's a member of their society. He has a ring with this same symbol on it."

"So?"

"Well, don't you remember? There was that theory in 1888 about Jack the Ripper. A lot of people believed that he belonged to the Masonic order."

TERRIFIED, BERTIE the church sweeper squatted behind a barrel in the sooty alley. No one crossed Slasher Tom and lived to tell the tale. Obviously, the man squaring off with old Slasher now hadn't been warned.

He advanced on Tom like a cat, stick in hand, dressed in a black cape and hat. Quite the proper gentleman he looked—except for his eyes. There was nothing proper about his eyes.

Bertie shrank lower, a cold hand of fear gripping his chest. Evil, he thought, and he breathed a little faster. Oh, Slasher, you might be for it this time.

"You failed," the man said simply. "I don't tolerate failure."

Slasher Tom muttered something unflattering. The man smiled. Bertie slunk deeper into the shadows.

Slasher kept a knife up his right sleeve. His beady eyes were locked on the man's face. He didn't realize his adversary also had a knife, because this man kept it up his left sleeve. Poor old Slasher.

Bertie heard a horrible, strangled cry, torn off at the source as the man's knife plunged into Slasher Tom's throat. Slasher's own knife fell from his lifeless fingers. His body, however, didn't quite fall to the ground. It landed on a snowy rubbish pile in a pool of steaming blood.

Bertie had seen people die before. He'd seen them turn blue and choke, seen them get shot and trampled and stabbed. He'd seen killers and drunks and men who murdered for tuppence. But he'd never seen a man like this one anywhere in his life. This man's eyes shone brightly in the murky afternoon light, glittered like shiny gemstones. And there was saliva on the corners of his mouth.

His face was all painted, too, but not like the toffs and rich folk normally did it. This was different, overdone, wrong. It gave Bertie a creepy feeling in the pit of his stomach to look at him.

Overhead, Bertie heard a soft scrape, then saw a clump of snow skitter along the sloped roof. The man looked sharply sideways, narrowed his eyes, then pulled his knife smoothly from Slasher's throat. He didn't bother to wipe if off as he strolled toward Bertie's hiding place.

"Good afternoon," he said pleasantly.

Bertie couldn't find his voice or his muscles. He could only plaster himself to the wall and watch in horror and dread as the bright-eyed man drew nearer.

SIR GERALD MUST BE a Freemason. Jack the Ripper had probably been one. Morgan had known about Jack. He hadn't known about Sir Gerald.

"Sir Gerald belongs to three clubs and two secret organizations devoted to sex and drinking. When did he join the bloody Freemasons?" Morgan demanded, though not of Cassie specifically. "None of my sources told me he'd joined, so it's either a recent membership or Sir Gerald's managed to keep his involvement unbelievably quiet. It's leaning to the right," he added in passing.

He was referring to the Christmas branch Cassie had delivered to his room thirty minutes ago in an attempt to divert him. So far her ploy had failed miserably, but she refused to admit defeat.

"You can't brood forever, Morgan," she said reasonably, straightening the bough on the mantel. "Sir Gerald must be a Freemason or he wouldn't have one of their pins. Unfortunately, his belonging to their society doesn't prove that he's Jack. It simply means he could be, which is something you've suspected all along, anyway, so what's the problem?"

He mumbled something about having missed an important clue and losing his touch, and kept right on pacing.

Cassie had the branch propped between two stacks of books. It still looked crooked, so she snapped off a few of the smaller twigs to give it the illusion of straightness.

She'd brought all kinds of things to Morgan's room. Ribbon, thread, colored string, beads, berries—mistletoe.

Not that he'd notice if she hung half a ton of it from his ceiling beams, she reflected. Turning, she planted her hands on her hips. "Morgan, for heaven's sake, will you stop pacing."

Absorbed in thought, he grunted at her.

"All charm now, aren't you?" she said, then squared her shoulders and went to block his path.

It didn't surprise her that he almost knocked her over. It did surprise *him*. He looked startled for a moment, then—Well, actually, she wasn't quite sure how to describe the expression that flitted across his face. Uncertain, maybe? Startled?

Of their own will, her fingers snared his cravat, holding firm when he would have pulled away. "You're wasting energy, Morgan," she insisted, "to say nothing of making me dizzy. It's Sunday afternoon and everyone's out. Why don't we talk?"

Surreptitiously, he eased himself free. "About what?" he asked, and she recognized the wariness in his tone.

"Anything except Jack."

An uneasy light entered his brown eyes. "Fine." He straightened. "I'll have Bartholomew bring us some coffee, then, shall I? Barth—"

Cassie took a step closer, just enough to disarm him. "No, I don't think so," she said.

"Umm..." He darted a glance at the door as if it were his sole means of escape.

Encouraged, she grinned. "Something wrong, Morgan?"

"No," he said, and brought his gaze swiftly back to her face.

"So why don't you kiss me, then?"

He stared at her as if he couldn't possibly have heard her correctly. "What?"

She articulated each word. "Why don't you kiss me?"

"What, you mean *here?*"

"It's as good a place as any, don't you think?"

His hands came up to ward her off. He took a precautionary step backward as he spoke. "Look, Cassie, we've been through this before."

"No, we haven't. Not really. But it's okay, Morgan. You don't have to kiss me if you don't want to."

His eyes narrowed in suspicion.

And so they should, Cassie thought, giving her head a defiant lift. "I'm a twentieth-century woman," she said. "I'll kiss you."

And placing her hands on his shoulders, she caught his startled mouth with hers.

A feeling of astonishment raced through her body, leaving her jolted and faintly breathless. How could this second kiss be better than the first?

His response was immediate. Morgan only resisted the idea. The act, once she got past his defenses, became a phenomenally erotic thing. Too much for her to handle, maybe.

His hands, reluctant at first, moved deftly to her waist and hips, drawing her closer into his fully aroused body. She hadn't expected that and caught back a small gasp of surprise.

"Problem?" he asked, raising his head just enough to look at her.

"No," she lied, then pressed her thumb to his full lower lip. "Stop frowning, Morgan. You'd think someone was torturing you."

He made a sound deep in his throat, then covered her mouth again.

Cassie had lived in a liberal society long enough to know what was almost certain to evolve from this. She should have fought it—after all, she'd only meant to kiss him—but her sudden overwhelming hunger for him stopped any protests cold. He was always so aloof, so unreachable, so determined to avoid any sexual entanglements, and yet now it was Morgan who was kissing her, Morgan who crushed her breasts against his chest so hard that it hurt.

Ah, but it was an exquisite pain. Her breath uneven, her fingers dug deeply into his shoulders.

His mouth was hot and demanding—persuasive, too—and his tongue delved past her lips with something bordering on compulsion.

Cassie tangled her fingers in his hair. God, she could feel every part of him, feel the heat and desire that burned in him, and still she couldn't resist his hair. The texture of it fascinated her—the long ponytail that fell over the warm skin of his neck and the shorter curls on the sides and top... There must be something wrong with her.

Whatever it was, she didn't care.

Morgan's breath was hot on her cheeks. Cassie closed her eyes, savoring the moment, loving it, not wondering once if what she was doing was right.

She thought fleetingly of birth control, but thank heaven, time travel must have made him cautious, as well. Suddenly—and for the life of her she had no idea how they'd gotten there—they were standing in front of an open cupboard where half the contents were now strewn onto the floor.

When he found what he wanted, he nudged the door shut with his elbow, regarded her for a long troubled moment, then whispered a resigned "Oh, damn," and spirited her across the floor to his bed.

One simple no, and he would stop, Cassie knew instinctively. One twist of her head away from his searching mouth, one balled fist pushing at his chest, and he'd be gone.

Did he want that easy out? she wondered vaguely. Or did he want her? Of course, he could stop himself if he really wanted to. Morgan knew how to say no as well as she did, maybe better, though Cassie doubted it.

The excitement she'd experienced earlier resurfaced again. Excitement, eagerness—impatience.

He was being too gentle, lowering her onto the cream-colored eiderdown that covered his narrow bed. Didn't he understand? She wasn't a china doll. She wouldn't break, no matter how fragile she might appear to him.

For once, however, Cassie didn't press the matter. Not this time.

Far off in the London night, she heard a Christmas carol. Something classical, subtly different than the songs she knew, but recognizable in its swell of pure voices.

Flights of angels, she thought blissfully, then closed her eyes and arched her back as Morgan's fingers worked the tiny buttons of her bodice. She could hear his mind swearing, "Bloody clothes," and agreed, but she preferred to let him undress her without aid. Better for him; more delicious for her.

There were no tender endearments, but then Cassie didn't expect any, wasn't really sure she wanted them. He had better things to do with his mouth, and love—if, in fact, it was love she felt for him—wasn't a question she was prepared to consider right then.

His lips moved against her breast, his mouth and tongue trailing a hot, wet path to her hardened nipple. She had his shirt partly undone. Now, as a moan of pleasure rose in her throat, she longed to forget patience, tear the shirt from his back, then grab him and drag him fully on top of her.

Her whole body throbbed from wanting him inside her. If it were possible, she would have crawled right under his skin. For all his lack of verbal encouragement, her desire for him mounted with every passing second.

His long fingers moved along her rib cage to her waist. He'd tossed aside her fichu. Her dress and petticoats followed. Cassie saw them float through the shadows and land in billowy white heaps on the floor. That left only her chemise, and he was kissing her erotically through that fine layer of fabric, drawing her nipple firmly into his mouth and flicking his tongue across the sensitive tip.

Her breath came in spasms. She waited for the fear that should rightfully accompany it, but nothing of that emotion surfaced. Her own fingers fumbled for his fly buttons, located them, then got completely sidetracked.

Oh, God, she thought, groaning inside. She couldn't want him this much. But her brazen hands closed on him, proving to her and to Morgan that she did, and that they'd waited quite long enough.

Casting emotional caution aside, she pulled him down onto her until the full, hard weight of his limbs crushed hers.

He was so sleek and sinewy, his skin the color of pale gold in the dusky light thrown by the coal fire.

The carolers' voices rose and fell in perfect harmony. She heard Morgan's rough breathing, felt the damp silk of his hair on her neck and shoulders, the wet heat of his mouth on her throat and face and cheeks and knew she whispered something urgent in his ear. But it was all a blur to her now—the words, the sweet, faintly religious music that spoke of kings and angels and a blessed child.

And the star... Cassie pictured it in her mind. It seemed to appear and shower her with its golden warmth. Or was that Morgan exploding inside her?

Her hips arched off the bed. With his mouth, he swallowed the cry that emerged from her throat. His hands held and stroked her, his body rocked her. She was shivering, and not from the cold. Her hands clutched at the slick skin of his shoulders. His breath, hard and ragged, came into her mouth.

She remembered whispering a disbelieving "No!" when it was over, because it suddenly occurred to her that the moment had passed and she'd been too lost to recognize it.

"No," she said again, more fiercely. "Don't go."

He held himself above her for a moment. She saw his eyes close and heard him release a heavy sigh. "Oh, God, no," he groaned. "Don't tell me..."

Cassie's muscles froze. "Don't tell you what?" she demanded tremulously.

But all he did was drop his head facedown onto her shoulder and mumble something unintelligible.

Although she couldn't make out the words, she sensed it had nothing to do with love. Not on his part, anyway. And not on hers, Cassie told herself resolutely. So that was it, then. No problem. What had happened between them was in no way related to love.

So why, then, she wondered, did her skin feel suddenly chilled and her heart encased in a fine layer of snow?

LEADEN FEET CARRIED Desirée through the dark streets to his home. He wasn't there, she knew that, and still she was terrified. What if someone caught her? He might return unexpectedly. What if he caught her?

No, she mustn't think like that. Sneak in and look. See what there is to see. Try to find something—anything—that she could use against him.

She crept through the side door. The corridors lay steeped in darkness. She hated the dark, but doubtless he would love it. You could kill so easily in the dark. After all, hadn't she been attacked at night? Survived, yes, but now her worst fear had come to pass. He knew about her, and he wanted her dead.

It was his bedroom she sought, and she found it with no trouble. No one barred her entrance. Nothing stirred around her. Yet.

A film of perspiration formed on her upper lip despite the chill that penetrated the casements. Candles fluttered in their sconces, but that was commonplace even when no one was present. Removing one, Desirée moved stealthily about the room.

His furniture didn't interest her. Neither did his books. The armoire and dresser held nothing of interest. Everything was neat and tidy. Except...

Without realizing it, she'd crawled deep into the armoire. Her open palm rested on a short board. She must have pressed a hidden spring because the board suddenly dislodged itself.

Heart climbing into her throat, she eased the board up. There was a box beneath it, a most curious thing. Even after she brought it out into the dim candlelight, she couldn't decide what it was.

"Don't touch that!" a furious voice boomed out.

She spun to confront it. The box clattered to the floor. She saw it land next to the cheval mirror. More importantly, though, she saw Jack, or at least she saw his outline.

"You slut." He advanced menacingly, the personification of evil to Desirée's frantic mind. "How dare you invade my home."

She couldn't remember how to breathe. Her muscles turned to rubber, then ice. The shadow grew larger as he approached. His hands reached for her. She felt his icy fingers wrap themselves around her throat. Something flashed in front of her—a knife?—and then came an even more sinister flash of teeth. He was smiling at her!

"No!" she choked, beating on his wrists. The struggle unfolded in the mirror. His grip was relentless. She was going to watch herself die!

His fingers squeezed harder, but it wasn't a lethal grip, just enough to bruise. He wouldn't strangle her: even in her blind terror Desirée understood that.

She started to scream. He shook her hard to cut her off. She flailed and clawed and finally tore one of his hands from her throat. She wasn't sure how she broke free of the other, but she did, and the moment she did, she ran, past the armoire and the mirror and the dropped box. She ran straight through the door and down the long hall to the nearest exit.

Her mind was an hysterical blur. Escape, she thought desperately. Flee and hide.

Darkness loomed before her, a great pit of icy nothing. She could lose him inside it; she must. Please, she prayed, don't let him catch me. Then she plunged headlong into the thickest shadows she could find.

Slowly, the sounds of pursuit began to fade. She'd lost him in the night. Oh, but she would have to take care now, be quiet, walk cautiously. Footprints in the snow were a dead giveaway.

Her chest heaved. Her breath emerged in huge shuddering gasps. She gathered her cloak about her quivering shoulders and called herself a fool.

She couldn't defeat Jack. She wasn't cunning enough for that. In fact, she wasn't cunning at all. She was only clever enough to know that she didn't dare go home tonight, just as she hadn't been home any night since the attack.

Closing her eyes briefly, she passed a weary hand across her forehead. Strange that her gloves should leave a sticky trail on her skin. Now, why—?

Her heart gave a sudden horrified lurch as her gaze fixed on her fingers. Gray gloves stained with something dark and sticky.

"Oh, no," she denied, shrinking away from the gruesome sight. "Not that. Please, not that!"

But the coppery odor was unmistakable.

She pictured herself struggling with Jack, twisting at his wrists, tearing his hands from her throat. The blood smell filled her head. He'd killed again tonight, and now the blood was on her.

She began to tremble. "'Out, damned spot!'" she quoted from *Macbeth*. Panic made her voice vibrate as it rose in volume. "'Here's the smell of the blood still: all the perfumes of Arabia will not sweeten this little hand.'"

The trembling increased until finally it consumed her. A scream climbed into her throat. Throwing back her head, Desirée released the sound to the winter night.

Chapter Thirteen

December 15, 1790

Midnight. London spread out silently around Cassie as she walked through the snow-covered garden behind Amblewood House.

Cloak clutched tightly about her body, she went to a bench near the edge of the rose arbor and looked up at the night sky. Only a few stars glittered above the rooftops. The Christmas carolers were long gone, Morgan was fast asleep, Lady Mary and Sir Gerald had decided to spend the night away from home, and Cassie was disconsolate. Not because of what had happened with Morgan, although she wasn't sure she'd intended to make love to him; but because he hadn't spoken more than ten words to her afterward. Even then he'd only grunted at her. Well, except for those few fateful words he'd uttered: *Oh, God, don't tell me...*

What did he mean? Don't tell him *what?* Cassie dropped like a petulant child onto the marble bench. Did he regret making love to her? She'd gotten no sense of that from him at the time. It had certainly seemed urgent enough, to say nothing of soul shattering.

Of course, it might be that he didn't want to get involved, that he was either afraid of relationships or that he simply had no time for one.

Because, really, what was time to a time traveler? For all she knew, he might have the ability to return to his own century five minutes after leaving it, no matter how long he chose to stay in another era. If she wanted to get really depressed about this, she could even return to her old theory about him having a wife and children tucked away somewhere.

Cassie, however, preferred a more positive view—namely, fear. Somehow it suited Morgan to be, if not frightened, then at least reluctant to become emotionally involved. Trust her to fall in love with that type of man, she reflected with a sigh.

And it *was* love, she realized. She loved Morgan in spite of his moods and his snappish temper, his impatient attitude and the fact that half the time he forgot that she was alive.

Well, maybe he didn't go quite that far, but he had an annoying tendency to ignore her, and anyone else not relevant to his current train of thought.

Giving her hair a defiant toss, Cassie rose from the cold bench, determined not to dwell on the negative. In her mind, she heard the carolers singing their Christmas hymn. Like Morgan, their crystal voices suited the era. Still, she wouldn't mind a little upbeat "Jingle Bell Rock" about now, the Hall and Oates version, a slice of New York soul to remind her of her home, some four thousand miles and two hundred years away.

"You're getting morbid again, Cassie," she warned herself, then took a deep breath and gathered her cloak more closely about her shoulders.

One street over, a carriage clattered by. She heard the clop-clop of horses' hooves on the snow and the jingle of their harnesses.

A shiver passed through her. It seemed unnaturally quiet tonight. Her boots crunched loudly on the snow; her satin dress rustled every time she moved. Not a puff of wind stirred the branches; no snow fell from the sky. Even the house struck her as eerily lit. It cast a macabre shadow against the indistinct outline of the old city.

That did it, she thought, wiping her clammy palms on her cloak. Spooky thoughts were starting to creep in. Time to go back and seek out either her own or Morgan's bed.

Cassie's breath steamed like a white vapor around her. Her cloak snagged on the holly bushes she passed. In her wake, the tiny white-tipped branches shivered and cracked.

A frown touched her lips. Was she pulling enough for the branches to crack?

Cassie snatched her head around, but the garden behind her remained still and silent. It was only her imagination working overtime. For all his depravity, Jack didn't strike her as the type to lurk in garden shrubbery.

Nevertheless, she breathed a sigh of relief as she drew closer to the house.

From the path, she regarded Morgan's window. It brought to mind an image from *Wuthering Heights.* She might be Cathy's ghost out here, beckoning to her lover. Except that Morgan wasn't really her lover, this wasn't her time or his, and Emily Brontë hadn't even written her classic novel yet.

The frozen snow crunched underfoot. Her fingers and cheeks tingled with the cold. A cloud of white vapor enveloped her head. She slipped once but regained her footing by grabbing a sapling trunk beside her. She was about to release it when it suddenly occurred to her that saplings didn't have woollen bark. And they definitely didn't breathe.

A white cloud engulfed her again, cutting off her vision. But then, she didn't have to see clearly. She knew what loomed behind the cloud.

Her heart gave a panicky lurch, then started pounding in her throat. She spun from the figure before it could grab her and began to run. The house stood directly in front of her; the door was right there.

But suddenly so was a wall of black. It materialized out of the darkness so swiftly she never even had time to scream.

Short, angry breaths hissed from between Jack's teeth. His fingers clamped themselves like a vise to her throat. Cassie couldn't see his face, or anything else for that matter, but she knew it was his left hand that held her.

Jack the Ripper!

Stark, ghastly images of blood and death swam before her eyes, of knotted handkerchiefs and jewels and a prostitute named Ruby buried in the snow, of a cameo buried in the folds of a white linen handkerchief. Jack wrote taunting notes; Julian Stockwell wrote secret notes. Jack slaughtered women and might be a Freemason. Sir Gerald had a Masonic pin. She'd seen blood on Sir Gerald's stockings, and more blood still on Dr. Peach's clothes and bedding. Sir Patrick had erased something from a brick wall. Ignatious Athelbert had dreams and took drugs and spoke of death. Procopius Rowe went in disguise to sleazy taverns and started fights over prostitutes.

Pressure on her windpipe brought Cassie's mind back.

"Death, lovely death," Jack whispered in her ear. "You'll die soon, slut. But not here, not where we might be interrupted. I want to take my time when I kill you."

Having uttered those ominous words, he wrenched her sideways, snapping her neck, yet not loosening his grip.

Cassie scratched at the steel bands of his fingers. If he didn't let her breathe, she would die here, and then she really would be a ghost like Cathy.

Outrage momentarily blotted out her terror. No, I won't die, she swore, and somehow got a grip on his arm.

He wasn't expecting this form of resistance. It caught him off guard. Cassie seized her opportunity. Using all her weight, together with what leverage she could manage, she flipped him. Two seconds later he was a shapeless black mass lying on a patch of snow and bushes.

Her vision spotty, she began to run. "Morgan," she choked, but her voice failed her.

She'd almost reached the door when her feet were suddenly torn out from under her. Jack had tackled her by the ankles. He held her fast, despite her attempts to kick free.

The wall of Amblewood House rushed toward her. Her head collided painfully with the bricks. She felt her body being dragged roughly backward. An angry snarl filled her mind. The sound echoed, then began to fade. So did the pain. Shadows poured in. A knife glinted above her, and then Jack's teeth.

He had many teeth, Cassie thought hazily, yet no discernible features, only splashes of red paint on his white cheeks and eyes that glittered madly in the weak light.

She fought and was rewarded with a vague impression of color before she lost consciousness. Blue. Jack's eyes were blue. They were also utterly, completely mad.

"LEAVE ME ALONE, Bartholomew," Morgan said, burying his face in the arms he'd folded on top of his desk.

Bartholomew fidgeted in the doorway. "But Sir Gerald's ringing for you, Mr. M."

Scowling, Morgan raised his head. "At five o'clock in the bloody morning? What does he think he is—a robin?"

"I think he just got home, sir."

Morgan made an impatient gesture. "I thought he spent the night at Ramsgate."

"Well, Lady Mary did, but Sir Gerald must have decided not to. Flora, the upstairs maid, says he's in a queer state." Bartholomew's darting eyes scanned the room. "Uh, where's Miss Cassie?"

Morgan grunted. "Upstairs asleep, probably." He aimed a warning finger at Bartholomew's face. "Say one word, and it'll be your last until Christmas."

Bartholomew nodded, still wringing his hands. The jangle of the kitchen bell continued.

"Oh, God," Morgan groaned, resigned. "I'll have to go. Bring up some tea, Bartholomew—preferably laced with Valium," he muttered, casting a quick glance at the ceiling. Standing, he reached for his coat. "After you've done that, send a message to Millicent Parsons for me. Tell her I said, 'No, thank you.'"

Bartholomew nodded blankly. "Is that all?"

"No, fill the tub with hot water, then go and wake Cassie. Tell her I have to talk to her before Lady Mary returns."

The hesitant grin that split Bartholomew's homely face had Morgan rolling his eyes. "Just do it," he repeated before the smaller man could offer a comment.

"Yes sir. Should I take her flowers, too?"

"No, you bloody well shouldn't," Morgan snapped, then waved an impatient hand. "Now go on, get out of here. And don't forget, tea first."

"I won't." Bartholomew shifted his weight. "You know, Mr. M., it's a funny thing, but I thought I saw someone down in the garden late last night."

Morgan began brushing his coat. "Oh, really? And who was it?"

"Well, I'm not sure who, but there was this shadow, and it ran down the path like a giant bat. Then I heard a thump. Then a few minutes later I thought I saw..."

"Yes?"

"Well, it looked like Sir Patrick's coach sitting in Welp's Lane, except there was no crest on the door."

"And then?"

"Nothing, sir. When I looked again, it was gone."

"Right." Morgan finished brushing his coat. "Chances are, then, that you were either dreaming again or what you saw was a legless Sir Gerald returning home and attempting to find the door."

Relieved, Bartholomew smiled. "Yeah. That makes sense, doesn't it. I'll fetch the tea straightaway."

Morgan made a distracted sound in his throat and fingered a sprig of mistletoe on his desk. Then he glanced at his bed. Cassie hadn't been there when he'd woken up. When had she left? Why did it matter to him that she'd gone? And more to the point, why, when he thought of her, did he start to shiver inside?

SOMETHING BURNED AGAINST Cassie's cheek. She emerged from the darkness slowly at first, then with a jolt of remembered terror.

Jack!

She sat up sharply, head throbbing, unable to focus her eyes.

Except for the fire that roared in a huge open hearth, the room around her was dark. It was also blessedly empty. The shadows on the stone walls revealed no human shapes lurking inside. In fact, the only thing visible was a small piece of parchment lying on the floor beside her.

Swallowing the dryness in her throat, Cassie reached for the parchment, every movement an agony and she suspected, every second precious. But the black scrawl looked familiar, and she was still far too groggy to stand.

She ordered her aching eyes to focus on the scrawl. Jack's writing, her mind told her, set down by an agitated hand.

"I must leave you for a time," it read. "But you may trust that I will return. A fire burns to keep you warm and alive in your temporary prison, for I wouldn't want you to die of exposure. No, no my two-faced sister whore, by my hand shall you die. Kill Mother's trollop daughter, red-haired daughter, slut inside."

Poetry again in the last two sentences.

Crumpling the note, Cassie hauled herself to her feet and stumbled up a set of stone stairs to the door, but it was at least three inches thick and locked tight.

Head bowed, she leaned on the heavy iron frame. The room had overtones of a cellar. It contained no windows and only the one door bolted and doubtless chained on the outside.

Shoving the hair from her eyes, Cassie turned and stared at the parchment in her hand. Panic beat a tattoo in her head. There was no way out.

No, there had to be a way out!

Turning back, she pounded the door once with a balled fist. Then, defeated, she rested her forehead against it and prayed for God to help her. Because if He didn't, she was going to become part of history—and die at the hands of a raving, time-traveling maniac who called himself Jack the Ripper.

"I'VE BEEN RINGING for twenty minutes, Morgan," Sir Gerald announced loftily from his satin chaise. "Is the bell broken?"

"No, sir, it isn't," Morgan answered politely. "I hadn't expected you to be back until at least dawn."

"Oh, that." Sir Gerald scoffed at the early hour. "I couldn't stomach Ramsgate House all night. Too stuffy for my taste. By the way, you haven't seen old Procopius about, have you?"

Morgan nudged aside a pair of discarded shoes and picked up Sir Gerald's frock coat. No blood on it or his stockings. "I wasn't aware that Mr. Rowe was here, sir," he said.

"Well, he should be. He showed up at the door right after I got in. Said he had something important to do this morning and wanted to catch a few hours of sleep. I thought you might have tripped over him in the library or something. Oh, well, it doesn't matter. What time is it? Julian's coming by this morning, I think. He popped in at Ramsgate for an hour last night. Crashing bore of a party, he called it, and carried off old Ignatious, who was facedown in the dessert pudding. Not that anyone cared, mind you, after the fuss Iggy raised about some vision he claimed to have had." Sir Gerald's brow furrowed. "Now, what did Dr. Peach call it? A deluge?"

"A delusion, sir," Morgan said, folding his hands in front of him.

"That's right. At any rate, Ignatious was on for simply hours about blood and guts and some woman getting killed in one of those dreary buildings in Whitechapel or Stepney—down near the river, anyway." He jutted his lower lip. "Or was it near a cemetery?"

Morgan frowned, moving closer. "Excuse me, sir, but which woman was he talking about?"

"Who knows. Not a real one, I shouldn't think. Still, Julian scribbled a few notes just on the off chance. Dr. Peach gave Ignatious a glass of port, and that's when his head went down. Ah, good." He glanced cheerfully at the door. "Tea and muffins. My faves."

Casting a quick look at Bartholomew who rattled every dish on the tray as he entered, Morgan digested Sir Gerald's words. For some reason they disturbed him, though which ones most of all, he couldn't say.

His eyes rose to the ceiling. As long as he was up here, he wanted to check on Cassie. But it might also be a good idea to pursue Sir Gerald's Freemason involvement. Of course, that information could be ferreted out through his servant contacts, but a direct question or two never hurt.

He opened his mouth to form one, then closed it again when Bartholomew almost dropped the tray.

"Fumble fingers this morning, eh?" Sir Gerald said while Morgan shook out his napkin.

Eyes downcast, Bartholomew mumbled a faint "'Scuse me, sir."

"What, no jelly?" Sir Gerald demanded, moving on.

"I'll fetch it right away, sir." Bartholomew tugged with surreptitious insistence on Morgan's coat. "Mr. M.," he whispered hoarsely. "She's gone."

Morgan glanced back. Head bobbing, Bartholomew pointed upstairs, mouthing the words, "Miss Cassie, sir—she's not in her bed."

"What!"

Sir Gerald blinked at Morgan's ejaculation. "What?" he echoed, oblivious to the conversation. "Is something wrong, Morgan?"

"Not at all, sir." Somehow Morgan forced a pleasant tone. He even summoned a smile. Well, he curved his lips at any rate, then worked on not curling his fingers into a fist. "If you'll excuse me," he said with a polite bow. "A problem has apparently arisen in the kitchen."

"Of course." Sir Gerald waved him off with a wink of one blue eye. "Is it a pretty problem? Red-haired and all that? Oh, and never mind the jelly, Morgan." He yawned. "I'm feeling a bit sluggish. Think I'll turn in. If I'm not up by lunchtime, come and fetch me, will you?"

"Certainly, sir," Morgan answered, then shoved Bartholomew discreetly through the door. Once in the hall, he grabbed the smaller man's lapels. "What do you mean, she's gone?"

"What I said, Mr. Morgan. She's not in her room. Her bed's made, and she's not there."

Morgan swore under his breath, gave Bartholomew a frustrated shake, then released him abruptly. An idea hit him, farfetched and desperate, but worth a try.

"The East End," he said. "Stepney and Whitechapel. The cemetery." He stared at the servant's confused face. "You're sure she's not in the house?"

"Not unless she's in the attic, sir."

"Right, saddle my horse, then bring him around back."

Bartholomew trotted along beside him as he made for the rear staircase. "Do you have an idea, sir?"

"Yes, I do," Morgan said grimly, recalling the "dream" Bartholomew mentioned having. "And it's not a pleasant one, either."

6 a.m.

HE'D BE BACK FOR HER anytime, Cassie thought. She walked in circles around the cold room. The fire was dying; there was no more wood to burn. What was she going to do?

There must be something. Screaming was pointless. So was pounding on the door. She couldn't remove it from its hinges, or pick the lock, or tunnel out through the stone floor. She couldn't even climb up the chimney, because it was too narrow. She'd checked that possibility when the flames had dropped. That left little, except prayer and the small hope that there might be some way of thwarting Jack's plans for her when he returned.

Surely he had a weakness, some flaw she could exploit. She knew he would use his left hand to kill her; maybe there would be something in that.

Images raced haphazardly through her head. Knots in handkerchiefs. *Knot* meaning *not?* And the jewelry beside them, genuine gemstones. Not jewels? Not gems? She pictured Joelle's cameo inside her folded handkerchief and a woman buried in the snow—although that last image might not be significant—and, most recently, the message Jack had written her, containing references to a mother, capital *M,* a daughter and a sister. His mother, daughter or sister? Cassie wondered. It was difficult to say. But his ongoing fixation with prostitutes and a later obsession with red hair were certainly clear.

Cassie rubbed her temples as she walked, then halted when something clanged on the other side of the door.

Jack!

She whirled, panic clawing at her. The door opened outward; she couldn't hide behind it. Although the shadows offered little concealment, they'd have to do.

She chose the deepest one across from the fire. A series of muffled clangs reached her ears. She balled her fists and prepared to run. He wouldn't expect her to shoot past him, surely.

The iron ring began to turn. Breath held, Cassie gathered every scrap of courage she could muster. A loud creak filled the room as the door swung outward. Muscles taut with strain, she waited for her chance. Not yet, she thought, holding herself back. Not yet.

It stopped moving.

Wary, she counted the seconds. One, two—oh, God, where was Morgan in all of this?—three, four. She got to ten before she dared creep forward. A soft patter of footsteps outside receded as she approached. But that couldn't be right.

Screwing up the reserves of her courage, she flung the door back. The resulting crash, as it slammed against the stone wall, echoed through the building.

She peered out. No Jack. No one at all, in fact. Except...

Far ahead, in a corridor that probably dated back to the Dark Ages, she detected a flurry of motion, something black rounding the corner. Her impression was one of a long cloak and cowl, someone moving swiftly, steathily, purposefully.

Cassie pondered the mystery for a full five seconds, then gave herself a hard shake. It would be light in a few minutes, and Jack would return as promised; she had no doubt of that.

Run, her brain commanded. Run and don't stop until you get to Amblewood House, until you're back where you belong. Until you get to Morgan.

DARKNESS WOULD SOON give way to dawn, Jack realized. He had to go now while the night still lingered.

His failure earlier would turn to triumph when he killed Morgan's pretty friend. He would rather kill Mother's slut daughter, but not everything could be done at once. In time he would get them all.

The streets smelled in the notorious East End. The building came into view at last, a charcoal silhouette against a pearling sky. It had taken him too long to get here from his home. Dawn hovered on the horizon. He must do this quickly.

Head bent down; he slipped into the dank storehouse. There were a hundred such slummy buildings in the vicinity, a hundred more closer to the Thames. All were silent now, but soon the people would awaken—the people, the city, and the woman whose throat had been within his grasp last night.

No, he mustn't think about her now. He would confuse himself if he did. Kill the red-haired servant girl first.

His boot heels made a flat sound on the damp stone floor. He clutched his knife, which was sharpened and ready, and his surgeon's tools in their little pouch. He even chuckled a little at dear old Mother. Then he stopped in his tracks and stared, too stunned for a moment to accept the truth of what his eyes told him.

The iron door stood wide open!

Unaware that he'd moved, Jack rushed forward. This was impossible!

He darted through the open door and down the stairs, then halted, panting like a wild animal in the middle of the floor.

The room was empty. The fire was dead.

Jack's fingers curled into claws. That made twice now that she'd eluded him. But how could she have opened the door?

The answer was simple. She couldn't. Someone had released her. Morgan? No! Jack's head came up, nostrils flaring. This was the work of another one, the red-haired spy slut.

"Whore," he gritted in a vicious whisper. He whirled around, blue eyes blazing. "I'll kill you, slut sister, do you hear me?" he roared to the rafters. "I'll kill you if it's the last thing I ever do!"

Chapter Fourteen

Don't panic, Cassie ordered herself as she made her way through alleys and shadow-filled lanes. Jack can't possibly be lurking around every corner.

She had to go away from the Thames, she decided, away from Stepney and the sailors' bars, to the cemetery in Whitechapel. It was a ghoulish prospect, but at least she knew that area.

She recalled the first night she'd gone there. They'd found poor Ruby Fox, buried in a snowdrift like so much dead vegetation. God, but Jack was sick.

The cold numbed her fingers as she trudged on. Her cheeks stung, and her toes. She wasn't dressed for a winter hike. Still, freezing was better than being hacked apart by a mad butcher with a mother-sister-red-hair-prostitute fixation.

Sir Gerald had had problems with his mother and sister, she remembered. Dr. Peach had had trouble with his sister. The poet's mother and sister had allegedly been visionaries. And Christopher Crowley's mother was rumored to have been a woman of noble blood. Oh, but the actor had been with Desirée the night she'd been attacked. He couldn't be Jack.

Streaks of silver split the darkness in the lane she finally entered. She smelled rotting garbage and other less pleasant odors. She also smelled coffee and baking bread. Heaven, she thought, inhaling deeply. If only she could stop.

It was slippery walking in ruts and still too dark to avoid them, so Cassie hugged the brick wall on her right. Mounds of refuse had to be skirted, but otherwise she could follow the wall all the way to the street.

Ahead of her, she spied a tattered wool scarf, blowing in the breeze. She wouldn't have noticed it except that it appeared to be tied to something. Something that looked suspiciously like...

Cassie's heart gave a violent lurch. She hesitated, then crept closer. Spots of blood on the wool made her stomach tighten, but she bent and put her hand out, anyway. Her fingers unearthed a gray wool cap.

Oh, God, it was, she thought weakly, closing her eyes. The scarf was wrapped around a man's frozen throat. His slashed and frozen throat.

Horrified, she backed away. It made no sense. Jack didn't kill men.

But the evidence glared up at her; she couldn't deny it. Blood and body parts lay strewn in the snow. Jack had disemboweled his male victim, slashed his throat, then left him faceup and gaping at the empty winter sky.

Hand pressed to her stomach, Cassie retreated from the mutilated body. Revulsion slowly gave way to terror. Was Jack still here?

She wouldn't panic, she vowed. But she had to get out of this lane now, quickly, without fuss or sound.

Eyes riveted on the dead man, she backed over to the far side of the lane. She continued walking backward, casting furtive glances over her shoulder every few steps. She made it past the pile of old crates and the pools of raw sewage, past the garbage heaps and the litter and—

Her heel bumped against something and she looked down. A feeling of dizziness gripped her. How could there be two bodies in the same alley!

For the first time in her life, Cassie panicked. She didn't stop to consider, she just bolted blindly for the street.

A carriage rolled past, or was it a cab? Whatever it was, she couldn't quite catch the back of it.

She fell twice in the ruts—once on her knees, the second time flat on her face. The jolt scarcely registered. Thank God, her brain had gone numb. She didn't even feel sick anymore, merely mechanical. Maybe if she lay here long enough she would...

No, she refused to think like that. She wouldn't die. Run for safety, that's what she would do. Send a message to Morgan.

Dragging herself to her feet, she stumbled through the creeping dawn shadows toward a lit brick building. She didn't see the horse until the last minute. Standing benignly out front, it looked like all the other shapeless shadows. But this particular shadow was entirely real. Better yet, it was saddled.

"Cassie?"

Her name, an uncertain question, issued from the lit building. Her panic resurfacing, Cassie grabbed for the stirrup and reins. Did she know how to ride? For some reason, she couldn't remember.

Gloved hands caught her from behind before she could mount. She kicked at them.

"Cassie, it's me."

She knew the voice, but then, she probably knew Jack the Ripper's voice, too.

"Get away from me," she grated, and kicked again.

"For God's sake, Cassie." The hands yanked her down, squirming all the way. "It's me, Morgan."

Her back was pressed against his chest. He held her tightly. His warm breath came into her ear. Morgan, not Jack. Relief filled her. Or were her senses playing a cruel trick on her?

She twisted her head around, almost collapsing in relief when she saw his face. "Thank God," she breathed. And closing her eyes, she let herself be drawn into the sheltering heat of his body.

HE PLIED HER WITH CUP after cup of hot coffee. He sat behind her on the bench in the coffee shop, rubbed her arms and talked to her in a calm voice until the shudders that racked her subsided to the occasional tremor.

"He locked you in a cellar and left you this note." Morgan's fingers closed about the parchment she'd given him. "But he never returned, is that right?"

She shoved weakly at her tangled hair. "Yes. Someone snuck in first and opened the door. I don't know who it was. I think it might have been a woman."

He set his mouth close to her ear. "What makes you say that?"

"Body language, I suppose. Maybe I'm wrong. Stop grilling me, Morgan." She sounded exhausted and cross. With her fingers, she massaged her forehead. "I'm sure there was something more important I had to tell you. Is there brandy in this coffee?"

His lips moved in a frown against the soft skin of her cheek. His mind was only now beginning to function above a level of total desperation. "No. Do you want some?"

"Yes... No!" Her head snapped up and she grabbed his wrist. "Morgan, I remember now. The bodies! There are two men in the alley!"

"What? Where?"

"Out there." She pointed, then jumped up, yanking him off the bench. "They were like the women, exactly like the women, only this time he killed two men. But it's Jack's handiwork, I know it is."

And five minutes later, staring in disgust at the two bloodied and frozen corpses, Morgan knew it, too.

CASSIE RECALLED the scene that unfolded that morning better in retrospect. At the time it seemed more like a bad dream.

Morgan dispatched three peasant men he knew from the coffee shop to watch the building where she'd been imprisoned, although his hopes weren't high that Jack would be caught. Neither were Cassie's, unfortunately. By 8:00 a.m., she figured Jack would long since have come and gone, and in a rage she'd bet.

Sir Patrick, summoned to the crime scene with several other committee members, arrived in the company of Julian Stockwell. Again.

"Make sure you spell my name right this time," Cassie heard him growl to the reporter. "Stupid bugger, you got it wrong in your last column."

"Glory seeker," Julian retorted.

Both men looked rumpled, Julian more handsomely so with his black hair, slender features and deep blue eyes.

Blue eyes. The memory made Cassie shudder. Jack had blue eyes. So did Julian Stockwell. But then, so did Sir Patrick, Sir Gerald, Procopius Rowe, Dr. Peach and, when the light was right, Ignatious Athelbert. Only Christopher Crowley's eyes were hazel, and he no longer mattered.

Morgan had dark brown eyes, and those eyes had been watching her closely all morning. Pleased though Cassie was by the discovery, she wished she knew what he was thinking. Trust Morgan not to say, or even give her a hint. But, best not to dwell on her emotions, she decided.

Her photographer's defenses kicked in as the bodies were cleared of snow. She found she could regard them clinically, though not without the odd shudder of revulsion.

"Bertie, the church sweeper." Morgan identified the smaller man. "And Slasher Tom."

"Lovely name," Cassie remarked, then indicated Slasher Tom's feet. "What's that?"

Julian peered over her shoulder. "A dirty stocking." His brows went up. "Next to a pile of jewels. A ruby ring, a diamond brooch, sapphire earrings. Quite a cache for a sewer rat."

"Stolen, no doubt," Sir Patrick concluded.

Cassie studied the pile, then nudged Morgan's ribs. "Those sapphire earrings look like a pair Lady Mary owns."

His brow furrowed. "Are you sure?"

"Pretty sure, but I'm not a jewelry freak."

With a covert glance at Sir Patrick's back, Morgan bent to scoop the earrings up. "Find out" was all he said, then he smiled benignly past her shoulder at Julian and dropped them into her hand.

"We're looking rather guilty, Morgan," Julian said in a regal tone which he then shed. "Do you have any ideas about this? A stocking and jewels, a dead street thief and a church sweeper—two men this time, no women."

"Two disemboweled men, murdered by someone who used his left hand," Cassie said. "Those things are consistent."

Julian's eyes glittered. "You're very attached to your left-handed theory, aren't you, miss?"

"I suppose so."

"Sir Patrick's left-handed."

"Interesting, isn't it?"

"Well, I'm sure it will be to him." Julian scratched down a few notes.

His handwriting was nothing like Jack's scrawl. It was also illegible to her.

"Can you actually read that scribble?" she asked, and he laughed.

"Not really, no. I have to rely a great deal on memory."

"Maybe you'd do better with your left hand," Morgan suggested, returning his diverted attention to them.

"Ah, I see. You think I'm really left-handed." Smiling coldly, Julian wrote a recognizable version of his own name, right-handed. "Satisfied?"

Morgan merely raised an unimpressed brow and returned his gaze to Sir Patrick.

Procopius Rowe arrived in the lane at some point. Cassie didn't actually see him come, but suddenly there he was, flamboyant as always, and only half-drunk. She suspected he'd just rolled out of some woman's bed. However, seeing as it was almost noon, that didn't mean much. It certainly didn't prove he wasn't Jack.

The men Morgan had sent to watch the river building returned near one o'clock with nothing to report. Morgan accepted the news stoically, paid them, cast a final look at the stocking which had clearly been removed from Slasher Tom's left leg, and the jewels beside it, and urged Cassie toward the coffee shop.

Thirty minutes later everyone was there, including, of all people, Ignatious Athelbert, who stumbled in wild-eyed and disheveled, grabbed Julian's lapels and shouted, "You see, I told you last night this would happen! Sir Gerald and Dr. Peach laughed at me, but I warned you. In lane, near bodies buried nigh, more bodies soon to join them lie. I made a poem of it in my head."

"You make a poem of every bloody thing you say," Sir Patrick bellowed. "Get that rhymer out of here, Julian, or else pop his face in a coffee cup."

Julian disentangled himself with difficulty. The poet fell, sweating, into the nearest chair. Sir Patrick snarled at him. Procopius Rowe threw back his fiery red hair and laughed boisterously. Julian dusted off his coat.

Curious bunch, Cassie reflected, then did a double take as Morgan slipped a coin to a young peasant boy. His eyes were fixed on the reporter who was busy writing in his notebook.

The peasant boy hovered close at hand, his eyes expectant on Julian's bland face. Discreetly, Julian tore off the parchment, folded it, then gave it to the boy. His instructions for delivery were issued with the aid of a warning finger.

Cassie observed all of this while Morgan propelled her out the door. She considered questioning him, but decided against it. They exited the coffee shop several seconds ahead of the boy.

"Over here," Morgan directed. Cassie hesitated, then followed him to a nearby alley, thankfully not the one where she'd found the dead men.

A few minutes later, the boy appeared. Bright-cheeked, he surrendered the parchment to Morgan.

"Skinflint only gave me a ha'penny to run this halfway to Piccadilly," he said with a cocky swagger. "I reckon sixpence is a better deal, Mr. M. What's it say?"

Morgan's eyes skimmed the writing. "None of your business," he murmured. "Who was supposed to receive this?"

The boy squinted one eye. "I was to meet a bloke with white hair at the rag shop on Beekham Road."

"Lame Daniel?" Morgan mumbled, preoccupied.

"Yeah, d'you know him?"

"Nope. You can go now." When the boy didn't move, he said, "Well, go on, get out of here. You've got your money."

"I see you love children," Cassie observed. She couldn't read the note over his shoulder. "Who's Lame Daniel when he's not running a rag shop?"

Morgan tapped his tooth as he reread the message. "That particular child makes Dickens's Artful Dodger look like a piker, and Lame Daniel's what you would call a go-between."

"Ah, then shouldn't we find out who he's going between?"

"Not unless you want a knife in your neck." His frown deepened. "What do you make of this?"

" 'More bodies discovered,' " Cassie read. " 'Two men. Plebs, but A.L.M. and girl suspect connection to previous deaths. Fair warning from scene. Suggest problem be nipped in bud. Sir P. desirably ineffective. Might be wise time to move.' "

She went over it again. "It sounds like a warning," she said finally. "Doesn't it?"

In lieu of an answer, Morgan pulled her sideways into a low doorway. "Our friend's leaving."

Cassie wished he wouldn't stand so close. It was distracting. "Julian?"

"And Procopius. Oh, and Sir Patrick, too."

"Eenie, meenie or minie?" Cassie asked, easing herself away from him.

Morgan took a covert look around, then gave her a gentle shove. "Eenie. Come on. I want to know who Julian Stockwell's writing secret messages to, and I want to know why."

THEY FOLLOWED the reporter's serpentine trail to the narrow, somber-looking Billingsgate building where he lived. Christopher Crowley, arriving from the opposite direction, waited at the door and walked up with him. They separated in the upper landing.

"He knows someone's trailing him," Morgan said to Cassie.

Judging by the looks Julian was casting over his shoulder, she had to agree. "And here I thought we were doing such a good job. Hey, wait a minute, where's he going?"

The question wasn't even out of her mouth before Julian disappeared down a rear staircase. If he hadn't slipped and fallen on the street, they might not have caught him.

He glowered as they approached him. "All right, why are you after me?"

Morgan produced the parchment. The sight of it caused Julian's eyes to narrow.

"You're an impertinent bloody butler, I'll give you that," he snarled, then winced as he tried to stand. "You've also made me break my ankle."

Morgan fell easily into his charming butler role. "Oh, I am sorry," he apologized with exaggerated solicitude. "Can I help?"

"Damned right you can." Julian stuck out an arm. "I should send for the peelers," he muttered as they recrossed the street.

"The what?" Cassie asked.

"Peelers." He waved her off. "Police. Never mind. I thought you were anarchists or something. What are you doing with that message I wrote? It should be in Piccadilly by now. Oh, God, not him," he groaned suddenly. "Go left, Morgan. Left."

But it was too late. Ignatious Athelbert toddled toward them, eyes dull, feet dragging. "Dead like a fallen snowflake," he was mumbling. He spied the threesome and blinked rapidly. "Are you injured, Julian?"

"Twisted ankle," Cassie supplied.

"Broken," Julian insisted.

"Do you want me to send for Dr. Peach?" Morgan asked.

Julian stiffened. "That quack? I'd sooner let the addict here treat me. Open your door, Ignatious," he barked. "I'm not hopping up a flight of stairs until my ankle's wrapped."

"In rags?" Morgan suggested with a sly sideways look.

His shot hit home. Julian shook free of his hand and hobbled across the poet's garishly decorated room to a red satin sofa.

A sort of Nubian brothel was how Cassie would have described the decor. Ghastly porcelain Egyptian servants bearing urns and trays dotted the perimeter of the room.

Red was the dominant color, with splashes of black and gold thrown in for good measure. Even the carpet was bright red.

"I'm waiting," Julian said, glaring at Morgan.

His was not, Cassie reflected, the attitude of a man in league with a crazed killer, which was the theory she'd devised while they'd been following him.

Morgan started forward. Cassie could envision his expression. When he wanted to, Morgan could look downright villainous. "What I want," he said levelly, "is an explanation."

"*You* want an explanation," Julian gaped, astonished. "For what?"

"This note." Morgan held the parchment up as he advanced.

Julian bristled. "I'm a reporter."

"Yes, you are. But this message has nothing to do with your job at the *Times*."

"Oh, doesn't it?"

"No."

"Personally, I'd answer his question," Cassie said, fingering one of the statues. "I've never met anyone who knows more lowlifes than Morgan, and those type of people tend to get rough."

"So now you're threatening me?"

Morgan halted. "No. I'm asking you to explain this note."

"And I'm telling you, it's none of your damned business."

"Right." Curving his lips into a false smile, Morgan turned to Cassie. "We'll just go and dig up some of Slasher Tom's friends, then, shall we? Come along, Cassie."

Julian swore. "Nuisance butler. What are you, Morgan—a spy?"

"Not at all, sir," Morgan said pleasantly, reverting to the polite butler.

Julian wasn't convinced. "Well, you must be something." He paused, then said, "Oh, all right. If you must know, I'm working for the King."

"But he's..." Cassie started to say the king was mad, but stopped herself in time. She wasn't sure if George III had gone mad by 1790 or not. Instead, she substituted a hasty "He's not interested in street crime, is he?"

"Of course he is," Julian retorted. "He can't let old Pitt's parliamentary committee show him up, so to speak. The lords want to know what's happening on the streets, too, you know."

From a corner chair, Ignatious laughed, a low nervous laugh. "Foolish lords, they have but to ask me."

"Yes, well, they tend not to put much stock in opium-smoking poets who claim to have the second sight," Julian said wryly. "Agents are the preferred source of information."

Morgan narrowed his eyes. "So you wrote this note to the King."

"Yes."

"We can check your story, you know," Cassie reminded him.

Julian's dark blue gaze impaled her. "I realize that, miss. And while we're on the subject, just who are you with your fine hair and skin and your makeup that's more subtle than anything I've seen in my, if I do say so myself, rather extensive travels? You're not really from America, I'll warrant."

"Oh, but she is," Ignatious protested. His sunken-eyed stare made Cassie's skin crawl. "She's a colonial, born and bred."

"And here we thought only your mother and sister had the gift," Morgan remarked, studying him.

Ignatious shrank back in his chair. His cheeks were gaunt and sallow, his eyes verging on bitterness. Or was it desperation? His expression changed so swiftly, Cassie couldn't be sure what she saw.

"Forget the peelers, we should be sending for the bailiff," Julian muttered, grimacing as he probed his sore ankle. "The man's a bloody loon."

"So's Jack," Cassie said.

"Who?"

"The one who's been doing all the slaughtering."

Dipping her hands into the pockets of her cloak, Cassie located the earring Morgan had given her. Her fingers brushed lightly across the smooth cold sapphires, diverting her from the conversation.

Did the earrings belong to Lady Mary? she wondered, casting a quick look at Morgan's profile. Because if they did, there was really only one way a man like Slasher Tom could have obtained them. It was doubtful he could have infiltrated Lady Mary's private suite at Amblewood House. Which left Sir Gerald as the possible thief, and a few extremely disturbing questions about his nocturnal habits.

December 16, 1790

"I DON'T UNDERSTAND, Mr. M.," Bartholomew said late the following afternoon. "Why would Jack kill this Slasher Tom? And even if he did, why were Lady Mary's earrings lying beside the dead body?"

Morgan rolled his eyes. "In order," he said as if speaking to a child, "to either frame Sir Gerald for the murders, or as a double bluff because Sir Gerald is, in fact, Jack and earrings were used as payment to Slasher Tom for attacking Desirée Deveau last week." He started to pace. "The question is, why would Jack hire someone to kill for him?"

"To confuse things?" Cassie suggested from the partition. She glanced behind her. "Uh-oh, heads up. Mrs. Dickson's back from the cellar."

"And Sir Gerald's ringing for you, sir," Bartholomew added. "He wants you to dress him for the Cumberlands' party tonight. I heard him say that Jenkins hasn't been doing it properly."

Morgan snarled as he put on his coat. "You're sure those are Lady Mary's earrings?" he asked Cassie.

"Positive. She wanted to wear them tonight, so I gave them to her. She recognized them right away."

"Good, fine." He straightened his waistcoat and cravat. "So either Sir Gerald is Jack or someone's trying to make it seem as though he is. We're really getting on with this."

Coming up behind him, Cassie pulled the ponytail from under his collar. "Don't be so gloomy, Morgan. At least we know that Julian was telling the truth when he said he was an agent for the King. Your palace contacts were quite definite in their confirmation. Not that it proves he isn't Jack, but at least it's something."

Since being close to her made concentrating difficult, Morgan walked around to the far side of the table. He tapped agitated fingers on the top. "Yes, well, I'm also convinced that it was Slasher Tom who attacked Desirée's coach—although I still can't imagine why Jack would hire someone to murder for him."

"To give himself an alibi?" Cassie theorized.

"Possibly. But all that does is put Christopher Crowley back in the running."

"And frames Sir Gerald," Bartholomew inserted brightly—and with no idea what he was talking about. He was too busy shifting his beaming gaze between Morgan and Cassie to let logical thought creep in.

Sliding him a look from under his lashes, Morgan offered a dry, "Shut up, bunny brain, and get the tea tray ready."

"Right away, sir. There's the bell again."

"I hear it. By the way, did you send my message to Mrs. Parsons?"

"Yesterday morning," Bartholomew confirmed.

Morgan felt Cassie watching him. "I've been meaning to ask you about that," she said. "Who is this mysterious friend of Lady Mary's, and why do I get the feeling she knows you quite well?"

Morgan was saved the necessity of a reply by the arrival of a pockmarked teenage boy in a tattered coat and breeches. Cap in hand, he faced Morgan breathlessly.

"I came from Dr. Peach's place, sir," he said.

Morgan brushed his cuffs, not expecting much. "Yes, what is it?"

"It's about that toff who was stabbed, sir—the one who got the doctor all bloody the other night. Far as anyone can tell, his name is Sir Robert Geoffries and his arm got scratched in a duel."

Morgan kept his voice level. "What?"

"His arm got scratched—"

"Yes, yes, I heard you. I presume it was a large scratch."

"No, sir. That's the funny thing. It was small and hardly bled at all. And since you were asking, I was told to tell you that the doctor didn't go straight home after he fixed up Sir Robert. He went to Heatherington Hall, but on the sly, if you take my meaning."

"And what's at Heatherington Hall other than a Scottish laird, a stocked wine cellar and six French maids?"

"Well, sir, as far as Dougall could count—Dougall is the doctor's valet's cousin's brother-in-law's uncle who drives for the old laird—there were twelve other men that night. One of them was the laird, and another was Dr. Peach, who arrived in a cab. The doctor stayed for about fifteen minutes, then went home." The boy leaned forward. "But then, sir, he went out again. Alone. No driver or anything, says the stableboy. Took his own horse, saddled it and everything."

"Yes, and what time did all of this happen?"

"Well, the duel was at nine o'clock, but the doctor didn't get to his place until just before midnight. Can't say about the rest of it, sir. Too many people involved to be sure."

After the boy, duly paid and pleased with himself, had left, Cassie said, "So Dr. Peach could have attacked Jane Brede, gone to Sir Robert's home, patched up his arm, dropped in on a very weird-sounding party at Heatherington Hall, gone home, then ridden out and murdered Ruby Fox. He probably had enough time to do it, you know, and his laundress did say she thought he came in around dawn." She frowned. "Of course he might have gone back to that Heatherington Hall place, and just didn't want anyone to know about it. Because, if you ask me, that little gathering smacks of a coven meeting, and no self-respecting doctor of medicine would want his name linked to a black mass, especially if there was any bloodletting involved."

"Oh, be quiet," Morgan snapped, drumming his fingers on the table.

"On the other hand," Cassie persisted, deliberately difficult, "there's also the little matter of him having to steal the coach he used to chase Jane Brede. That would have taken some maneuvering."

Morgan waved that problem aside. "For all we know, he could have stolen the coach and pair earlier and sheltered them in a convenient spot."

"Which is to say he could have done it. Which in turn means he could be Jack."

A grunt was Morgan's only response—together with a careful avoidance of her eyes. He didn't need to be reminded of Cassie's delicious curves, or the softness of her skin and hair, or of the sleepless hours he'd spent last night, tossing and turning in his empty bed. Empty partly because Cassie hadn't pressed him to share it and partly because he was too pigheaded to know a good thing when it reared up and slapped him in the face.

"Message, sir," Mrs. Dickson announced roughly, curling her lip at Cassie as she handed Morgan a grimy parchment. "It's from one of those committee bloke's porters."

Morgan broke the ratty seal.

"I gather from your expression, it's not an invitation to the Cumberlands' party," Cassie said in a meaningful voice.

His mind occupied, Morgan missed her sarcasm. "No, it's about Sir Gerald. It seems he is a Freemason, after all. He joined their society five weeks ago upon the recommendation of his good friend Sir Patrick Welland."

"Really?" She sounded impressed. "Sir Patrick, the left-handed Freemason, and Sir Gerald whose grandmother's earrings were found next to the body of one Slasher Tom. That *is* interesting."

"Very," Morgan murmured. Bringing his mind back, he straightened his clothes. "Right. We're off, then."

"To where?"

"Astley Manor, where the Cumberlands live."

"You mean we're going to crash the party?"

"Yes," he said in a doubtful tone. "But I wouldn't look so pleased about it if I were you."

"I'm not pleased, Morgan," she said with a shiver. "I'm terrified. I'm also coming with you," she added quickly before he could suggest an alternative. "I just have a feeling, that's all."

"That Jack's going to be there? He will."

She shivered again, and he had to curl his fingers to keep from taking her in his arms. "No, it's not that. This feeling has to do with the possessions he's been arranging beside the victims. It seems almost desperate to me."

Morgan frowned. "What, you mean a cry for help?"

"Something like that. Otherwise why would he be doing it? Why put a pile of jewels next to a stocking?" She sank into Morgan's chair, propping her chin up on her hands. "I wish Sigmund Freud were here. I wish I'd studied psychology at university. I wish we could catch him."

"So do I," Morgan said, forcing himself not to look at Cassie's lovely throat. Because every time he did, he saw blood. Her blood.

He made a vicious sound deep in his own throat. Over his dead body, he swore. His and Jack's.

DESIRÉE DIDN'T KNOW whether to go to the Cumberlands' party or not. She knew Jack would be there. And he was getting bolder and smarter and madder by the minute. Dear God, the things that man would do if he ever went completely over the edge.

At least Cassie was safe. She'd seen to that, if nothing else. Well, no, she'd also tracked down the men Jack had murdered in the lane, for all the good that had done.

Jewels and an old stocking. She closed her eyes to combat fatigue and a throbbing headache. Would anyone ever understand? In the way a child might paint a crude picture, the truth was there for all to see.

Her mind uttered a silent wail of frustration and pain. Why didn't someone—anyone—see it!

Chapter Fifteen

"There you are, you little tease." Sir Gerald's unexpected appearance at the door of Lady Mary's suite startled Cassie. He closed the doors behind him. "No need to disturb my grandmother for a while yet. She's sipping a glass of tonic, and I believe the doctor's planning to pay her a call shortly." His eyes glinted in lewd appreciation of Cassie's rounded neckline. "That gives us a chance to get better acquainted, my pretty little vixen."

"I'm not a vixen, Sir Gerald." Cassie endeavored to twist free of the fingers he'd wrapped around her arm, but his grip was unrelenting and painful. He propelled her firmly down the staircase and all the way to the library before she broke away. Naturally, there wasn't a soul about.

"Morgan will be waiting for you in your room, you know," she said, rubbing the red marks his fingers had left on her upper arm.

Sir Gerald smiled a long, wolfish smile made infinitely more sinister by the deep shadows that fell across furniture and floor. "I'm the master here, Cassie, not Morgan." He licked his pink lips. "Now, come here, you gorgeous thing."

She evaded him by ducking swiftly sideways. "I'm not a thing, either," she told him, her eyes searching. Where was the damned door? "I'm a woman."

"You're a servant."

"That doesn't make any difference."

Twin dimples appeared in his cheeks. "Damned right," he declared.

Something about the glazed light in his eyes set her nerves on edge. She ran damp palms down the skirt of her cream satin dress, but had to do it on the move. He was very quick—and apt, she knew, to lunge.

"Look, Sir Gerald," she said, putting a small table between them as she worked her way toward the door. "You may not understand this, but I'm not like other women you know. Not that I think you have the right to harass them, either, but this sort of rutting-boar behavior is just not tolerated where I come from." She glanced behind her. Twelve feet to go. "In fact, it's considered a crime."

"Not here it isn't," Sir Gerald said, undaunted.

Cassie used the sofa as a barrier, easing her way along it, but keeping her muscles poised in case he decided to hurdle the back.

Eight feet.

Cassie looked nervously at Sir Gerald's shadowed face. She hadn't realized how blue his eyes were, or how nimble his lanky frame could be when ordered.

Was he Jack? she wondered, slipping from sofa to plant stand.

She glanced down, then swiftly up as he reached for her. She thought he might be trying to grab her with his left hand, but she didn't feel quite brave enough to find out for sure.

Another sofa loomed, draped in dusty darkness. This part of the room was especially badly lit. Unfortunately, it also contained her one and only means of escape: the door.

Palms resting lightly on the carved top, she inched her way along the couch. Sir Gerald laughed as if it were a game. Four feet left.

She was about to make a run for it, when someone's fingers suddenly shot out to ensnare her wrist. A tiny scream escaped from her lips.

"What's this, then?" a man's voice boomed.

His face appeared opposite her own. She flinched automatically. She saw a beard and long red hair, or would have if she hadn't been so busy trying to wrench free.

Sir Gerald seemed as startled as Cassie. "Good God!" he exclaimed. "What are you doing here, Procopius?"

Procopius Rowe laughed loudly. "Reposing on your sofa, my friend. What else?"

Sick of being treated as though she were slave labor, Cassie pounded on the M.P.'s wrist. "Let me go," she ordered.

"No, wait." Sir Gerald pointed at Procopius's hand. "Hold her there. I've been—" His eyes widened in shock. "Good Lord!"

The last was a response to the fist Cassie shoved into Procopius's unsuspecting throat. He gurgled and dropped her hand. Sir Gerald looked on, astonished.

Backing away, Cassie groped for the door. "You two will have to play your games alone. I'm leaving."

An indignant Sir Gerald straightened. "Bloody cheek. Who do you think you are? You get back here this minute."

"Stay away from me," she warned when he started around the sofa. "Or I'll..."

"You'll what?"

She lifted her head defiantly, her fingers still searching behind her. "I'll send for the peelers."

Sir Gerald drew back. "The what?"

"Peelers. Bobbies." She ground her teeth. "The police."

Recovered, the M.P. looked on in faint amusement while Sir Gerald screwed up his face. "Don't think I've heard them called that before, but it doesn't matter." He flapped a dismissing hand. "You're a servant in my household, and you'll damned well start acting like one, or I'll send you off with old Procopius here."

"To my little East End den of iniquity," the M.P. said with a wink. "I like women who fight. Sweetens the taste of victory."

They were mad, perverted, sexist creeps. Worse than that, they were both moving toward her.

Whirling, Cassie dived for the door and yanked it open, snatching the key from the lock before she ran across the threshold. One twist on the other side and she was safe. Well, safe for the moment, anyway.

It unnerved her to hear Sir Gerald shrieking for her to release them, and beneath that Procopius Rowe's eerily soft chuckle.

An icy tremor spread upward from Cassie's stomach. Two completely different reactions, she thought, her eyes glued to the door. And for the life of her, she couldn't say which one of them struck the deepest note of terror in her mind.

"YOU DID WHAT!" Morgan said unbelievingly as they stood in the second-floor corridor where Cassie had found him. He stared at her in that intense penetrating way of his for about ten seconds, then baffled her completely by glancing over the banister and saying quite clearly, "Good, fine. Here, take the tea up to Lady Mary. I'll deal with the oversexed baronet."

He left her with a tray of tea and buns, and absolutely no idea whether he was pleased or outraged by what she'd done.

Later in the kitchen she didn't ask, and he didn't say. In fact, no one mentioned the incident at all. Which Cassie reasoned was Lady Mary's doing. No doubt Sir Gerald would have fired her in a minute. Unless Morgan had somehow talked him out of it.

There was little time for her to ponder that mystery or, indeed, any other. Lady Mary wanted to look her regal best for the Cumberlands' Christmas party. That meant Cassie had to pull out every piece of silk she could find and dress the woman's white wig and fancy hat with jewels and feathers.

"Pay no attention to Dr. Gloomy," Lady Mary said flatly, and slapped at Dr. Peach's hand as he tried to take her pulse.

"You're overdoing it," the doctor insisted in a huffy tone. "You shouldn't attend this party."

Why were his eyes on her when he said that? Cassie wondered uncomfortably. And why couldn't she erase the image of blood on his shirt and breeches or the picture her mind drew of him sacrificing virgins at a black mass?

Thirteen men gathered at the home of a Scottish laird. A coven? The way Cassie saw it, if Jack wasn't the devil, he was certainly a dutiful disciple, and while it might be irrelevant, Dr. Peach's eyes were very, very blue.

The night progressed slowly. Cassie and Morgan left Amblewood House at eight o'clock, five minutes after Sir Gerald, Lady Mary and a strangely subdued Procopius Rowe. The doctor preceded them all in his own carriage.

"Evening, Mr. Morgan," the Cumberlands' housekeeper called out as he ushered Cassie into the kitchen of Astley Manor. "Party's just starting. You can go up the back stairs to the upper landing. It circles the whole ballroom. You'll see everything from there."

Morgan's smile was polite. "Thank you, Mrs. Tubbs."

"Is there anyone in this city you don't know?" Cassie asked as they climbed.

She didn't expect an answer and he didn't give her one. His mind was already fixed on the task at hand. But Cassie didn't want to spy in silence while she struggled not to notice how incredibly sexy Morgan looked in his long black coat with its caped shoulders. She didn't want to think about his mouth that drove her crazy or the fact that he was standing so close behind her she could feel every single part of his body.

Well, not quite every part. He very neatly managed not to touch her with the one part of his body she wanted desperately to explore.

Frustrated, she gave in and focused her attention on the party below.

The hall was richly decorated with holly and ivy and shiny gold bows. Christmas punch flowed liberally. Red, of course, Cassie noted with a shudder.

All the suspects put in an appearance. Even Julian Stockwell showed up. "Playing on his limp, I see," she remarked, fingering the candy bar she'd stuffed into the pocket of her cloak. "Men are such babies."

Morgan arched a meaningful brow. "And how many times have you broken your ankle?"

"His ankle's not broken," she scoffed. "It isn't even sprained. He didn't start limping until he got within range of those women." She leaned forward. "My God, is that Ignatious at the door? He looks terrible. And Sir Gerald looks like a thundercloud," she added smugly. Before Morgan could comment, she removed her hand from her pocket. "Have some chocolate?"

He made a strange face. "What is it?" he asked, his expression one of great skepticism.

"A coconut bar. Haven't you ever had one?"

"It looks like... Never mind."

With a little urging, he did eat the bar, but Cassie found it odd that he didn't recognize candy. Weren't there any sinful indulgences in his century?

For all its grandeur and strong Yuletide atmosphere, the party turned out to be uneventful. The night, however, didn't end with the party.

This time it was Morgan who came to Cassie—reluctantly, she knew, but he came, and he stayed until dawn. Once while he was stroking her damp hair, she thought she glimpsed a softening in his eyes. She saw a young boy there for a minute, lost, a little unsure—and still a huge mystery to her. For once in her life, though, Cassie set her questions aside and settled for holding him.

IT WAS LIKE THAT for the next three days. No one got murdered—well, actually they did, this being a rather brutal time despite its surface elegance, but it was all stabbings and shootings and poisonings. Nothing that could relate to Jack.

Desirée dropped in twice to see Lady Mary. Both times, her artfully made-up features were drawn and pale. Cassie told her about Morgan's theory that it was Slasher Tom who'd attacked her carriage rather than Jack, but the news didn't mollify her.

"He wants me dead," she whispered on the second afternoon, while Lady Mary talked to another friend and only Cassie could hear her. "He'll murder a hundred, a thousand, ten thousand. And the tragedy is, he'll never stop, because his mind is broken."

"Whose mind is broken?" Cassie asked, but Desirée shook her head.

"I don't know his name," she murmured.

She did, though, Cassie thought. She knew—she just wouldn't admit it. Why? Was she protecting someone? That made no sense. You wouldn't protect someone who wanted you dead.

"UNLESS HE'S HER brother or something," she theorized that night in the kitchen. "But who could her brother be? Nor Sir Gerald or Dr. Peach. Do you know anything about her background, Morgan?"

He glanced over as he poured two cups of tea. "Only that she married a Frenchman."

"Did you know him?"

"No, he died before she met Lady Mary."

"She's close to Lady Mary," Cassie mused. "I wonder if Desirée would confide in her."

But Lady Mary had other things on her mind when Cassie went up to help her prepare for bed.

"You mustn't rile my grandson," she said the moment they were alone. It was the first reference she'd made to the incident in the library. "He's still brooding about it, although I believe Morgan has more or less gotten him to view it as a jape."

"A what?"

"A joke, dear, a joke."

Cassie sighed as she removed the old woman's powdered wig. "It's a whole different language here," she murmured.

"Yes, well, it was bound to change some." Lady Mary hobbled toward her bedroom. "England and America are an ocean apart."

An ocean and two hundred years, Cassie reflected.

"But back to my grandson." Lady Mary climbed into bed with difficulty. She looked very old and frail tonight. "I think if he wanted to, he could be a rather dangerous young man."

"I suppose anyone could be if they put their mind to it," Cassie said. "Tell me, Lady Mary," she asked carefully, "is your grandson right- or left-handed?"

The old woman smiled. "He's like me—neither and both. Many people are these days. Gerald's uncle, my other son, was the same way. It's rather convenient for a surgeon, I always think."

Cassie's heart thudded against her ribs. "Sir Gerald's uncle was a surgeon?"

"Yes, though not, I confess, the most skilled member of his profession. However, style isn't everything. He had no sons of his own and wanted Gerald to follow in his footsteps, but we thought that an unwise idea. The sight of blood has always had an adverse effect on my grandson. He goes white and starts to shake." She eyed Cassie sternly. "But that wasn't my point. My grandson is unpredictable, not unbalanced. He wouldn't harm anyone deliberately. He simply resents certain aspects of his childhood." A gnarled hand came out to squeeze Cassie's cold one. "Do watch yourself around him, my girl. I should hate to see you hurt. You must remember, however, that Gerald is my grandson. My first loyalty will of necessity be to him."

December 19, 1790

JACK SAT ALONE in his darkened room. He hadn't come up with a plan. He had no victim in mind. He understood nothing except that he must kill her. It was his one and only thought, his obsession. Kill the traitorous red-haired slut.

Tomorrow night. Yes, at the Hammonds' Christmas party. That would be perfect.

His fingers curled in his lap, first on his right hand, then on his left. Write a taunting note. Kill. In that order.

With his left hand he caressed the cold steel blade of his knife. With his trembling right he picked up a quill....

December 20, 1790

Jack's note read:

> When shall we three meet again, Morgan? Soon, I expect. But this night I'll spend unto a dismal and fatal end.
>
> None of woman born will elude me. I am young in deed and shall remain so until she is dead. The eye of childhood fears a painted devil. She took everything

from me. But it was you, Mother, who created her. You brought her into this world. Slut sister. Hurt but wanted. And where did that leave me?

No, they must all die. She must die. Soon it will be done, Mother. But for now a false face must hide what the false heart doth know.

That note haunted Morgan more than its predecessors. He recognized lines from *Macbeth,* mixed in with Jack's vindictive words. The weak rhymes were in keeping with Ignatious Athelbert's style of poor poetry, but then everyone knew that, so anyone could have imitated him. In the same way, everyone knew that Christopher Crowley was playing Macbeth at the Haymarket Theatre.

Did everyone know that Lady Mary owned a pair of distinctive sapphire earrings? Probably, though he hadn't paid much attention.

And what about the other jewelry found near the victims? Lady Annabelle's emerald choker had been a gift from Sir Gerald.

"Knot," Cassie said, her head bent over a piece of parchment. She was attempting to solve the mystery of Jack's postmurder arrangements, still as baffling to them as his latest note. "Not. Not emeralds?" she guessed. "Not rubies and diamonds?" She scribbled on the parchment as Morgan paced the kitchen floor. "Not genuine? Not real?"

"What's not real?" Bartholomew asked in his customary childlike fashion.

"Well, she doesn't know that, does she?" Morgan said impatiently.

"Something about Jack, maybe?" Cassie said, then she sighed. "But I guess we already knew that, didn't we? As for Joelle's cameo inside her handkerchief, the best I can come up with is that he's saying there's something hidden."

"His identity, for starters," Morgan muttered, staring at the floor as he walked back and forth.

"Or some other secret. He hates his mother and sister."

"And quotes Shakespeare, specifically *Macbeth,* and picks on women with red hair when he can...."

"And if your theory's right, probably hired Slasher Tom to attack Desirée," Cassie added.

"Then put Lady Mary's earrings and a stocking next to his body," Bartholomew finished for them. His expression went from triumphant to confused. "Why did he do that?"

"For God's sake, Bartholomew, if you're going to ask asinine questions, at least keep them to yourself," Morgan said, exasperated.

Shoving the parchment away, Cassie stood and stretched the small of her back. He closed his eyes so he wouldn't see the way her breasts pressed against the heavy satin of her mauve dress. "Don't be so grouchy, Morgan," she reproached. "Bartholomew's only trying to help. You should be grateful. Is it time to go yet?"

"Just about." He knew he sounded even grouchier now, but she was driving him to bloody distraction. He tended to think about her first and Jack second, and that could be lethal. Would be lethal, he felt sure, before long. Jack hadn't killed for three or four days now, and his note reflected that pent-up store of homicidal energy. Tonight he'd vowed to spend unto a dismal and fatal end. Morgan shuddered, still not looking at Cassie.

"It's all bits of things, isn't it?" she said, rereading Jack's words. "Mostly lines from *Macbeth.*" She indicated one of them. "This is a strange remark. 'None of woman born will elude me.' We're all of woman born."

Morgan glanced over. "He probably plans to kill every woman throughout time."

"Maybe," she said thoughtfully. "I'm not sure about that, though."

Morgan was only sure that it was time to bundle Sir Gerald and Lady Mary off to the Hammonds' Christmas party. At his suggestion, they were attending with friends from Kensington, leaving their coach and driver free for him and Cassie to use. Bartholomew, too. Morgan wanted someone watching the rear exit tonight. Because Jack was in the mood to kill, no doubt about it.

Reaching for his coat without enthusiasm, he tugged it on.

Behind him, Cassie pulled his ponytail from under the collar. "We'll catch him," she promised. "I know we will, Morgan."

She didn't, though. That was the problem. No one could predict the actions of a madman. Unless...

He turned suddenly. "Bartholomew, go upstairs to the study and find Desirée Deveau's address."

DESIRÉE'S HOUSE STOOD in total darkness. No one responded to Morgan's knock. She must have given the servants the night off. So why didn't Cassie's instincts like that simple explanation?

"I think Desirée's been hiding since the attack," she said as Sir Gerald's coach pulled into the Hammonds' elegant sweep of drive.

"I imagine she has," Morgan agreed, and opened the door. "Don't let anyone see you," he instructed Bartholomew, who hopped out into the bushes. "Keep your eye on the back of the house and let me know immediately if any of our suspects come out that way. Got it?"

"Got it, sir."

"All right, go on then."

Closing the door, Morgan arranged himself in a corner of the coach where he wouldn't have to touch Cassie. She would have been upset if she hadn't sensed he was tempted. And if she hadn't been so uneasy herself.

"All that *Macbeth* stuff," she said, offering him a piece of her last Hershey's bar. "I think he's trying to frame Christopher Crowley."

"Or he's trying to make us *think* he's framing Christopher Crowley."

"Well, that's no help, Morgan."

He made a distracted sound in his throat, a signal to Cassie to stop talking—unless she intended to talk to herself.

He'd made her dress warmly for this excursion and had brought along plenty of hot tea. Evidently they couldn't sneak into this party, not without risk of getting caught, and Morgan didn't want to risk that, so here they would sit until someone inside made a move.

Sir Gerald's driver, Wilkie, returned from the kitchen at nine-fifteen to report that all the suspects were present.

"What about Mrs. Deveau?" Morgan asked.

"No sign of her, sir. But you must be cold. I'll watch for a while if you want to pop in and have some of Mrs. Sinclair's coffee and fruitcake."

No one had to twist Cassie's arm. Before Morgan could object, she had him by the hand and was dragging him out of the coach. "Thanks, Wilkie," she said with a smile. "We'll tell Bartholomew where we are."

Naturally, Morgan knew the kitchen staff. It earned him and Cassie a double portion of cake, with a bowl of thick cream on the side. Morgan sent his portion out to Bartholomew and took absent bites of Cassie's.

Cassie didn't blame him for being restless. Her own nerves had been frayed since she'd read Jack's note. There were undercurrents of sickness in it that defied interpretation. He'd started out writing to Morgan and ended with a message to Mother.

But for now a false face must hide what the false heart doth know.

It wasn't a direct quotation. Was that important? she wondered. Certainly the jewels and stocking beside Slasher Tom's body were.

The hours crawled by. Busy kitchen staff came and went. So did Morgan and Cassie. They'd just arrived for their third cup of coffee when Bartholomew rushed toward them through the new-fallen snow.

"It's Mr. Rowe, sir, the M.P. He's leaving."

Morgan let the kitchen door close, shutting out the chatter and the warmth. "Alone?"

"No, sir." Bartholomew panted. "With a woman, a red-haired woman."

"Are you sure?"

"Positive. I saw them come out."

"All right, stay here." Looking around, Morgan thrust Bartholomew into the kitchen and grabbed Cassie's hand. "Come on. We'll have to follow them."

The powdery snow made driving difficult. Oil lamps on the streets emitted only a feeble light. A few more years and they'd have gas lamps in London, but for now it was all oil. The equivalent, Cassie thought, of a candle in an extremely large cave.

Morgan tapped a gloved finger on the seat. "He's not in a big enough hurry," he murmured, then called up to the driver. "Catch him, Wilkie."

"Do my best, sir."

His best was excellent. They pulled abreast of the carriage, which Morgan recognized as belonging to the Kinboroughs of Kensington, within five minutes.

"What in bloody hell's going on out there?" Procopius roared at his bemused driver. Two faces topped with red hair appeared at the window. "Morgan, is that you?" the M.P. demanded. "What are you playing at?"

Cassie saw Morgan start to answer as he approached the door. Then his attention was drawn to another part of the coach and he veered off.

The woman with Procopius—if she could be called a woman, since she couldn't have been more than eighteen—giggled uncertainly. "Mr. Crowley was right when he introduced us tonight, sir. Interesting things do happen in your company."

Cassie drew nearer. "Mr. Crowley introduced you?" she repeated.

"Ah, the servant with the fist of iron." Procopius regarded her, mildly mistrustful. "To what do we owe this honor?"

"Well, actually..." Cassie began. She got no further than that. Morgan snatched up her arm and spun her about before she could finish.

Thrusting a stiff piece of parchment into her hands, he offered the bemused pair a smile and a polite "Sorry to disturb," then propelled Cassie back to Sir Gerald's coach.

"Morgan, what...?"

"Read it," he said. Raising a gloved fist, he pounded on the roof. "Whitechapel, Wilkie, as fast as you can."

"Whitechapel!"

"Read the note, Cassie."

He struck a match as he spoke, holding the flame over the black scrawl she'd come to know so well.

Decoyed, Mr. Clever Butler. Try again. Except by the time you read this it will already be far too late. Another whore will be dead. I'll leave her body for you to discover in the same place I left them for your predecessor, old Kroat, a hundred years hence.

It isn't over, Morgan. It will never be over. But you won't win, because I'm close to her now, so very close. No more clues from the whore who's been spying on me. She'll be dead. Your friend will be dead. They'll all be dead. Victory to me at last as I dance upon Mother's cold, cruel grave.

Ashes to ashes, hear the child cry. Pretty girl, Mother calls: Take their money for I.

How sad that Mother couldn't understand. Her daughter was never as clever as her son, Jack.

Chapter Sixteen

Horse and carriage flew through the London streets with Jack wild-eyed and excited in the driver's seat and poor, terrified Lady Elisabeth Fontaine trussed up inside.

Letting out a reckless laugh, he slapped the reins hard, driving the horses on. "To Whitechapel," he shrieked. "My home from home from home. I'll be infamous there one day, a regular Jack the Ripper."

It was a large, unwieldy carriage. Jack managed to control it, but he couldn't control what he didn't know, and he didn't know that he and Elisabeth weren't alone tonight.

Desirée crouched in a darkened corner like a frightened animal. She heard Jack's rantings above the rush of wind and snow. She felt the cold seeping into her bones. She couldn't see Lady Elisabeth and wasn't sure she wanted to.

It was doubtful she could stop Jack from killing her, but maybe there was something else she could do, a more permanent solution.

Desirée didn't want to kill; she'd never wanted to do that. And yet, if it was the only answer...

A horrified shudder started deep in her belly and spread outward to her fingers and toes.

Jack emitted a roar, and she tensed, shrinking deep into her corner. This man couldn't be cured. He acknowledged no sickness. He must be destroyed. It was the only answer.

A frozen blade, razor sharp, pressed against her skin. Yes, Jack, she thought, I have a knife, too.

But did she have the courage to use it? Could she overpower him, or would surprise be the better way?

Her head throbbed just thinking of all the dreadful possibilities. She'd survived her mother's abuse; she had strength. She could do anything she set her mind to.

But murder her own flesh and blood? Oh, no, that was too ghastly to contemplate.

The sound of Jack's laughter filled her head.

"Whitechapel dead ahead," he shouted. "It won't be long now, slut."

Desirée wanted to cry. Instead she burrowed deeper into the shadows and prayed for guidance.

December 21, 1790

THE WIND WHIPPED blinding snow into Morgan's eyes. Whitechapel was too big an area for two people to search, especially in the dark.

"He wants us to find her," Cassie shouted above the wind as they waded through another rubbish-filled lane. "He must or he wouldn't have left that note."

"He'd have left it, anyway, as a taunt," Morgan told her wearily. Then it hit him. "He'll do it on one of his future sites." He grabbed her hand. "Come on. It'll be light soon."

Whoever Jack had targeted tonight, she'd be dead already, Morgan knew. Jack was no time waster. But he was mad, and madmen made mistakes. If he focused on that thought, there might still be hope.

"Marie Jeanette Kelly," he mumbled as they climbed into the carriage. Where had she lived? He told Wilkie to drive south for three blocks, turn left and stop.

"Marie Jeanette Kelly," Cassie repeated slowly. "Wasn't she Jack the Ripper's last victim, in 1888?"

"And the most brutally murdered," Morgan confirmed. "She was killed in her flat."

"By Dr. Gull or the Duke of Clarence, or so a lot of people believed." Cassie dusted snow from her hair. "Do you have any idea who Jack was in 1888?"

"Left, Wilkie," Morgan called up, then made a negative motion with his hand. "I wasn't chasing him then."

"So what if we catch him here in 1790? What happens in 1888? Will there still be a Jack the Ripper then if he's caught now?"

"I'm afraid so." Morgan had no idea how to explain this. "Jack travels through time, Cassie. Once he leaves that time his actions become part of history. Whether he goes forward or backward from there makes no difference."

"Could you go to 1888 and try to catch him again?"

"No."

"Why not?"

"Because there are rules in time travel similar to those in physics."

"Isn't Jack breaking those rules?"

"Not really, although he's destroyed every moral one I know." Morgan pounded a gloved fist on the roof. "Stop here, Wilkie. Wait here," he told Cassie.

She obeyed reluctantly, hovering in the carriage door while he forged a path through the ice and snow to a shabby building on the corner. Flats in later times, they were flats now, dark and gloomy, but with nothing to indicate that a murder had taken place.

Massaging his temples with his thumb and middle finger, Morgan forced his tired mind to function. They'd searched the streets, the lanes and now the flats. What did that leave?

His head snapped up. The junkyard. Of course.

"The horses can't take much more, sir," Wilkie said, through his frosted wool scarf. "I'd best take them to a livery and warm them."

"Take us to the junkyard first," Morgan instructed. "There's a livery half a block away."

"It's getting light," Cassie observed as they jolted along.

She had to be half-frozen. *He* was, Morgan reflected, giving her a covert sideways glance. But if he touched her, he'd lose his concentration, and her life was in danger, too. The longer Jack remained at large, the greater the risk that he would attack Cassie again.

Strong winds buffeted the carriage. Wilkie pressed on through the dismal dawn, finally halting the horses in front of a tall fence. "Junkyard, sir. D'you need help with the latch?"

Cassie was already hanging from it, Morgan noted with a flicker of grim humor. No thought given to the fact that Jack might be standing on the other side with a big knife.

Catching her waist, he lifted her down. "All it needs is a kick," he said, and aimed his foot at one of the boards. The gate groaned and popped an inch. They wedged it open just enough to slip inside.

There was another gate at the rear of the yard, also open, Morgan noticed. His eyes swept the discarded pieces of furniture and old barrels. People sometimes slept in these places, though not as often in this kind of weather.

He motioned behind him with his hand. "Stay close," he said.

Cassie picked up the hem of his coat and hung on, her eyes fearful as they probed the black shadows.

The wind swooped down like a giant bird, tearing at everything that wasn't frozen in place. Nothing stirred except the loose snow. London hadn't awakened yet, so the shops on either side remained in darkness, with only a trickle of smoke rising from their chimneys.

Cassie halted abruptly. "What's that?" she demanded, pointing ahead of them.

Morgan squinted. "A broken bust," he replied, and masked a sigh of relief. "Watch where you step."

"I am," she said, then promptly lost her footing and fell. She ended up in a clump of frozen feathers, unharmed but checking swiftly beneath her for dead bodies.

Morgan helped her up. He understood her case of jitters. Something about this place unsettled him. Maybe it was because he knew about the horror that would take place here in less than a century. Or maybe Jack was lurking in the vicinity, a foreboding thought with the shadows still so long and thick.

They worked their way through the yard to the rear, where the junk was piled highest. A crack of wood, audible above the wind, drew Morgan's attention, but when he looked he saw nothing.

It came again seconds later. Cassie crowded close to his back, her hand on his arm. "I saw something move," she said. He felt her tremble slightly. "Over there."

Morgan followed her gaze to a heap of lopsided rain barrels. "I don't see..." A frown touched his lips. He did see, actually, but he couldn't have said what it was.

One of the barrels rolled off the pile, landing with a plop in the snow. A sound like rats' claws scrambling over wood erupted from behind, and suddenly a figure in a black cloak and cowl materialized.

Morgan moved quickly to cut off its escape. He heard Cassie clambering up over the barrels and swore at her rash behavior, but didn't stop.

The figure's cloak got snagged on a broken metal ring. By the time it tore free, Morgan was there, tackling it to the ground.

"No, don't," the person under the cowl wailed. "Please let me go."

Morgan's brow furrowed in a blend of confusion and disgruntlement. "Desirée?"

"He'll kill me," she cried, twisting underneath him. "Don't you understand?"

"Morgan, look!"

At Cassie's shocked exclamation, he glanced left. On the snow lay a woman's mutilated body, stiff and staring, the blood on her throat frozen solid. At her feet sat a knotted handkerchief, to the right of that a jumble of unsorted possessions.

He climbed off Desirée, but kept a firm hold on her arms. "Who did this?" he demanded, shaking her.

She appealed to Cassie. "You're a woman, you understand. Men are so much stronger than women physically. A woman's strength is in her mind. We can endure pain that would break a man. He hates that about us. He hates women. That's why he cuts up their wombs. He sees it as a symbol of womanhood."

Morgan shook her again. "Who is he, Desirée?"

"Please tell us," Cassie urged. "It was you who arranged the possessions at his victims' feet, wasn't it? Why didn't you just tell someone who he was?"

Desirée's face went deathly white. "I couldn't," she whispered, her body rigid. "I didn't know who to tell. There aren't any street-corner bobbies. There isn't even a real police force in London. Besides, he can outsmart anyone here. If someone got too close, he'd just leave and start murdering women somewhere else."

Tears formed in her dark eyes. Bloodshot eyes, Morgan noted. He made the mistake of relaxing his grip when she grimaced in pain. A second later she'd wrenched away.

Gloved fists pressed to her cheeks, she stared at Lady Elisabeth's knotted handkerchief. "You won't see it, will you? He's *not* what he seems."

"Not real," Cassie murmured.

"Not real!" Desirée cried. "Mad. Homicidal. He hated Mother. He blamed her for my being born. He blames me for everything else."

Morgan's eyes narrowed. "Then you're Jack's..."

"Sister," she hissed, backing away. Tears streamed down her cheeks. "I'm his flesh and blood, all he has in the world. But don't you see, he's all I have, too."

Choking, she jammed a fist against her mouth, then spun and ran. Morgan lunged for her but missed. At the gate she paused briefly, her fingers strangling the boards. "He has to die," she rasped, her voice husky with pain. "It's the only answer. I have to make sure he dies!"

"Desirée, no don't!" Cassie shouted, but it was too late. Desirée was through the gate and running for her carriage, which was parked several yards away.

"She's going for him," Morgan said when they reached the other side. "Watch her. See which way she turns. I'll get Wilkie at the livery. If she gets to Jack before we do, he'll kill her for sure."

"THAT'S HER CARRIAGE, I think," Cassie said, twenty minutes later. She motioned to the right, then paused and looked up at the tall, narrow buildings crowding around them. "We're in Billingsgate. Isn't this where Julian, Ignatious and Christopher Crowley live? Yes, it is," she answered her own question. "Look, Morgan, that's the house. I don't see Desirée's carriage, though, do you?"

Morgan grunted. "She probably ditched it on a side street."

Inside her gloves, Cassie's palms felt clammy and cold. Her stomach was tied in knots. The sky had lightened just enough to see, but the eerie shades of dawn coupled with icy blasts of wind and snow chilled her right through.

She pictured the dead woman's chalky features, then ruthlessly shoved the image aside. Wilkie would contact the authorities while she and Morgan located Desirée.

She had to have gone inside the building. That meant Jack must be one of three men. But which one?

Desirée knew which one. She'd left clues at the murder scenes—here, and all through time, Cassie realized with a start. That meant Desirée was a time traveler, too. Wonder if her butchering brother knew that?

They entered through the rear door. It was like creeping into a tomb. Everything was still and silent. A long, drafty staircase rose to the right. The poet's door stood straight ahead. She didn't know which flats belonged to Christopher Crowley and Julian Stockwell, but they must be at least one flight up.

The floor beneath Morgan creaked. "*Macbeth,*" he mumbled under his breath. "Bad poetry. I'm missing something."

Cassie tugged on his coat. "Which way?"

"Well, I don't know, do I?" he retorted impatiently.

She held her temper. "We can't just stand here all day, Morgan. Aren't your instincts giving you anything?"

"Not much." He started to tap his tooth with his thumb, then paused and lifted his head. "Wait a minute." He wagged his fingers as if trying to recall something. "What did Desirée say back there? Something about not calling a bobby to help her."

"Because there's no organized police force here," Cassie finished.

"My God, that's it!" He closed his eyes. "How could I have been so stupid? It was right there."

"What was?" Cassie didn't understand.

Morgan started for the stairs. Although she wanted to scream, she followed him.

"Bobbies," he said. "And peelers, Cassie. They're derivations of a man's name. But not a man from this time. In 1790, there are no such things as bobbies or peelers."

"But Julian said..." Her eyes widened as comprehension dawned. "My God," she whispered in disbelief. "It's Julian, isn't it? Julian Stockwell is Jack!"

HE HEARD THEM COMING and crouched low by the wall. His tramp of a sister had burst in on him moments ago, knife in hand, sobbing that it had to be done. Still half-asleep, he'd fended her off. Now she was the one who slept, and he had the knife.

"I'll be back for you," he'd promised, then he'd run out to the landing and hidden.

He'd known Morgan would come, because she'd said his name. She'd said Cassie's name, too. Yes, another female he must dispose of. Red-haired and smart—God, how he hated that combination.

Palms slick with perspiration, he waited for them. *Julian Stockwell is Jack,* Cassie had whispered. The great revelation, and every word of it true. But only half a truth. There was more, so much more.

The sleeping slut, for instance, his sweet sister, Mother's beloved child. Well, Mother was long gone, and soon his dear sister would be, too. And Cassie. And Morgan. And anyone else who tried to stop him.

Jack's secret must never be revealed.

A SHIVER OF UNBRIDLED terror crawled along Cassie's spine. She felt breathless and light-headed, but doggedly put one foot in front of the other and continued climbing.

Out of the blue, her mind flashed a picture of Slasher Tom's body, of the jewels and the dirty stocking placed at his feet. Jewels and a stocking? Julian Stockwell? It was a stretch, admittedly, but no more so than some of the knock-knock jokes she'd heard as a child.

She concentrated on the term *peelers,* the tip-off. "Where did it come from?" she whispered to Morgan. "And when?"

Eyes trained on the upper landing, Morgan said quietly, "Sir Robert Peel organized the first London police force in 1829. Initially, his men were known as Peel's Bloody Gang, but later people started calling them peelers and bobbies. If I hadn't been so distracted the other day, I'd have noticed Julian's slip."

Desirée had made a similar slip, Cassie reflected. So she definitely knew time travel. It must have been Desirée who'd placed Joelle's cameo inside her handkerchief, whatever that meant. What a dreadful situation, to know her brother was a murderer. No wonder she'd been so distraught.

Cassie pushed all thoughts of sympathy from her mind as they reached the upper landing. Only a few windows admitted light to the building, not that there was much light to admit, or that it mattered in any event, since there were no names on the doors.

"We could ask Ignatious where Julian lives," Cassie suggested.

Morgan started to shake his head, then stiffened as something dark and squat moved in the shadows ahead of them.

"Here now, what are you doing sneaking around?" a man's voice barked.

A wild screech couldn't have startled Cassie more. She jumped back, collided with the banister and stood there clinging to it, even after he ventured into the light.

"Well?" he demanded. He was small and grizzled and gray. Toothless, she noted, and unarmed except for the chamber pot he held in his arms.

Morgan recovered first and smiled at him. "Good morning," he said pleasantly. "We're looking for Julian Stockwell's room. Do you know which one it is?"

For some reason, Cassie expected to have to buy the information, but the man merely eyed Morgan up and down, then sniffed loudly and jerked his head to the right. "Down the hall, third door. Don't know as he'll be pleased to see you, though."

"Why is that?" Morgan asked, his composure perfectly intact.

"Because of the woman. She came tearing in here ten minutes ago. Barged right into his room."

Prying her fingers from the railing, Cassie ventured forward. "Did you hear anything after that?"

"Probably could have if I'd put my ear to the door, but I didn't. It's no business of mine what Mr. Stockwell does."

"Wouldn't you know Julian would live in the one place in the world where the neighbors aren't nosy," Cassie said when the man was gone.

"He probably chose this building for that specific reason." Morgan set his left hand on the knob. In his right, he held the Magnum. "Ready?"

Tightening her muscles, she nodded.

He swung the door wide and brought the gun up. Cassie waited. Then, when nothing happened, she peeked over his shoulder.

"He's not here," she exclaimed softly. "How can he not be here?"

Morgan crossed the threshold, using his body to keep her behind him. "Desirée?" he called warily.

No one responded.

Julian's flat was one large sectioned-off room with a bed, a dresser and an armoire on the opposite wall, cupboards and table on the left, and a sitting area in front of the smouldering fireplace.

"No Christmas decorations," Cassie murmured, rubbing her arms for warmth. "It's awfully Spartan. I'd have expected more flash from Julian, more of life's comforts."

"Yes, well, you might remember that he isn't Julian," Morgan said, lowering the gun as he prowled the room.

Either it was extremely cold in here or there was something odd about the atmosphere. Cassie's skin positively prickled, yet when she looked, no one stood at the door.

It must be nerves, she decided, and all the unanswered questions plaguing her. Where was Jack? Where was Desirée? Had he killed her? Shuddering deeply, she shoved her thoughts away and began going through the drawers. Like the room, however, they contained only the bare essentials.

Finally, she stood. "There's nothing here, Morgan." She felt his shoulder brush against her back. "At least if there is, I don't—"

Her body went rigid suddenly. Morgan wasn't behind her. He was across the room next to the window.

She spun. For a moment she saw only her own reflection in the mirror. But then Julian—no, Jack—chuckled and stirred in the shadow beside her. Before she could order her muscles to move, his arm snaked out to grab her.

"Morgan," she managed to choke.

"Hello, Morgan, my nemesis," Jack greeted.

His smile grew wide; Cassie saw it in the mirror. She couldn't see Morgan, but it didn't matter. Jack would want to kill her first, anyway.

The pressure on her windpipe was painful but steady. She could breathe, and if she could breathe she could think, despite the knife blade he pressed to her throat.

"Put the gun down and walk to the middle of the room," Jack instructed. "Slowly. That's right. We wouldn't want the pretty whore hurt, would we?"

His eyes were red and glazed. His cheeks glowed pink in the frosty dawn light. His hand clutching the knife trembled slightly.

"Should I kill you now, slut?" he whispered. "Or wait?"

His black hair grazed her cheek. Too terrified to respond, Cassie stared at him via the mirror. He looked maniacal, not like Julian at all. But had she ever really studied Julian feature for feature? If she had, she might have noticed the faint resemblance he bore to Desirée.

"Let her go, Julian," Morgan said calmly.

"Call me Jack," the man holding her snapped. His entire body began to shake with suppressed fury. The tremor in his hand grew more pronounced.

Seizing her opportunity, Cassie grabbed hold of his left wrist and twisted hard. The knife fell, and she kicked it toward Morgan. Then she wriggled out of Jack's forced embrace and stumbled over to the mirror.

His outraged roar filled the room. When Cassie's vision cleared, she saw that Morgan had the knife. Unfortunately, Jack had also had a gun, and it was aimed directly at Morgan's head.

"You're starting to irritate me, Mr. Future Cop. Or should I say peeler?" His mouth curved into a ghastly smeared smile. "Oh yes, I know where I made my mistake. But you understand how difficult it is to keep everything straight. I'll bet your slut understands, too, doesn't she? Is she from your time, Morgan?"

"No," Morgan said in a level voice. "She came through the corridor accidentally. Let her go, Jack. She can't hurt you."

Frantic, Cassie scrambled over to where he stood. She had the very strong feeling that Jack was about to blast Morgan out of time for good.

"Wait," she begged, as his finger started to squeeze the trigger. "Where's—" she searched for a question. "Where's Desirée?"

Jack's narrow face mottled, purpling beneath the layer of rice powder that clung to his forehead and chin. He was disheveled, hastily dressed, his shirt and stockings smudged. But not with blood, Cassie realized. With something more pink than red. Desirée's lipstick, maybe?

"You killed her, didn't you?" she whispered, unable to hide her revulsion.

Jack was sweating heavily. "No," he said. He gripped the gun tightly in both hands. "I should have, but I haven't. Not yet. She would have killed me, though. She broke in here with a knife. She was going to stab me. She didn't want to do it, she said, but that was a lie. Mother put her up to it. I can hear her now. 'Kill Jack,' Mother would say. 'We don't need him anymore. You were the child I wanted, Desirée, my pretty daughter. Lure the men to me, pretty one. Bring them to Mother so she can drug them and take their money. Leave us alone, Jack. You're of no use to me now. I have my darling Desirée, my prostitute of sorts.'"

Jack was panting, making horrible gasping noises. His slender body heaved. If she hadn't been numb with fear, Cassie would have marveled that a man's countenance could change so drastically in the space of one short speech.

His blue eyes blazed with fury, and his whole body seemed to have puffed up. His hair was completely out of its ponytail, a mass of black curls framing angry, twisted features.

"Inch backwards," Morgan said, scarcely moving his lips. He kept his gaze steady on Jack's face. "There's a door behind us, and stairs beyond that."

Cassie knew better than to look. Escape was her overriding thought. Get away from this man or get shot.

"It was all Mother's fault," Jack charged. "Her son was of no use to her. She knew Jenny Diver, the pickpocket, and Elizabeth Brownrigg, the murderer. She whipped us the way

Elizabeth used to whip the foundlings who worked in her so-called hospital. But Mother never used a hospital as a front for her cruelty. No, she beat her own children, first me, then the slut."

"So you come from this time, then." Morgan's tone sounded almost conversational. With his hand on Cassie's hip, he nudged her toward the partially opened door.

Jack laughed. Sweat stained his collar and armpits, even though there was no heat in the room. "Does that surprise you, Morgan? That a foe from the past could grasp the concept of time travel?"

"Not really, no."

"I have old Kroat to thank for that," Jack went on, his eyes glittering like lit sapphires. "He came here when he was young. On a lark, he called it. But he was sloppy and stupid, and a coward. I figured out that he came from the future. I threatened to kill him, so he talked. He told me all kinds of things, Morgan, about how others from his century traveled through time, searching for new recruits, people indigenous to a certain era who could fill historical gaps for them. But I wasn't about to be anybody's walking textbook. I wanted to travel, and I have traveled, thanks to Kroat's time box. But I'll always like this time best."

"It has its good points," Morgan murmured. An imperceptible nod told Cassie that she should prepare to move, while Jack's arms were sagging and his bleary eyes were trained on an invisible point over Morgan's head.

"Stupid Kroat," he said softly, rocking back on his heels. "He was stuck here for two years before anyone from your time pinpointed him. Meanwhile, there I was, flying about with his black box." His forehead wrinkled. "I never could make the box take me to Mother, while she was alive. I heard it had a fail-safe device built in, which was good, I suppose, since I also heard that if you go back into your own past, you die instantly."

"Because one person can't occupy two spaces in the same time," Morgan said under his breath. "Now," he whispered to Cassie.

She pivoted and raced for the door. Her icy fingers yanked it open.

"The bolt," Morgan said when they reached the other side.

Cassie helped him wedge a heavy bar into a pair of iron rungs as Jack's fists set up a cacophony on the planks. Then suddenly the banging stopped.

"No," he said in an ominous voice that made Cassie's blood run cold. "I won't let you escape."

An eerie chuckle filled her head. A chuckle and the sound of a key being turned in the lock.

Chapter Seventeen

"I liked it better when he was hysterical," Cassie said shakily. "Morgan, I can't see. Where are the stairs?"

"Right in front of you. Hang on to my coat."

And if he fell...?

No, she wouldn't let herself consider that possibility. Morgan was her lifeline, her love. They would get out of this.

It seemed as though they descended the narrow, slippery stairs forever, but it could only have been a few seconds. Together they shoved open the warped door at the bottom and stepped into a frigid room with two windows set up high near the ceiling.

"We must be in the cellar," Morgan remarked.

He lit a match, his last. Cassie fumbled for a candle in the wall sconce. As soon as it was burning, she began to hunt for the door that would lead them to the street.

"There," Morgan said. "On the far wall."

But Cassie's eyes had fastened on something quite different, several things, actually, including a number of large chests brimming with clothes and costumes.

"This must be where Jack keeps his disguises," she said, preceding Morgan to the street door. Intrigued despite her terror, she cast apprehensive glances at the overflowing trunks. "I assume he uses disguises sometimes." A violent curse from Morgan drew her attention back. "What's wrong?"

He banged a gloved fist on the planks. "It's locked." Snatching his head around, he searched for an alternative.

Cassie doubted he'd find one. She stared at the bolted door, her heart hammering in her ears. He'd trapped them down here. He was going to— Catching herself, she pressed her fingers to her temples and whispered a vehement "No. There has to be something." Her head came up. "The windows!"

Morgan made a disgruntled sound in his throat. "Too narrow."

"We could break the glass and yell for help."

"We won't be alive long enough for anyone to respond," he told her, peering up the chimney.

Setting her candle down, Cassie ran back to the stairway door. Naturally there was no bolt on this side. On the other hand, there was no sign of Jack on the stairs. "We could—" she began.

"No, we couldn't," Morgan interrupted irritably. "We're locked in from both directions, remember?"

"Then we'll have to find a weapon of some sort, won't we?" She dug into the nearest trunk, tossing out boots, pants, bustles and waistcoats. "I'm not going to be one of Jack the Ripper's victims, Morgan. God, he isn't even from the future."

"Meaning?"

"Meaning *we* are, therefore we should be more inventive than him." Frustrated, she pushed off from the edge of the chest. "These are all clothes."

"Try the dresser," he said, pressing his ear to the street door.

Cassie yanked open the top drawer. "Nothing," she said, fighting tears. "A twentieth-century passport, a wristwatch..." She hesitated. "I wonder what he did with Desirée?"

"She's probably dead by now."

"He said he hadn't killed her yet."

"He hasn't killed us yet, either, but he will if we don't find a way to stop him."

Shuddering, Cassie resumed her search. Shirts, cravats, trousers, stockings—it was the same thing drawer after drawer. She found a makeup case and other assorted boxes, but no gun. One of the smaller boxes slipped from her fingers and popped open. "Contact lenses," she said, shoving back her hair. "Just what we need."

She yanked open another drawer. "Lingerie," she muttered. "So he's a transvestite, too." She halted and glanced back sharply at the contact lenses. "Wait a minute, these are tinted."

Any further observation flew from her mind as a commotion erupted on the other side of the door. She heard a roar, and suddenly Jack burst through, the breath heaving out of his chest.

Cassie's knees trembled at the sight of him. He was mad, uncontrolled, waving the gun wildly. Her hip collided with the open drawer as she tried to ease away.

"Move another inch, slut, and you're dead," Jack growled. "And you." He swung the gun to Morgan, who'd made his way over to the dresser. "Stop right there."

Cassie risked a few more steps, though she wasn't sure why. If it was to draw attention to herself and away from Morgan, her ploy worked. Jack's face turned deep red.

"I said, don't move," he shouted and brought his left arm up.

She didn't see it snake out, didn't even glimpse the hand that slammed like a brick into her jaw. A searing bolt of pain shot through her cheek and neck. The blow sent her sprawling backward into one of the chests.

Clothes cushioned her fall but did nothing to dull the fiery ache in her face. She scrambled up, even so, or tried to, ignoring the stabs of pain that momentarily blinded her.

"You utter bastard," she heard Morgan snarl and knew he would go for Jack's throat.

She was right. The blunderbuss hit the floor and discharged. Cassie smelled gunpowder, then spied a gaping hole in the wall three feet from her head.

With renewed defiance, she untangled her limbs from the dresses and stumbled out of the trunk.

An iron poker lay next to the grate. Wrapping her fingers around it, she ran to where the two men fought. "Duck, Morgan," she shouted, bringing the rod around in an arc that caught Jack's shoulder and sent him crashing into the wall.

He was up again before Morgan could retrieve the gun. "Whore," he roared. He gave her a weighty smack with his right hand and grabbed Morgan again.

Although she saved herself from falling this time, Cassie wound up hanging over another open chest, her hand braced on the wall, her face inches above the contents.

She spotted a lavender silk dress and lace gloves. And just beneath those things a red wig. Her mind flashed a sudden picture of a woman in Lady Mary's sitting room, a beautiful widow with red ringlets, wearing a lavender silk dress.

Her breath caught; her head snapped up sharply. "Tinted contact lenses," she whispered, shocked. "Bustles and corsets and lingerie." She pushed off, gripping the poker again. No, she thought dizzily, it couldn't be. She was imagining things. They didn't look that much alike.

Putty, a small voice in her head reminded her. Actor's putty could alter features. They'd found putty under Lady Annabelle's fingernails.

Eyes still blurred with pain, she located the men. Morgan had Jack pinned to the wall. Jack bit him, then kicked him in the groin.

"Future poofs," he derided, then shrieked and ducked sideways as Cassie swung the poker at his head.

He moved with superhuman speed, diving to the floor and snatching up the gun.

"Get behind the mirror," Morgan said roughly, pushing her.

"No, Morgan, wait!" She clutched at his arm. "I think he might be—"

"Shut up, slut," Jack ordered.

She opened her mouth, but this time it was Morgan who said softly, "Shut up, Cassie." His eyes were fixed on Jack.

"Look to your right," she whispered desperately. "In the trunk. The wig, Morgan. It's red. And he had brown contact lenses in his dresser."

"What?" Morgan's head came around.

"Shut up," Jack said, levering himself to his feet.

Cassie nodded emphatically at Morgan's disbelieving stare. He glanced at the trunk, then returned his gaze to Jack's contorted face. "Yes, of course, we'll shut up,"

Morgan said calmly, forcing a polite smile. "Desirée, isn't it?"

Jack blinked rapidly. His lips thinned to a white line. "It's Jack," he insisted harshly and lifted the gun higher.

"Are you sure?" Morgan gave Cassie a small sideways shove.

He wanted her to hide behind the mirror, but she had a better idea. Risky but worth a try. While Morgan held Jack's attention, she crouched down and slid the red wig out of the trunk. Then, taking care to move slowly, she crept over behind Jack.

"Your sister's here with us, Jack," Morgan said, fully aware of Cassie's actions. "We saw her just a minute ago."

"No, you didn't." Jack pressed trembling fingers to his forehead. "I knocked her out. She's unconscious."

"She was unconscious," Morgan agreed, taking a bold step toward him. "She isn't anymore."

From another chest, Cassie extracted a black cloak. She would have to be very fast and hope that Morgan was ready.

Screwing up her courage, she surged up, plunking the wig onto Jack's unsuspecting head and tossing the cape over his shoulders.

He whirled as she'd expected. However, some sixth sense must have warned him about Morgan, because he spun back.

"Keep away," he ordered in a shuddery voice. The gun swung like a pendulum between them. "Keep—keep away from me."

"We're not going to hurt you," Morgan promised.

Jack's head moved left.

"We want to help you," Cassie said.

His head moved right. It started to move left again, then stopped. He craned his neck, peering mistrustfully into the mirror before him. "Desirée," he murmured. His voice altered, rising to a polished female pitch. "Yes, of course, I'm Desirée. Jack..." Wide eyes suddenly turned to impale Cassie. "You have to get out of here. He'll be back for us, for all of us."

The wig was starting to slide off. Desirée must have felt the movement. Before Cassie could catch it, the mass of red curls tumbled to the floor. In the mirror, it was Jack who now stared out at them.

Cassie honestly didn't know what to do, so she held her breath and prayed. Jack blinked twice at his reflection.

"You can't let your brother kill you, Desirée," Morgan told her quietly. "You said it yourself—women are mentally stronger than men."

"Yes," Desirée whispered, clearly confused. "Stronger."

"You're Desirée," Morgan said. "Say it out loud."

"I'm..." She faltered.

"Desirée," Cassie repeated softly, replacing the wig.

"Desirée," she whispered. "I'm..." Slowly, eerily, her expression shifted. She dropped the gun and produced a knife which she held, unwavering.

Cassie's feet were glued to the floor. Her heart banged against her ribs. A feeling of horror spread through her body as she stared at the sharp metal blade.

Smeared lips curved into an ironic smile. "Goodbye, slut," Jack's voice said. Then he laughed wildly—and with both hands, plunged the knife deep into his victim's throat....

Chapter Eighteen

Sir Gerald gaped in amazement. "So, what you're saying is that Julian Stockwell's real name was Jack, but he was also Desirée. And it was Jack who actually killed Desirée." He beamed as if proud of himself, then paused and jutted his lower lip. "Nope, I still don't understand."

"Oh, do be quiet, Gerald," Lady Mary ordered. She fixed him with a stern glare. "And remember, once this incident is cleared up to the satisfaction of all concerned, you have a great deal to answer for yourself. Joining the Freemasons behind my back, carousing until all hours, spilling red wine on your stockings—I thought it was blood. Morgan did, too, I'll wager. And you, young lady," she rounded on Cassie, "posing as a maid. You're no more a maid than Morgan here is a butler.

"And not a word from you, Morgan," she warned, holding up a gnarled finger. "Don't you open that polite mouth of yours and 'yes, ma'am' me. I had a nice long chat with Millicent Parsons today while you and Cassie were out hunting murderers. She's partial to sherry, you know. It took me a full bottle to get the truth out of her, but I did it." She aimed the tip of her cane at Dr. Peach. "And not a word from you, either. If I die, I'm going to die doing the things I've always done and enjoyed. Now, I want silence from everybody while I get this story straight."

"Lady Mary, please . . ." Dr. Peach began.

"Shut up," she snapped, then smiled sweetly at Cassie. "You may correct me if I'm wrong, my dear, but only you. I'm over my shock now and ready to accept any truth.

"Julian, or Jack as you call him, was mad. He thought himself to be both a man and a woman—at different times, of course. He disguised himself as Desirée, duping all of us with clever makeup and mannerisms. He worked as a reporter when he was Julian, and he also worked as an agent for the King. A clever ploy, I must say. As Jack, he killed women representative of a sister he never really had. As Desirée, he left clues at the murder scenes, because the woman in him felt guilty for what the man was doing. But as Desirée, he knew better than to go to the authorities, because Desirée, while she might not consciously have been aware that she and Jack were the same person, certainly suspected that this might be the case." Lady Mary arched her white brows. "Am I correct so far, my dear?"

Mutely, Cassie nodded.

"Good. Now on to this brother-and-sister business. You say that according to a journal you and Morgan discovered in Jack's flat, it became clear to you that his mother used to dress him up as a girl. She then sent him out to lure rich men away from their clubs and into dark alleys. These rich men would be both stupid and sick, I presume, but that's a separate issue. In time, this so-called girl became a separate entity—Jack's sister, so to speak. She was 'born' so that his mind could cope with all the horror in his life—a mother who beat him, being dressed as a female, baiting men—and yet despite what Desirée's presence accomplished, in the sense that Jack himself was no longer made to suffer these indignities, he was also jealous of her because it was the little girl that his mother really loved. The boy meant nothing to her.

"And so, for years Julian has been leading this triple life. As Jack, he saw his red-haired sister as a whore and set out to destroy her. But he was confused, knowing yet not understanding that he couldn't physically kill her. So he settled for killing other women instead, prostitutes on some occasions, because that's how he viewed Desirée, and women of means more recently, because that's how Desirée presented herself to us."

"Good Lord," the doctor exclaimed, mopping his heavy face. "I've never heard of such a case in all my life."

"It certainly does tax the old brain box," Sir Gerald agreed. He leaned back on the sofa, waving his wineglass. "So what are you, then, Morgan, if not a butler?"

"He's an agent for the King," Lady Mary judged. "That would be my guess. In a different capacity than Julian, of course, but an agent nonetheless." Her eyes twinkled. "And a slyboots, I might add. He almost became engaged to my dear friend Millicent's daughter a few years back. However," she added at Cassie's startled expression, "things didn't work out as Julia—she's Millicent's daughter—intended, so naturally there was no announcement made."

Still smiling, Lady Mary raised her wineglass. "Now, a toast. To Morgan and Cassie. Long life and health to both of you, wherever you might travel. To the end of a nightmare and all of our losses therein. And to a happy Christmas four days hence. We shall enjoy the festive season more, knowing that a mad murderer no longer terrorizes the red-haired women of old London town. To life, my friends." Her sparkling gaze landed on Cassie's face. "And to changing times."

December 22, 1790

"SO YOU'RE LEAVING for good, then." A dejected Bartholomew looked up at Morgan from the kitchen table. "You won't ever be back?"

He sounded so abject that Cassie almost wanted to cry. Although, if she was honest with herself, she had a much more personal reason for resorting to tears. Morgan's job here was finished. That meant he'd be going home now. At the very least, he would be off on another assignment—right after he sent her back to London, 1993, that was.

Since she didn't want to think about that, or Jack, or any other unpleasant thing, she walked over to where he stood making a note in his journal and asked point-blank, "Where do you come from? And who's Julia Parsons when you're not almost getting engaged to her?"

Morgan would never change, she realized with a flicker of amusement. He looked disconcerted for a moment, then recovered and straightened his waistcoat. She noticed that he also took a backward step away from her.

"Yes, right. Well, Julia is just a woman I know. She lives in Essex."

"Ah, the same place where you told Lady Mary you were born."

"Exactly."

"So you took Julia Parsons's home as your own."

"Not exactly."

"Then what—exactly?"

He glanced over his shoulder at the partition he was about to bump into. In her peripheral vision, Cassie saw Bartholomew grinning broadly at Morgan's apparent discomposure.

"I do come from Essex, actually," he said uncertainly.

"Yes, but in which century?"

His dark eyes narrowed on her face. "Are you sure you want to know?"

"I wouldn't ask if I didn't."

"I think it's the twenty-third," Bartholomew volunteered.

"Oh, shut up," Morgan murmured without any real sting.

Bartholomew continued to grin hugely.

"Oh, all right," Morgan relented at last. "I'll tell you." He shook a warning finger at her. "But this goes no farther than the partition, do you understand? That goes for you too, Bartholomew," he added, not looking over.

"Anything you say, Mr. M."

A thought suddenly occurred to Cassie as she studied his expression. Pressing her palms to his chest, she felt his heartbeat beneath the velvet of his embroidered black vest. "You're not from the future at all, are you, Morgan?" A smile lit her face. "You fit this time so well, because you were born in it. That's how you really know Millicent and Julia Parsons, isn't it?"

He regarded her with faint mistrust. "And if that's true?"

Cassie opened her mouth, but couldn't think of anything clever to say, so she asked instead, "Do you have parents?"

"My mother's still alive."

"Do you ever see her?"

"She was remarried ten years ago."

Cassie tilted her head consideringly. "To a Scotsman, I'll bet, huh?"

Morgan's expression was answer enough.

"So you won't be spending Christmas with your mother, then?" she pressed.

"Why?"

Cassie slid her hands from his chest to his shoulders. Then, when he didn't resist, she slid them around his neck. "I just thought it might be nice to spend it here, that's all. Jack's gone and you know Lady Mary wants us to stay."

"Yes...." he said slowly, drawing the word out doubtfully.

She pressed herself against him. "Well, it would be a wonderful experience, Morgan. I'd love to see what Christmas in 1790 is all about. And there's no reason for me to rush back home afterward, either. I mean, you can send me back anytime, to the point where I left, or close to it, at least. So no one would ever have to know I'd been gone, even if I stayed away for a month, or a year, or even two years."

"Cassie..."

"Well, it's true, isn't it?"

"Yes, but..."

"And you're not engaged to Julia, and I did help you catch Jack. I even figured out what Desirée meant when she hid Joelle's cameo inside her handkerchief."

"And that is?"

She kissed the corner of his mouth. "Cameos have women's faces on them, Morgan. She hid the cameo inside a handkerchief. The woman was hidden, the same way Desirée was hidden inside Jack. Clever, huh?"

"Not bad," he conceded. Then he glanced at Bartholomew and made an impatient gesture. "Well, go on, make some tea, then. Obviously we're going to be here for a few more days."

"And then?" Bartholomew asked expectantly, while Cassie's finger traced the outline of Morgan's jaw.

"Well, I don't know, do I?"

"What about Camelot?" Cassie suggested.

His eyes came down. "What?"

"Camelot. You know, King Arthur."

"For God's sake, Cassie, there wasn't really a Round Table."

"But there was an Arthur. And you can't just dump me back in 1993. Not just like that—it wouldn't be fair."

"Well..." The tension seemed to drain from his body. "No, I suppose it wouldn't." A reluctant hand came up to stroke her cheek.

"Anyway," she said, nudging him with her hip. "We can take Bartholomew with us as a chaperon."

He frowned. "You want to take Bartholomew to the Dark Ages?"

"Until you're sure, yes."

He started to say something, then thought better of it and let his hands encircle her waist. "Somehow," he said dryly, "I don't think that's going to take very long."

The last thing Cassie heard was Bartholomew whistling cheerfully as Morgan's mouth covered hers. In a distant part of her mind, she wondered how the people of Camelot would react to such an unlikely threesome.

Epilogue

December 3, 1993
From an entry dated December 27, 1790

"So that's how we spent Christmas and Boxing Day in 1790. Cassie loved it. So did Bartholomew. Lady Mary was both delighted and suspicious. Although she never came right out and said anything, I think she's curious about me, and about Cassie, too. She's not curious about Jack.

"It doesn't matter. Jack the Ripper no longer exists. 1888 will never forget him, and certainly several other centuries now have their own version of the man, but as a mad time-traveling human, Jack is dead.

"Cassie believes that Desirée killed him, even though his final words, 'Goodbye slut,' indicate to me that it was Jack who killed Desirée. Still, it's a moot point, one of many unanswered questions throughout time.

"Tonight the Peregrines host their final party of the holiday season. Cassie plans to get me drunk just to see me unguarded, she claims. Maybe I'll indulge her. I might even tell her I love her. That depends on how unguarded I get.

"At any rate, we leave tomorrow, Cassie, me and Bartholomew, our dubious chaperon. If there is a Guinevere, I have a strong feeling that Cassie will want to have a chat with her.

"It could be worse, though. She could have asked to meet Mr. Charles Dickens. One has to wonder how people would have reacted to a female Artful Dodger...."

Dead silence reigned in the parlor when Mr. Flint stopped eading.

"Is that all of it?" an enthralled Mr. Pit asked, pouring he last of the wine into his glass.

"That's the last entry," Mr. Flint said. Closing the worn ournal, he set it on the table, then stared at the black leather over with its flaking gold Florentine trim. "What an inriguing read," he remarked finally. "Fiction, of course, but ascinating nevertheless."

Mr. Pit sipped his wine nervously, not as convinced as his riend of the book's fantastical nature.

"You don't suppose..." he started to suggest, but Mr. 'lint waved him off with a wave of his wool-gloved hand.

"It's impossible," he scoffed. "Utter bosh. It must be."

A knock on the door prevented further discussion on the ubject. Mr. Flint hastened off to answer it. After a monent's hesitation and another uncertain look at the journal n the table, Mr. Pit scuttled after him.

Mr. Flint was just opening the front door when he reached he hall. A flurry of snow and wind blew across the threshld.

"Good evening," a man's polite voice greeted. "I'm your ew tenant. I believe you're expecting me."

Mr. Flint smiled, motioning him in. "Yes, of course, sir. orgive me. My nephew made the arrangements, and my iend, Mr. Pit, and I have had rather a strange evening. lease, come in."

With an acknowledging nod, the new tenant entered. Mr. it studied him over the rim of his wineglass. He was a oung man, somewhere in his early to mid-thirties. His hair as dark and curled away from his face. His eyes were also ark, and extremely intense, Mr. Pit noted. He was lookg around already, taking in every aspect of the old house, seemed.

He carried a knapsack over his shoulder, wore a long ack coat with the collar turned up and moved with a deded sense of purpose.

"Come into the parlor," Mr. Flint invited. "It's not a fit night out there for man nor beast. Here, stand by the fire and have a warm. My nephew didn't tell me your name."

The man's eyes circled the room before coming to rest on Mr. Flint's round face. He shifted the weight of his knapsack, his lips curving into an absent smile.

"Morgan," he said simply. "Anthony Lazarus Morgan."

Mr. Flint almost choked. Mr. Pit did. Then his startled gaze fell on the man's knapsack, and his coughing attack grew worse.

Out of the pocket stuck a black book with gold Florentine trim—a brand-new book, by the look of it. Yet, new or not, it bore a striking resemblance to...

Mr. Pit's heart skipped a beat as he glanced at the table. The journal they'd just finished reading was gone. It was nowhere in sight.

Mr. Flint noticed too. He stared at Mr. Pit in a blend of awe and disbelief. Both men turned shocked eyes to Anthony Lazarus Morgan, but the enigmatic smile hovering on the corners of the man's lips told them nothing.

In a deft move, he reached around and pushed his own book deeper into the pocket of his knapsack. Then he offered pleasantly, "I'm told this house once belonged to a woman by the name of Lady Mary Peregrine...."